Sky's Shadow

Sky's Shadow

A Tommy Dapino Thriller

TED
GALDI

ONE

The black Cadillac Escalade with aftermarket rims seems like a drug dealer's car. Excitement tickles Danielle's stomach.

An eight-year-old girl sitting on the ground of the homeless encampment looks up at her with wide eyes and asks, "What happens next?"

"I forgot it's time for me to eat dinner, sweetheart."

"Does she get away from the wolves?"

"I'll finish telling you the story later. Promise. The end will surprise you."

The child smiles, her dirt-speckled cheeks dimpling. Danielle, thirty-three, winds through the tents to her boyfriend Len by the Escalade.

He rocks on his feet and says, "Their stuff sounds downright ruthless, babe."

"Tar?"

"Tar and fentanyl. New batch. Just released from some gang narco lab in Tijuana."

"I've never done—"

"Yeah. This'll be special. Your first time. With me."

"I don't know."

"We came out here to be free, right? No better way to feel free than with fentanyl."

"But so many ODs and—"

"Don't overthink it. I love you. Do you love me?"

She gazes into his face, wishing it were her ex-fiance's. And lies, "Of course."

"Then be free with me."

Len's smile doesn't rouse much in her. But at least gives her some self-worth. "Yeah, whatever, okay," she says.

"Ah. Beautiful. They don't want to sell it out here. So many cops, you know? They'll drive us somewhere safe."

He leads her into the Escalade, three others from their tent village in the backseats. Up front are two mid-twenties Mexican men, the one at the wheel with a tattoo of a boa constrictor around his neck, the other a retro NBA jersey jammed with veiny muscles.

The car starts moving. Nobody talks. Within fifteen minutes, the San Diego cityscape is lost behind trees. The driver turns off the road. Deepens into the woods. His head-lights shine onto a clearing. He stops and kills the engine.

He and his partner step into the darkness. Len approaches them, Danielle and the others following.

"All right," Len says. "Where's the stuff?"

The dealer with the snake tattoo says, "Trunk." But doesn't open it, instead leans against it. He glances at the time on his cellphone.

"Let's get to it," Len says, clawing at his arm. "Pop that trunk, bro."

The dealer chuckles.

"What's so funny?" Len asks.

"Nothing . . . bro."

"You want my money or not?"

"Here." The dealer reaches into his front pocket. "You get a sugar high while we wait." He removes a stick of gum and holds it out.

"What is this?"

The dealer unwraps the gum and puts it in his own mouth. "One more minute."

"What're we waiting for?" Len steps closer to him.

Danielle lays a cautionary hand on his forearm and says, "Baby."

"Have you ever seen anyone conduct business like this?" Len asks the three other buyers.

One shakes his head *no*. Another shrugs. The third seems too drunk to have listened to the question.

The dealer with the basketball jersey circles the group while the one with the snake tattoo watches his phone. The minutes on it change from 9:29 PM to 9:30 PM and he says, "Okay."

Guratt, a loud noise booms.

Len's forearm slides away from Danielle's fingertips. His face hits the Escalade's bumper, then the dirt. The back of his head is missing a chunk.

Danielle gazes over her shoulder. A gun.

The three other buyers scramble through the woods. The dealers, both clutching pistols, pursue them.

A voice spouting Catholic prayer silences when the snake-tattooed dealer fires. The sound of a corpse hitting the ground. *Guratt*, another gunshot, another toppled body. The dealer in the jersey pumps a bullet into the skull of a third.

Danielle's necklace flaps as she sprints. In her periphery the snake-tattooed man rushes toward her. She trips on a rock, skins her palms landing. His feet plant at her sides.

She looks up at him, says in a shaky voice, "Why're you doing this? We just wanted to buy some—"

"You did nothing wrong."

"Yeah, yeah I know. If something happened between you and my boyfriend in the past, I swear I wasn't involved."

"He did nothing wrong either. This is bigger than both of you. Fate brought you here for a reason you'll never understand. But you, I like you. You have kind voice. So I'll let you go free of this. Just promise you won't tell police."

"Of course not. Thank you, sir."

He extends his grip. "Let me give you a hand."

She reaches for it. He laughs and shoots her in the face. Then walks to his partner and watches a pair of headlights approach through the brush.

Danielle's left eye socket feels empty beside a mushy wetness. The bullet must've torn through her eyeball but missed the fatal parts of her brain. She wants to scream. But doesn't. They must think she's dead. She steadies the minor fluctuations in the elevation of her chest and stomach as she breathes.

From the corner of her one working eye she sees a white truck pull into the clearing. It looks like a box-back U-Haul without markings. The dealers drag a slain buyer toward it. The hatch opens. Two other men inside. White. The woods too dark to make out facial details.

The Mexicans hoist the corpse off the ground and pass it to the White men in the truck. Danielle peers farther into the vehicle for any clues to what's happening. She just spots some drink coolers.

The Mexicans approach her. While her eye is open. One grabs her ankles, the other her armpits. They carry her to the truck, the dust and wind wearing down her resistance to blink.

Just before she gives in, two new sets of headlights appear on the horizon, the Mexicans whipping their attention off her.

"Hey," the one in the jersey calls toward the truck. "Someone's coming."

The White men kick the corpse they were passed onto the ground. The Mexicans let go of Danielle.

"Shit," the one with the snake tattoo says as two incoming engines roar. "We need to leave. Now, now, now."

The Mexicans run to their Escalade. A White man jumps out of the truck and races around a corner. The one inside slams the hatch.

The Escalade's wheels spin, the truck's a couple seconds later. The vehicles accelerate, soon out of Danielle's sight.

A pair of ATVs skids to a stop near the dead bodies, atop them two teenage boys. "I told you that sounded different than fireworks," one says to the other.

"Holy crap. None of our friends will ever believe this story."

TWO

Tommy Dapino, thirty-one, walks into a lounge in Queens, New York. Josh, his next-door neighbor growing up and oldest friend, hand-signals to him from a table in the back. Tommy glimpses his outfit, smirks, and says, "What's with the vest and fedora? You look like a guy who gets rejected on *American Idol* ... then stalks all the judges."

"Come on, T. Just a little swag. This spot is trendy. The look works here."

Tommy sits his six-one frame in a chair across from Josh and eyes the decor. Funky light fixtures, red-leather couches, a wall of wine bottles. He says, "I liked this better when it was O'Shea's. Decent food. Good prices. This joint is trying to act too Manhattan for its own good."

"Nah. It's always packed. People like it. I even had my thirtieth here when you were ... away."

"Let's not talk about that, huh?"

"Right on. It's good to have you back, homie. Tonight'll be solid. I've got babes on the way."

"I thought it was going to just be me and you, catching up. I'm not really in the mood for any new people."

"Come on. I need you to be my wingman. I matched with this really cute nutritionist on Bumble. We've been messaging all week. She loves my jokes. Already sent me seven rolling-on-the-floor emojis. Tonight this can turn into something real, T."

"You're keeping a running count of her emojis?"

"I ... well ... anyway. She's bringing a friend. Maybe you hit it off with her."

"I don't know. Maybe. Whatever."

"At least just smile and try to make me look handsome by association." Josh checks the time on his phone. "They'll be here in nine minutes. Do I seem nervous? I seem nervous. I need to calm down. I need another glass of vino. Want one?"

"Bud Light."

Josh pops up from his chair and weaves his way through the crowd toward the bar. He bumps into a guy about four inches taller and forty pounds heavier, knocks the glass out of his hand.

The guy glances at the mess on the floor. "What the hell?"

"Sorry. I didn't see you. I was—"

"So you saying I'm not noticeable then?"

A bully. Tommy knows the type, came across plenty the last two years. A broken nose and black eyes on Josh wouldn't make for a good first impression on the nutrition-ist. His dating life has flailed since they attended their first spin-the-bottle game. Tommy still remembers the look on Josh's face when Laura Bancelli ran upstairs crying after spinning on him.

"Hey," Tommy shouts at the bully.

The group at the next table peeks at him standing. He squares to the bully, Josh stepping aside.

"What do you want?" the bully asks.

Tommy fans his hand in front of his nose and glances down at the spilt drink. "Whoa. That breath is flagrant. What was in your glass? Mule piss?" The spectators chuckle.

"Let's step outside. We'll see if you have the balls to tell me again there."

Tommy smiles, then right hooks him. The bully drops to the floor unconscious.

Gasps. A bouncer slams Tommy into the wall and says, "Dipshit. Let's go." He muscles him to the rear exit and pushes him into the parking lot.

"What the hell man?" Tommy says. "That guy was about to kick my friend's ass. I was helping him out."

"The only ass-kicking that went on in there was done by you."

"You didn't hear him? He said—"

"I didn't have to hear him. He was just talking. Talking is allowed. Punching other patrons out isn't. I'll remember your face. I'm putting you on the blacklist. This is a nice establishment. We don't need guys like you—" He keeps yapping, but Tommy slips on his headphones, drowning him out. Then flips him off and walks away.

After twenty or so minutes on foot through Queens blasting Nirvana, he arrives at his building and takes the stairs to his fourth-floor apartment, an "Assistant Maintenance Supervisor" placard on his door.

He enters and flips the light switch. The small living space's only furniture is a bed and secondhand cloth chair. He fills a cup with sink water and pours it over the soil of his plant on the windowsill. Since the weather was cloudy the last three days, he runs his fingers over the leaves to make sure they feel okay.

He sits on the chair and turns on the TV. The streaming service gives him dozens of recommendations for movies he's never heard of. Instead of taking a gamble, he settles on *Ghostbusters*, a favorite from his childhood he's seen about fifty times.

About ten minutes into the movie, his phone rings. "Hello," he answers.

"I think there's a family of bats trapped in my wall," Mrs. Kevel says, a resident in apartment 2F who calls him at least twice a week with some building-maintenance problem that's imaginary.

He closes his eyes. Huffs. "Yeah. I'll come down." He pauses *Ghostbusters* and steps into the hallway.

His phone rings again. He wonders what inventive nuance Mrs. Kevel decided to add about the bats. But her name isn't on his screen, rather a number not saved in his contacts, one with a 619 area code.

"Yeah?" he answers.

"Is this Thomas Dapino?" a man asks.

"Who wants to know?"

"I'm Detective Browing with the San Diego Police Department. You were listed as an emergency contact for Danielle Dapino on a former employment record. This is her brother, correct?"

"Yeah. Is she under arrest? What, possession?"

"No, no sir. She didn't commit a crime."

"Why's a detective calling me if she didn't do anything?"

A pause. "She's dead."

THREE

Tommy sits in a San Diego funeral home in the only suit he owns. Across from him is a closed casket. Despite the booze and drugs over the years, Danielle retained her beauty, but won't be taking it to the grave. Tommy turns to the man next to him, her ex-fiance, and says, "The funeral director told me half her face was missing."

"The whole thing is just sickening. I haven't been able to eat more than a cracker."

"Remember those eyes?"

"I fell in love with her the moment I saw them."

"This scumbag didn't even let her keep her eyes."

Tommy recalls those crystal-blue ones of hers. And the time when he and Josh were fourteen and snuck out of the house for a party. At one AM they attempted climbing back in through a window. The curtain rushed to the side, those eyes of Danielle staring at them. She could've told on her little brother but didn't. Instead she made him and Josh grilled cheese while they recounted the details of their first high-school party.

A woman enters the funeral home Tommy at first doesn't recognize. Big, black sunglasses conceal her face, the visible portions tight, as if pulled back by a recent plastic surgery.

His mother.

A part of him feels she lacks the right to even be here. She is responsible for the event that drove away his and Danielle's father, leading to her excessive drinking, which then led her to drug addiction, which then led her into the woods with those dealers.

His mother removes her sunglasses and gazes at him, the first they're seeing each other in about a decade. She waves. He does not wave back.

After the service, Tommy walks out of the funeral home into the first restaurant he sees, some open-air cafe that doesn't look too expensive. He sits at the bar and peers out at the street, the sun shining on all types of passersby. A young couple with a stroller. Three teenagers on skateboards. A man walking a dog. A woman in a business suit. Everyone wears a variation of the same carefree smile.

Tommy asks the bartender, "Are all these people as happy as they look or is it some sort of an act you guys play on the West Coast?"

"Let me guess . . . Philly?"

"Queens."

"First time to Cali?"

"First time out of the Northeast. Shot of whiskey. Jack."

"You on vacation?"

"Do people usually order shots of whiskey before noon on vacation?"

The bartender chuckles. "First one's on me. You eating?"

"Cheeseburger. Medium rare."

The bartender keys in the order on a terminal. Tommy notices a framed photo beside it of the Twin Towers, "America Strong" along the top.

"Been to Ground Zero?" he asks.

"The owner. He put it up. Visited the memorial a few years ago."

"I knew guys who were there. That day."

The bartender passes him the shot and leans forward as if to hear more.

"I was too young," Tommy says, "but a few of the older guys in my ladder company told me all about it. Every detail. Every last detail."

"You're a New York City fireman?"

Tommy drinks the shot. "I was."

"I've got mad respect for firefighters. Society couldn't run without you guys."

Tommy lifts his shot glass. "Couldn't without you guys either."

"True that."

Tommy checks his phone screen and sees the time is 11:45 AM, when Danielle's ex-fiance mentioned authorities would be making a statement on her murder investigation. "You mind turning the TV to channel nine and putting on the sound?" he asks.

The bartender does both. On the screen above the liquor bottles is a live press conference. A Black man in his fifties walks to a podium. On it is the seal of the FBI, now apparently running the search for Danielle's killer. A reporter in the crowd asks, "Agent Gabor, any leads yet?"

"We don't have any names quite yet. But I have confidence we'll apprehend whoever took the lives of these five innocent San Diegans. Next question."

After a couple minutes, Tommy says, "This guy is so full of shit."

"What he say?" the bartender asks, drying a glass.

"Nothing but vagueries and platitudes. Trying to hide the fact the FBI has no grip on this case. Pathetic."

"I'm sure they'll figure it out. They're the FBI. They figure shit out. That's what they do."

"No. They do what politicians and their corporate

donors want. And I doubt this case is high on the priority list. After the initial media attention dies down, so will FBI resources. You'll see."

"Hey man. Don't knock the FBI." The bartender points at the 9/11 photo on the wall. "They took down a lot of would-be terrorists after that."

"Of course they did. Because it was a priority." Tommy nods at the screen. "But the murder of five non-tax-paying men and women who lived in tents isn't."

"Oh yeah, yeah. I read about this online. Those people buying drugs in the woods. I grew up here. And never seen it this bad. The city needs to do something about all them."

"What the hell is that supposed to mean?"

"Bums. There's too many of them. They're filthy. Leave used needles lying around."

Tommy stands. "What're you saying? They don't deserve justice for being slaughtered just because they took drugs?"

"Easy, dude. No. I was just making a general statement about the homeless problem in the city."

"I bet you've made a mistake in your life. Just like them. Does the city need to do something about you too?"

The bartender holds up his hands as if in surrender. "Look, I—"

"What're you suggesting the city even do? Get them off the street and put them where? The ocean? Is that your plan? Did you even think any of this through or do you just like the sound of your voice when it's coming out of your ass?"

"I'm sorry, let's—"

"Shut up. Cancel the burger." Tommy pulls a twenty-dollar bill from his wallet and tosses it on the bar. "And I'm paying for that shot. What do I look like to you, some charity case? I look like someone who can't afford my own shot? You don't know me."

Tommy marches out of the restaurant. He walks to his rental car, a Chevy Cruze, climbs in the driver's seat. On the passenger's are a toothbrush, toothpaste, and half-full bottle of water. After paying for a cross-country plane ticket, his checking account was so low he slept in here last night instead of a hotel. He takes a deep breath. Cools down.

Soon he has to drive back to the airport to catch his flight to New York. But he decides not to make that trip. If he wants any justice for his sister the vagrant, society won't deliver it for him. He must get it himself.

FOUR

Tommy, hoping a dose of caffeine will burn away the fog of whiskey lingering in his head, steps out of a coffee shop with a large cup. If he is going to do what the FBI has failed to so far, find Danielle's killer, he'll need not just a plan, but one better than theirs.

He slips on his sunglasses and walks toward the water. Calls Josh.

"How was the service?" Josh asks.

"Police case files."

"Huh?"

"Can you get them?"

"What do you mean?"

"You know, like hack one for me. On the internet."

"Why do people who don't work in tech assume we're all magicians? My cousin once asked me to hack him the winner of the upcoming World Series so he knew who to bet on."

"So you can't do it?"

"Break into a government database and nab a police case file? It's possible if their firewall is vulnerable. But it's almost definitely not. Plus, it's highly illegal. Why—"

"Danielle."

"For—"

"Her last words."

"Why do you want her last words?"

"She's my sister. I don't know. It'd be cathartic to hear the final thing she said."

"I've never heard you say the word cathartic once in your life until now."

"So?"

A pause. "What're you up to?"

"Nothing."

"Why would her last words be in a police file?"

"A detective called me a few nights ago to tell me the news and ask if I had any helpful information. After I told him no, I asked him if Danielle . . . you know . . . suffered. He said probably. Said she didn't die right away like the other four, but on the way to the hospital."

"All right. But how—"

"I'm sure a cop questioned her in the ambulance about what she saw that night. Probably how they know this whole thing involved a drug deal."

"Yeah. I guess. But I can't help. I heard the FBI is involved now. If I get busted even attempting this, I'll get dick-slapped with all sorts of federal charges."

"All right. I'll figure something else out. See ya."

Tommy hangs up. An aircraft carrier comes into view. A massive docked warship with fighter jets atop. On a sign, he sees the boat is the USS Midway, the site a military museum. He stops on the pier, staring up at the ship. And has a long sip of coffee.

A murder over a narcotics deal isn't a federal crime. Some development in the case must explain the FBI's involvement. The authorities may not have leads on the shooter, but they have something, some nugget of information compelling enough for federal intervention. If Tommy can get that case file and find out what's already known, he may have enough raw material to mold a plan.

He lifts his arm for another sip of coffee. His eyes fixate on his sleeve. In his funeral outfit, a black suit, tie, and shoes with a white shirt, he looks like an FBI agent.

He smirks. He can use this.

FIVE

Tommy walks toward a six-story building, "SAN DIEGO POLICE DEPARTMENT" imprinted above the entrance. He steps into the lobby, officers buzzing about with varied insignia on their sleeves, and locates a divisional directory on the wall. His eyes stop on "Homicide Unit."

He takes an elevator up a few floors and arrives at a reception desk. Two employees behind it, a man in his mid-forties and a woman in her late twenties. Tommy decides to focus on the female, employ some flirtation. He saunters over to her and smiles.

"Can I help you?" she asks.

He eyeballs the personal items around her workstation. A framed photo of a cat. A small cactus. A pink trinket box with an Oscar Wilde quote on the lid, "Be yourself. Everyone else is already taken."

"The truth is rarely pure and never simple," Tommy says.

"Excuse me?"

He nods at her trinket box. "Oscar Wilde. Another of his quotes."

Her eyes widen. "Oh. Yes, yeah. Of course. Duh. You caught me off guard. Most people that come in here don't want to talk about Wilde. And you are?"

"Thomas. I'm with the FBI. Just got assigned to Agent Gabor's team. The five-person homicide in the woods." He shakes her hand.

"Kristen."

"Pleasure, Kristen. I'm here to see Detective Browing. Agent Gabor wanted me to get up to speed on the SDPD's end of the investigation."

"He's in back. I'll call him, tell him you're—"

"No need. I have his number." He walks out of her earshot, finds in his previous-call log the number Browing contacted him from a few nights ago, and dials it.

"Browing," the detective answers.

"Hi. This is Thomas Dapino, Danielle's brother."

"Thomas, yes. How you holding up?"

"It's tough. But getting through it. I'm out in San Diego for the funeral. Figured we should talk in person before I went back to New York. The other night I was so stunned by the news I wasn't thinking straight. My mind didn't recall things it should've, things that could be helpful to your investigation."

"That would be great. Our address is—"

"I'm one step ahead of you. Already here, at reception. Why don't you just peek your head out, then I can follow you back to your office and we can talk in private there? Black suit, brown hair, six one."

"Give me a sec."

Tommy hangs up, strolls back to the receptionist.

"So . . . how long you been with the bureau?" she asks.

"Just a few months. A big adjustment going from Quantico to actual fieldwork. I love it though. Couldn't see myself doing anything else. Still getting used to San Diego. Maybe you can show me around sometime?"

"For sure."

"Thomas?" a deep male voice says over his shoulder. In the doorway is a heavyset, late-forties man in suspenders.

"Detective Browing?"

The man nods.

"Great to finally meet you," Tommy says to him, then waves at the receptionist.

Browing makes small talk as he leads Tommy into the Homicide unit, its walls lined with tall filing cabinets, each drawer marked via an intricate alphanumeric codification system. Browing turns into his office, sits at his desk, on it a mug with the title "DAD OF THE YEAR." He collects a notepad and pen and asks, "So what can you tell me?"

Tommy sits across from him. "A guy with a long beard could be involved," he lies.

"Your sister mentioned a man like this? In what context?"

"It wasn't the last time I spoke to her. It was a few months ago, when she still had her apartment. We were talking about something else. A show. And she said every now and then when she was on her couch watching TV, she'd see this guy with a long beard peeking at her through the window."

"Anything else she mention about him?"

"A bandana. He wore a bandana."

Browing's pen scribbles down the page. "Did she call the police?"

"He didn't verbally threaten her or anything. So no, not that I know of. But she was definitely freaked out. Said he had crazed eyes."

"You think this man had something to do with her murder?"

"I don't have any proof. But he sure sounds mentally unstable. It's possible."

"Interesting."

"Anyway, that's all I have. Hopefully it's enough to help."

"I'll look into felon profiles in our database, see what

sort of matches come up on that physical description. Thank you, Mister Dapino."

Tommy stands. "Don't mention it." He shakes Browing's hand and journeys back to the lobby.

"That was quick," the receptionist says.

"Just a meet and greet. He referred me to the SDPD case file for all the details." He pretends to check the time on his phone. "I was hoping to squeeze in some lunch before I went back to the office. I know we have copies there, but I really want to dig in now, do some reading while I eat. If it's not too much trouble, would you mind printing me out one?"

"Not at all."

She types on her computer for about a minute, then walks through an entryway. She returns with a stack of papers secured with a clamp and hands them to Tommy, still warm from the printer. On the top sheet is a Post-it note with her phone number.

"Thanks so much, Kristen," he says. "I'll . . . text you."

"Def. Bye."

He tucks the case file under his arm and leaves.

SIX

Tommy sits at a table in a city library a few blocks from the police station reading the case file, the sun glistening through the domed-glass ceiling onto him and the dozens of others in the three-leveled interior.

Around his hand is a necklace the funeral director gave him this morning, the one Danielle was wearing the night she died. Its charm is two different-sized circles. Tommy guesses the smaller one is supposed to represent Danielle and the larger one the society she was outside of, that no longer accepted her.

According to the document, he was right about her. Even with a bullet in her head, she found the strength to make a brief statement to the officer who rode in the ambulance with her. He's proud about this. Though Danielle had a hippie streak, she was no flake. She was tough when she had to be.

Her statement lacks names, addresses, or license plates for any potential suspects, but does have a description of the man who shot her, apparently a member of a gang based in Tijuana, his most distinct feature a tattoo of a boa constrictor around his neck.

Tommy clenches his jaw thinking about what he said to Danielle before pulling the trigger. Then logs onto the public computer in front of him and conducts a Google search for "gangs in Tijuana." Almost all the recent-news results mention "Los Hombres del Vacio" in their titles. He clicks on the first article, from the *Los Angeles Herald*, headlined, "Atop of a Hill of Bodies."

He learns a large cartel left Tijuana last year, prompting an organized-crime power vacuum. Bands of outlaws battled for control last summer. One called Los Hombres del Vacio emerged the winner. Since then it's accumulated numbers, today dominating all illicit business in Tijuana. Tommy now understands why the FBI is leading Danielle's investigation. An international criminal enterprise is involved, lifting the case into federal jurisdiction.

A beam of overhead sun strikes the computer screen, obscuring the text. Squinting, he fights through the glare as he reads about last summer's turf war. Los Hombres del Vacio became known for a tactic they call "the stump."

When they capture an enemy like a rival or rat, they carve away at the body and seal the wounds to keep the person alive for a week. First they cut off the feet, then the hands, the genitals, the legs, and the arms, the victim chopped down to just a torso and head, conscious in this state for as many as two days before bleeding to death.

Tommy's heartbeat picks up. If Danielle's killer is a member of a Tijuana gang, it's almost certainly this one. And if he heads there to find him, he'll be up against "the stump." Tommy runs a hand through his hair. A voice in his head says not to go. But a second voice, a little louder, insists he must.

It reminds him he's been up against danger of this caliber before when he was a fireman. Like these gangsters, a raging fire lacks a conscience. It destroys while disregarding human life. If Tommy could survive a burning building, he may be able to survive gangland Tijuana.

He logs off the computer, collects the case file, and leaves the library. He gets in his car and drives south. In about thirty miles he reaches the San Ysidro Port of Entry, zooming under a sign with big red letters announcing "MEX-ICO."

SEVEN

Special Agent Clyde Gabor stands at the head of the room in the FBI San Diego field office dedicated to the massacre in the woods four nights ago. The case lead, he addressed the press this morning. Across from him is a junior agent just assigned to the investigation, twenty-six-year-old Jordana Quick.

He nods at a map on the wall behind him, eight red tacks stuck to it, and says, "These are the locations in eight recent missing-persons reports in San Diego County with homeless subjects."

"Police didn't make a connection between these incidents until now?" she asks.

"Addicts made the reports. About their missing addict friends. If you're the filing officer for any of these disappearance claims, you're probably assuming a drifter just ... drifted away. Hopped to another tent, another town, whatever. Cops had no reason to guess murder was involved until they saw what happened to those five people in the woods. Seems like these first eight cases were hardly investigated, let alone linked."

"What would prompt someone to go around San Diego killing homeless people?"

He takes a deep breath. "Not robbery. The victims are penniless. I don't think the motive is psychological either. You know, quenching a thirst for blood. Nothing ritualistic about the carnage the other night. No, seems we're looking at something more complex."

"Like what?"

He points at one of the eight red tacks in the map. "Mission Hills. When the team interviewed people in the encampment where this incident's subjects resided, a man said on the day of the disappearance he saw a White male in a box truck hand a Latino male in an Escalade cash. Danielle Dapino mentioned two White guys, two Latino guys, and those two vehicles in her statement. A transfer of cash tells me some sort of a business relationship is at play here. The White guys must be in charge, paying the Latinos to do work for them."

"Where do the homeless drug abusers fit in?"

"That I don't know."

"Did we put together a sketch of the Caucasian in the truck?"

"Unfortunately the witness was too far away to make out anything beside race and gender." Clyde points at another red tack. "But we have an age range here. A female in the Chula Vista encampment said a few months back two men in a white box truck tried luring her inside with the promise of drugs. She was about to get in, then thought she noticed big knives inside, got nervous, and declined. Said the White men were between forty and fifty, but was drunk during the encounter, and couldn't recall any facial specifics."

"So we have nothing but generic physical descriptions?"

"On the Caucasians. But on one of the Mexicans we have a detail that's actionable. A boa-constrictor tattoo Danielle Dapino saw on his neck."

"Two Mexican gangsters in their twenties. Two middle-aged White men. What's bringing them together on this?"

"No clue."

"The one with the tattoo, Mexican authorities don't know who he is?"

"I passed the description to the FBI's federal-police liaison in Mexico City. No matching records in their criminal database. Which means he's smart, careful to stay out of jail. Even so, I'm sure some police came across him once or twice on the street and have the potential to ID him. But as you're probably aware Agent Quick, many officers south of the border fall victim to the financial imbalances in their districts."

"They take bribes from gangs to keep their mouths shut. Yeah, I get it. What about the DEA? Don't they have undercover agents embedded in Mexico? Did you see if they had any intel on this guy?"

"I checked. No luck. Los Hombres del Vacio operates out of Tijuana, not a traditional narcotics empire like Juarez, where most DEA resources are concentrated. They're a newer gang we don't know much about."

Letting out a long exhale, Jordana leans against the wall. "What now?"

"Pack a bag. Me and you are going to Mexico."

"Give me an hour," she says, heading for the door.

About a minute after she exits, his phone rings. He answers it, "Gabor."

"Hey. It's Browing."

"How's it going, detective?"

A pause. "To be honest . . . not great."

"This case already isn't going great. You're calling me to tell me it just got worse? How is that even possible?"

"It's not about the case. Well, it is. Sort of. Either way, it isn't good. Felt I owed you a call so you're aware. I screwed up."

Clyde starts pacing. "Is that right?"

"More our receptionist. But you can't really blame her. She was tricked. We both were."

"A reporter?"

"A brother."

"Hey, Detective Browing, as a Black man, I've got to tell you, that's not really how you should refer to someone you—"

"No, not brother as in Black guy. A biological brother. Of one of the victims. Danielle Dapino."

"He tried to trick you? What for?"

"A few minutes ago Kristen, our receptionist, comes to my office swooning over some FBI agent I apparently just met with, asking me what I knew about him. So I tell her there was no FBI agent I just met with. And she describes the guy. And I tell her he was Thomas Dapino, Danielle's brother. Then she tells me he pretended he was working with you. And here's the bad part . . . he asked for a copy of the case file. And she gave it."

"What'd he want it for?"

"I don't know."

Clyde speaks with him for a bit longer, collecting all the details from Thomas's station visit, then says, "All right. Thanks for telling me. I got it from here." He ends the call, exits the case room, and sits at his desk.

On his computer he pulls up an FBI web portal connected to every public-records database imaginable and enters "Thomas Dapino" into the search bar. A handful of Americans with that name come back, a few from New York, one around Danielle's age. Clyde selects that result.

Staring back at him is a driver's license photo of a young man with brown eyes, olive skin, and a defined jaw. Clyde can tell from the tops of his shoulders he's in shape, outlines of lean muscle showing through his shirt.

Clyde eyeballs his driver's license data, then navigates to his public records. The first is an employment history from the New York City Fire Department. He was a firefighter at a ladder company in Queens for seven and a half years. Until he was terminated.

The second record is from the New York State Department of Corrections, its start date a bit after the dismissal date from the fire department. He served two years in Attica maximum-security prison, released last month.

An ex-convict is now in possession of sensitive FBI information. Wanting to find out the reason, Clyde picks up his phone and calls the ladder company in Queens where Thomas worked.

A male voice with a heavy New York accent answers.

"I'm looking for whoever is in charge of the firehouse," Clyde says. "Is a lieutenant in?"

After a minute or so, a male voice with a heavier New York accent says, "Lieutenant Connors. Who am I speaking to?"

"I'm an FBI agent in San Diego. Sorry to bother you. I was hoping to just ask a couple questions about a firefighter who used to work at your station."

"Which?"

"Thomas Dapino."

A moment.

"Lieutenant Connors?"

"I'm still here."

"Did you supervise Mister Dapino at all?"

"I brought Tommy up right out of the Academy."

"What was he like?"

"The best firefighter I'd ever seen. Once watched him go into a burning house by himself, move a five-hundred-pound beam off a mother and her two small kids, and carry the three of them out alive."

"Huh."

"Get this, did the whole thing with a broken arm."

"What about his attitude? Was he ever a disciplinary problem?"

"He joked around a lot. Was really good at voices, you

know, impressions. Would take turns doing the guys when we were hanging around the firehouse. Definitely a ball buster. But in a . . . good-spirited way. Never broke the rules."

"How did a kid like that end up in a maximum-security prison?"

Clyde makes out a groan on the other line. "I was just his boss. I'm no shrink."

"Anything could help. It may be relevant to my case. The murder of his sister."

"Word of that got back to Queens. Terrible. Sweet girl, years ago she worked at the diner where I get my bagel every morning. Would always scribble little notes on the paper to-go bags with marker, like 'Stay warm' if it were snowing, that sort of thing. Anyway, Tommy was looking to take on more responsibility in the department. Wanted to keep fighting fires, but also get into the crime fighting side of things."

"Like a fire investigator?"

"You're familiar. At night he was studying for his certification."

"The FBI works with them on a lot of bomb-related incidents."

"Well, Tommy would've been a hell of a good one if you ask me. He isn't just physical, but smart. The sort of mind that's always turning, always questioning. That's what got him into trouble. There was a big fire in town. He didn't buy the official story of how it started. Felt it was arson. Let's just say he looked into it himself . . . a little too closely."

"What happened?"

"I wasn't there. Wouldn't be right for me to just pass you a rumor." A pause. "How is any of this relevant to his sister's murder?"

"He just showed up at a police station in San Diego and lied his way into getting a copy of the confidential case file. If he does something stupid like sell it to the press, it could jeopardize my entire investigation."

Clyde hears a noise through the phone that might be a chuckle.

"Is that funny?" Clyde asks. "You think he might leak it?"

"Oh no. Like I said, I've known the kid for years. And I doubt he wanted it for financial reasons."

"Why did he then?"

Clyde hears that chuckle-like noise again.

"Good luck with your case," the lieutenant says. "I've got to get back to work." He hangs up.

EIGHT

Tommy treads a sidewalk in Zona Norte, Tijuana's red-light district, the main territory of Los Hombres del Vacio according to the *Los Angeles Herald*. Though San Diego is close by, Tijuana seems a different world, the cities' sights and sounds nothing alike.

Many of the storefront doorways along the sidewalk lack signs, others sealed with metal rollup gates scribbled in indecipherable graffiti. Street vendors with carts pitch products in Spanish to Latin pedestrians and broken English to White ones. Prostitutes in skimpy outfits huddle in almost every alleyway.

Tommy's been roaming the city, acclimating himself, gathering ideas for a plan. He calls Josh.

"Sup?" Josh says.

"I need a favor."

"What?"

"Mail me my passport."

"You have a passport?"

"Don't act so damn surprised. Figured if I ever made enough money for that trip to Italy I always wanted to do, I could go."

"You know you're allowed to travel anywhere in the US without a passport?"

"I know that dumbass. I'm not in the US."

"Say what?"

"I'm in Mexico. They didn't check my documents on the way in, but Border Patrol definitely will when I try to get back to America."

"You decided to take a vacation to Mexico after your sister's funeral?"

"I'm not on vacation."

"Well, I don't see a business reason for a maintenance man from Queens to be in Mexico. So what're you doing?"

"The passport's in the closet of my apartment. In a bin on the shelf with my old baseball cards. Hang in front of my building, wait for one of the neighbors to come or go, and slip inside. I have a spare key under my mat. Go in, grab it, overnight it."

"I'm not sending you shit until you tell me what you're doing in Mexico, T."

A pause. "Screw it. I came here to kill the man who shot Danielle. Happy?"

"Christ. I knew you were up to something."

"I'll give you an address in Tijuana. Whatever it costs I'll Venmo—"

"Do you realize this is a horrible idea but you made the choice to do it anyway? Or do you actually think this is a straight-up good idea, like mixing peanut butter with jelly? With you, sometimes I really don't know."

"I don't need a lecture. Just mail the damn thing."

"The feds are on Danielle's case. Let them take care of this."

Tommy kicks a metal gate over a doorway, a thud radiating across the sidewalk, a couple people staring. "I'm not trusting this to the feds," he yells into the phone. "They don't know my sister. They're just logging hours for a paycheck."

"A little cynical, no?"

"No. People don't give a crap about anyone but themselves, their families, and a few close friends."

"Who are you even looking for? You know the person who shot Danielle?"

"I know he's from here. And I'm about to find out his name."

"How?"

"Hookers."

"As in hookers, hookers?"

"As in hookers, hookers."

"As in *Dangerous Delusions*, a new one-man play starring Thomas Dapino."

"Soliciting prostitution is legal in Tijuana, but that doesn't mean the girls still don't have handlers to find them clients and protect them from muggings, rough johns, whatever else. The guy who killed Danielle belongs to the gang that runs every vice in town. Drugs, gambling, prostitution. Tijuana's hookers must regularly spend time around these men, a good chance one will know the guy I'm after."

"Wait. Did you say gang?"

"Relax. I'm not going to question any gangster directly. I can get all I need from a prostitute."

"Approaching a hooker instead isn't much safer, homie. If this gang runs all prostitution like you said, they'd banish a working girl who crossed them, probably do a lot worse. Any hooker's loyalty is with them. If you say one wrong thing and she senses you're after her employer, she's going to clam up around you, but tell someone about you. And if that happens, she's the last chick you'll ever have sex with because you probably won't have balls after."

"I'm not having sex with her. I just need to talk. Are you mailing me my passport or what?"

"Not unless you bounce from Mexico as soon as you get

39

it. And skip this whole . . . I don't know what you'd even call it. Cracking a multiple homicide isn't a one-person job. The feds have bodies, systems, software. Promise me you'll leave this to them and I'll roll to your apartment right now."

"I can't make that promise. I can do this without the feds."

"Emotions are running high. Understandable. When you chill out and come to your senses, call me back and I'll send the passport. I love you, buddy."

"Love you too."

Tommy hangs up. He leans against the gate he kicked, folds his arms, and thinks. He'll solve the passport problem later. The moment he questions a prostitute, he'll no longer be an anonymous American tourist in the eyes of this city. Instead a man pressing down on its underworld. He must dedicate all his mental energy to staying alive.

He stops at a food cart for a burrito, savoring every bite as this may be his last meal. If things go wrong, sneaking around in the dark would be easier than the light. He'll approach a prostitute once the sun begins setting.

NINE

A reddish sunset wraps Tijuana as Tommy steps into an alley with three hookers, knee-length white socks riding their toned legs toward short plaid skirts.

"Evening," he says to the trio. "I'm looking for a date. And I'm looking for the whole package. Quality conversation included. Call me sappy. So . . . anybody speak good English?"

"I know English pretty okay," the one with dyed-blond hair says.

"And I know who I'm spending the next hour with." He holds out his arm. "A bilingual beauty."

She giggles, interlocking her arm with his. "You're funny, mister."

He hands her five twenties he took out of an ATM, his checking account now the lowest its ever been. "This work?"

She nods and slips the cash in her purse. "I have room we can use."

She leads him around the corner to a building. The security guard, a three-hundred-pounder with hair gel in his goatee, smiles at her and says, "Hola Gabby."

"Taking one upstairs, Coco," she tells him, pushing open the door.

They enter a strip club. Tommy's escort, apparently named Gabby, walks him past a performer in a trashy-nurse costume jutting her boobs toward men seated at the stage, then takes him up a two-story staircase to red-curtain-covered private cubicles.

She struts into one, inside a twin mattress with a mirror above it. "Get comfortable," she says. Tommy sits on the bed. "For a hundred, usually you get just BJ. But you cute. So you can put it anywhere but my ass." She wriggles out of her crop top, unhooks her bra, and begins unbuttoning his jeans.

He lays his hands atop hers, stopping her. "How about you just dance for a little?"

She shrugs, then sways her hips, way behind pace of the techno track playing.

"I was in this part of Tijuana last spring for a bachelor party," he says. "Was insane. We were mixing it up with this local dude. Was hoping to sync with him again. Maybe you'd know him. Like twenty-five. Shaved dome. Has a really intense tattoo. A boa constrictor going around his neck. About five eight, one seventy."

She stops dancing. "What about him?"

"You know him?"

"Why?"

"I want to buy something from him."

The song changes to a heavy-metal track with Spanish lyrics.

"I met him once," she says. "Like two months ago. He come into club while I dance. Spend lots of money. But not very nice to the girls. What you want to buy from a guy like that?"

"I'll be honest with you. He sold me and my friends some banging coke last time we were in TJ. If I knew his name I could try to look him up on social media and message him, see if he could hook me up again."

She taps her nose. "Plenty people you get good coke from in Tijuana. No need him, silly."

"I hear you. But his stuff was bonkers. You met him, you must at least know his first name, right?"

"I worked all night. No sleep." She yawns. "Too tired to remember name I hear two months ago. But my friend here will know. First name, last too. You really want, I will ask right now. One minute. Okay?"

"Yes, definitely. Thank you."

She walks out of the cubicle.

That was easier than he figured. All he needs to do now is relax for a minute until a pretty naked woman delivers him the gangster's name.

A minute passes.

Then two.

Then five.

She comes back. With her is a jacked guy wearing a half-zipped leather jacket with no shirt underneath. He looks mad. She looks scared.

She tells Tommy, "My friend Raul is manager of club. He know man you ask about. When I go to his office to see what man name was, Raul said he wanted speak to you." When she mentioned she was asking her friend for the info, Tommy assumed it was a stripper.

Not Raul.

If this guy manages a club with dancers doubling as prostitutes, chances are he isn't so much her friend but her pimp. A gold chain with a clown-face medallion hangs from his neck, the symbol associated with Mexican gangs as Tommy learned from his stint in Attica. He must be in Los Hombres del Vacio.

"You American?" the pimp asks.

"I am," Tommy says with a smile. "Hoping to lock down some good blow like most of the other Americans here."

"Blow, huh? Gabby says you bought some from my

buddy last time you were here. That accurate?"

"Best shit I ever had. Straight up. Got any on you?"

"So my buddy's seen you? He'd recognize you?"

Tommy's heart gallops. "Absolutely."

The pimp takes his cellphone from his jacket pocket and snaps a photo of Tommy's face. He clicks a few buttons. "Just sent him your pic. We'll see if he knows you."

The text reply will expose Tommy as a liar, then to gang payback. He can't just stand here waiting for that fate.

So he yanks the mirror off the wall and smashes it over the pimp's head. The hooker shrieks as he crumbles to the floor among broken glass.

"Puta," the pimp screams, blood pouring down his forehead.

Tommy runs out of the cubicle onto the stairs. The bartender on the first floor lifts a shotgun from under the sink. Cocks it.

"Shit," Tommy says to himself, retreating back to the balcony.

To his left the pimp is hurrying toward him. To his right is a dead end. His only option is an unmarked door.

Tommy opens it. Enters an office. Bolts to its window. He digs his hands under the blinds and slides open the pane, the summer heat on his face. Three stories to ground level. From his firefighter experience evacuating buildings, he realizes he's too high for a jump, a broken leg likely.

About six feet to the left of the window a drainpipe runs down the strip club's facade. That'll work.

He raises his feet to the bottom edge of the window frame, then springs off it. He soars and clasps the pipe. His legs pendulum right, then left, then grip the metal. He maneuvers downward.

His feet reach the alley pavement. He starts sprinting away. However, a body almost twice as heavy as his tackles him from behind.

"Stay still," the squashing man says. Tommy recognizes the voice's owner. The bouncer with the gel in his goatee.

In under a minute a gold clown-face medallion speckled in blood sways into view. The pimp kneels next to Tommy.

"Your time with Gabby is over, bro," the pimp says with a smirk. "And your time with me is just beginning. I hate to warn you, but my dancing isn't as good as hers." He laughs, then howls at the setting sun as a wolf would the moon.

TEN

Tommy can't feel his hands. The pimp zip-tied them behind his back, tight enough to cut off circulation, before throwing him in his BMW.

The pimp idles on a street corner just outside Zona Norte, his window down. A twentyish Latino in a baggy tee shirt and shorts comes out of an apartment complex with something under his arm.

When he reaches the car, Tommy sees it's a folded blue tarp. He and the pimp converse in Spanish. Though Tommy can't understand the language, he can tell they're deriding him, their eyes flicking in his direction as they sneer.

The pimp takes the tarp from his associate and drives east for about ten minutes. He parks in the driveway of a house with a brown roof, collects the tarp, and pulls Tommy out of the car.

The pimp knocks on the door. Silence beside the grate

of the pimp's teeth on a toothpick. The door opens. Standing before Tommy is a man with a boa-constrictor tattoo around his neck.

Danielle's killer.

Tommy's instincts tell him to attack. But he refrains. An offensive right now with tied hands would be a guarantee of his own death.

The pimp shoves Tommy into the house, then across the den. He opens a door to a boiler room. He unfolds the tarp and lays it on the floor, an ease to his motions as if he's done this before.

A metallic clang. The gangster with the tattoo drags a chair across the house, a similar ease to him. He positions it on the tarp. The pimp grasps Tommy's shoulders and pushes him onto the seat.

The gangster with the tattoo unsheathes from his waist a knife with a blade almost a foot tall. And Tommy deduces the tarp's purpose. To collect the profusion of blood about to spill from him.

His breathing speeds up. If he doesn't lie his way out of this in the next few seconds, that knife is sure to hack him into a stump.

"You a cop?" the gangster asks.

Everything Tommy knows about him is confined to Danielle's case-file statement, his mind rushing to recollect as much as possible. Gangbangers are predators. And the only thing a predator respects is an even bigger one.

"I'll tell you who I am," Tommy says, impersonating the voice of an Italian mobster he grew up around in Queens. He stands, looks down on Danielle's shorter killer, and says, "I'm your worst nightmare, douchebag."

The two Mexicans glance at each other, squinting.

"Looking for coke at the strip club was an act," Tommy says. "I wanted to find out where your ass was for a more important reason. I planned to roll up on you and deliver a message from my boss. Until this idiot in the leather jacket ruined my flow."

The pimp barks something in Spanish, likely profane.

"I work for Frank Lunezzi," Tommy tells the man with the tattoo.

"Lunezzi? I don't know no Lunezzi."

"You probably never heard of him because you deal in peanuts. He deals in steak. Tijuana is small. It's scraps. Frank Lunezzi is head of one of the mafia's five families in New York. Runs an organized-crime empire from there all the way to Cali. Call any one of your drug distributors in San Diego and ask them who my boss is. Go on."

The gangster says nothing, his unblinking eyes surveying Tommy's expression.

"Hello?" Tommy says. "When you got your head buzzed, did the barber shave out all the brains too?"

The gangster glares. Then removes his phone from the back-right pocket of his jeans and taps the screen as if to unlock it, his other hand steadying the knife on Tommy's throat.

Tommy tries to appear calm as an outgoing call rings, quieting the pump of air out his nose. A voice through the phone answers in Spanish and the two converse, Tommy making out "Frank Lunezzi" though not much else.

The gangster hangs up, slips his phone back in his jeans' pocket, and asks Tommy, "So what problem Lunezzi have with me?"

"He knows you killed those people in California the other night."

"What people?"

"Good try. He owns all sorts of businesses he launders money through. Got security cameras on the outsides facing the street. They're on twenty-four hours a day. One of these shops is in San Diego, less than a mile from the woods you were in."

"I don't know about no woods in San Diego."

"Well, Lunezzi's camera does. After the story broke on the news, he had some guys check out that night's footage. Spotted an Escalade driving toward the crime scene. So clear you can even see the victims' faces through the damn window. Not to mention a plate number. We dug into it. Tied it to a driver's license in Mexico. Yours."

"Bullshit."

"Hey, believe what you want to believe. But when dealing with the Italian mafia, ignorance never means bliss."

"Show me proof. Proof you get me on camera."

"Show me fifty grand. That's Lunezzi's message. The FBI doesn't know our tape exists. If we give it to them, they'll have enough evidence to extradite you. Or, you give me fifty thousand dollars in cash and this all goes away."

"Don't threaten us," the pimp shouts. "You have a knife to your neck. You don't make threats. We do."

"Sure, you can kill me," Tommy says. "But . . . my crew knows I'm down here. And if I don't make it home to New York, they have instructions to mail the video to the feds."

The one with the tattoo says, "Show me video. On your phone."

"It's not on there. It's on a thumb drive in my car. Happy to get it, upload it to the internet, then play it for you on my phone. But only if I can expect fifty large waiting for me when I come back."

"How do we know all of this isn't a lie?" the pimp asks. "Fine, our guy in Cali heard of Frank Lunezzi. But how can we be sure you actually work for him?"

"You can't. But is that really a set of dice you want to roll? If I am telling the truth, and you disregard it, your buddy here will spend the rest of his life in an American prison, maybe even get the needle."

Silence for a few seconds.

"Eleven o'clock," the one with the tattoo says. "I have cash in safe at my business office. Meet there. Calle Toro, number eight thirty-nine. But you come with no video, I stick this knife all the way up your ass and turn it in circles."

"If you cut these damn things off my wrists I'll shake on it," Tommy says.

The gangster lowers the knife from Tommy's throat to

the zip-ties and severs them. Tommy shakes his hand and says, "See you at eleven," though has no intention of showing up.

He steps out of the boiler room, exits the house, and takes a long breath of air, a pleasure he was close to never experiencing again.

His priority was getting out of that man's house alive. With that behind him, Tommy refocuses on his original goal. Killing him.

He glances over his shoulder, noting in his mind the number by the door. He treads to the end of the block and glimpses the street sign, making another mental note. If he is going to kill a gangster in his own home, he'll need the surprise factor on his side. He'll return to this address later armed with a plan.

He begins the long walk to his car parked near the strip club, his mind evaluating options for tonight's move.

ELEVEN

Tommy paces through Zona Norte's center, only a couple more blocks to his car. The sun low in the sky, darkness descending on the city, the nightlife crowd spills into the streets. A man with a smiling-face belt buckle in front of an open doorway promises Tommy he can buy anything he needs inside for a low price. Tommy ignores him. The man repeats himself, *stressing* anything.

"You're an asshole," a different voice says over Tommy's shoulder.

He turns to it. A Black man in his fifties. "I get that from people a lot. But usually I at least have to piss them off first. What'd I do to you, walk by too loudly? You have sensitive ears or something, man?"

"Cut the shit."

Tommy recognizes him. The face, the voice. On the television this morning. The FBI agent at the press conference. Clyde Gabor.

"What is this?" Clyde asks. "Some vigilante thing?"

"I came down here to fight. But not how you're envisioning. International karate tournament." Tommy strikes a kung fu pose.

"What is that supposed to be, New York sarcasm?"

Tommy looks around, wondering how he found him. Clyde points at a four-story building and says, "My partner and I have been conducting surveillance of gang members from the motel. I spotted you from your DMV photo. Was easy. Probably thought you were really slick after you left the police station? You fooled some cops. But you won't fool us."

Next to Clyde is an attractive girl in her mid-twenties with green eyes and straight black hair. Tommy glimpses her, then says to Clyde, "So I lied to a receptionist. You looking to arrest me? Lying isn't a crime last I checked."

"No. It just makes you an asshole."

"You seem tense. That guy back there with the weird belt buckle seems to be selling all sorts of stress-relieving goods and services, FYI. Maybe he can square you up."

"What you did today was irresponsible. Detective Browing has a job to keep a community safe. And you hit him with some bullshit about . . . what was it? A man with a long beard in a bandana. You ate up more than an hour of his afternoon with a scavenger hunt through the computer for Captain Kidd lookalikes."

"I wasn't consciously going for a pirate motif with that description, but now that you bring it up maybe—"

"You took time away from real work on another case. A real murderer out there maybe got away because of your distraction. Did that possibility even cross your mind? Did you take a second to consider the repercussions of walking into the Homicide unit of a big-city police department and spreading nonsense all over?"

Tommy looks away. Scratches his face.

Clyde says, "Not to mention, you apparently got the receptionist's hopes up about a date. Now she feels terrible you were just manipulating her."

"This was . . . instructive. Thanks for everything. But I've got to get going." Tommy slips his headphones in and walks toward his car.

Clyde steps in front of him. "I get where you're coming from, Dapino. I have a sister too. And if something like this ever happened to her, a desire . . . for revenge might come over me too. But you don't know what you're up against. The gangsters down here aren't like the ones back in America. They operate outside the law. They can basically do whatever they want to you without consequence. If you keep going down this path, you're going to wind up dead."

"You just outlined in detail the glaring level of asshole I am. Now you're trying to convince me you have my safety in mind? Which is it?"

"Let's talk in the motel. Someone out here could hear us. It's dangerous."

"Is that the reason or do you just want to get back under a fan? Those pit stains are screaming at me."

Clyde peeks at the armpit sweat marks on his shirt. "That's . . . look, it's hot. Who cares? We have more important things to discuss."

His partner fights back a grin. "Sorry," she tells him.

"You busted me, Dapino," Clyde says. "I perspire, just like everyone else. Congratulations. I'm trying to do you a favor here, trying to help you step out of this mess piling up around you."

"You're the one who can help me, huh?"

"That's right."

"I'm just some schmuck who doesn't know what he's doing and you, the big FBI guy, are here to show me the error in my ways and keep me safe. Is that it?"

"I wouldn't phrase it like that. But you're not far off."

"Well then, big FBI guy, someone as skilled and experienced as you, a member of such a distinguished law-enforcement organization, must have my sister's killer in custody by now. So when's the trial date? I definitely don't want to miss that."

Clyde bites his lip, nodding.

"Oh," Tommy says. "So nobody in custody yet. I suppose that's excusable. The main suspect though, the gangster with the boa-constrictor tattoo around his neck, I'm at least assuming the FBI has some identifying information on him by now." Tommy smirks. "Like . . . I don't know . . . his address." He starts playing his grunge rock and strides toward the car.

Clyde jogs up to him. Tommy pauses the music. Clyde asks, "What the hell is that supposed to mean?"

Tommy shrugs, steps around him.

Clyde says, "If you have information I should know and you're keeping it from me, you'd be obstructing a federal investigation. Not a good look for a guy with a prior. So tell me what you have before your ass ends up back in prison."

"You know what's not a good look? You being four days into my sister's case and finding nothing."

Clyde's partner says, "We have a lot more than what's in the San Diego Police Department's file you stole."

Tommy stops walking.

She says, "After we took the case over from Browing, we looked into events he didn't. The takeaways are all documented in the FBI file. Which you don't have."

"What sort of takeaways?"

"Danielle didn't die in an isolated incident. Something a lot bigger is going on here. We probably shouldn't tell you what we've learned. But if you play ball with us, maybe we can trade. What we know for what you know."

She glances at Clyde, as if for his approval. He huffs. But nods in agreement.

She asks Tommy, "So . . . swap?"

He holds his stare on her for a while, then laughs to himself. And runs a hand through his hair.

TWELVE

Tommy leans against a wall in the FBI motel room beside a surveillance telescope on a tripod. He watches Clyde on a phone call with a federal-police contact in Mexico City. Tommy's eyes drift to his partner, Jordana, sitting on the edge of the bed. Her legs are crossed in a fitted, pinstripe skirt, the shadows of the room bringing out the contours of her cheekbones.

Clyde hangs up and announces, "Carlos Ayala." He claps his hands.

"So my info checked out," Tommy says. "I held up my end of the bargain. Your turn."

Clyde clicks the keys on a laptop. "Just pulled up the FBI file. Have at it."

Tommy sits at the desk. Views notes on missing-persons reports and witness interviews. Soon learns his sister's murder was part of a baffling string of attacks all over San

Diego likely organized by one of the White men from the box truck.

"What was your intention with Ayala?" Clyde asks him.

"I already told you. I'm just down here for a karate tournament."

"Well, if you were banking on using your karate skills to kill him, don't." Clyde lights a cigarette. "He may have pulled the trigger on Danielle. But whoever is at the top of all this is even more responsible for her death. He ordered Ayala to pull it."

"So what, just because Ayala has a boss, he gets a pass? To me, sounds like both of these freaks need to go down."

"And the FBI will bring them down. We all just need to be smart about it."

"Smart like you were the last four days?"

"Things are different now. We have a name. Because of you. Thanks, really. And I can assure you it makes our job simpler. The roadblocks we hit the last four days are gone."

Tommy gazes out the window, the neon lights of Zona Norte bars bleeding through the curtain fabric. "Theoretically, if Ayala were to say step in front of a bus, how does that prevent you from pursuing the White guy he's working for?"

"Nothing can prevent us from doing anything," Jordana says. "Having Ayala around just makes strategizing easier. These crime-syndicate investigations work like chess games. We can leverage a smaller piece on the board to get closer to the big one."

"I was specific with you guys. Told you everything that happened at the strip club and Ayala's house. Appreciate the metaphor, but I'd prefer an actual explanation."

Clyde replies, "Agent Quick, the Mexican police, and I will question Ayala tonight. I'll threaten him the same way you did when you were pretending to be an Italian mobster. With extradition to the US. Except I won't be pretending. Once he's scared, I offer him a deal. He gives up the name of the leader, I take the death penalty off the table. Ayala still goes to trial in America. Still likely ends up in prison the rest of his life. We've got it from here." Clyde opens the door as if suggesting Tommy leave. "Thanks again for the address."

Tommy stares him down. "Don't mention it."

Jordana unzips a bag in the corner and pulls out a cellphone. She taps on the screen and hands it to Tommy. "This is a secure device. If you get into any trouble with Los Hombres del Vacio before you drive back to California and need help, I just put my number in the contact book. Don't hesitate."

He smirks. "Don't worry. Hesitation isn't a problem of mine." He exits the room.

THIRTEEN

Tommy steps out of the motel onto the crowded Zona Norte sidewalk, the sky the color of ash. He calls Josh.

"So you came to your senses?" Josh asks.

"I've got to kill two of them."

"Ugh. Two who?"

"One gangster and his boss."

"The boss isn't a gangster too?"

"White, likely American. I don't know who he is exactly."

"I know who you are exactly. A—"

"Crazy person? I don't care. Do you know how to break into a phone?"

"Whose phone?"

"Just . . . in general. If I got my hands on a cell piece and it was locked with a passcode, could you guide me to hack my way through it so I could see all the texts and stuff?"

"Ah, a twist. So I'll be bestowing my magical abilities onto you."

"It's not magic. People break into phones all the time."

"Yeah, like the FBI."

"I met them. They don't know what they're doing."

"What?"

"The two agents on Danielle's case. I found the guy who shot her. And they mooched his name off of me. They think this banger is going to rat out his boss if they flex on him a little. I knew cats like that in Attica. They don't rat."

"What does that have to do with a phone?"

"I kill him. Then nab his cell. You show me how to break into it. Chances are he'll have a bunch of messages from his boss. Once I peep them, I'll know who the top dog is. I go after his ass next."

"Sounds like you're going to get bit."

"Bite me."

"You're doing all this by yourself?"

"Dead up."

"No. Dead you. Let's say you murk this gangster. You'll still be trapped on gang terrain. Without a passport to escape. This guy's buddies will scour every corner of Mexico for you. And likely find you. Even if you grab his phone, tunnel into it, and see who the boss is, you'll probably never make it back to America to go after him."

Tommy cracks his knuckles. "Maybe. Still, not going to quit."

"I get that. And though I'm not encouraging any of this . . . any of it at all . . . if you're moving forward, I want you to do it in a way that maximizes your odds of living. You're my best friend, man. I want to see you again."

"I mean . . . yeah, same. What sort of way are you talking about?"

"I bet those two FBI agents would also be interested to see what's on the phone. They could—"

"No way."

"Listen, T. Just—"

"I'm not working with them."

"Did you even consider the benefits? One, they have

guns and a ton of training. If you cruise into gang territory with them on your side, it'll be an even fight. Two, they're feds, can talk to Border Patrol and get you back into America ASAP without a passport. And three, the FBI's decryption technology is as close to magic as you could get. If you pocket that phone, there's a small chance I can show you how to circumvent the passcode. But with them, it's a guarantee."

"They're feds. They stick with their dumb procedures. They're not into any cowboy shit."

"They learned the killer's name from you, right? And I have a feeling you applied a healthy dose of cowboy shit to get it. If they were as rigid about procedure as you're suggesting, they would've avoided your intel on sheer principle."

"I don't know."

"Think about it."

"Yeah, yeah. Peace."

Tommy hangs up. Then opens Google on his phone. He enters "Clyde Gabor" and, clicking on results from newspaper websites, learns he's led quite a few successful narcotics busts.

Tommy types "Jordana Quick" into Google. A post on the FBI website from a couple years ago lists her as one of Quantico's annual graduates. No newspaper articles show up. Tommy supposes that makes sense since she's younger than Clyde, likely worked just a fraction of the cases he has. But her youth should be cause for profiles on Facebook, Instagram, and other social-media sites. Google's returned none.

Before graduating from Quantico twenty months ago, Jordana Quick seemingly never existed.

FOURTEEN

Clyde opens the door to an interrogation room in a Tijuana police station. He, a Mexican cop, and Jordana file inside. Carlos Ayala sits in front of them on a chair, his feet up on the table. Clyde glimpses the policeman, expecting him to tell Ayala to get his boots off his table. But he says nothing.

"You speak English?" Clyde asks Ayala.

"Only learned so I can do business with Americans. I like doing business with Americans. They overpay."

"Who paid you in San Diego from the window of the white truck?"

"I don't know what you talking about."

"Your business partner. The man who hired you to shoot all those homeless people in the woods. What's his name?"

"Maybe you show me video recording of me with him and it make me remember."

Clyde smirks.

"Oh," Ayala says. "What the matter? You don't have video recording?"

"One of your victims survived. We have an eyewitness statement attesting a Latino with your snake tattoo was her shooter. She also cited an Escalade. A vehicle that happens to be registered to you."

"A lot of Latinos have Escalades. A lot have snake tattoos."

"Not a lot have both."

"But enough do to force you come up with even more proof. This survivor woman you talk about, she is still alive I guess? She will point me out in a lineup?"

"I'm giving you a chance here to save yourself from the death penalty. Are you really too naive to see that?"

"I'm not naive one. You are."

Clyde snickers. "How so?"

"I know who I am. I live as nature intended. You a faker."

"Nature intended you to be a murderer?"

"Murder is bad name invented by people for a very natural thing. Look at animal kingdom. Animal kill each other all the time. Part of life."

"Humans aren't animals."

"They are. Just smarter kind. But smarts can be bad. With smarts comes denial. Regular animals no live in denial."

"Well, I'm not a murderer like you. I have nothing to deny."

Ayala leers at Jordana, licks his lips. Then turns back to Clyde and asks, "How many times a day you think about putting your dick in your little assistant?"

Clyde slams his fist on the table. "Watch it shithead."

"Simple question. How many times a day? Two? Five?"

"She's not my assistant. She's a federal agent. She can come down on your slimy ass just as fast as I can."

"See, you no want to answer. You change subject. You get so mad about question because you know you do what I ask about. But no admit. It only natural to want to shove dick inside something that look like that. You have a lot more to deny than you pretend."

"I assure you I'm not pretending about a lethal injection in the US."

"Look at you, doing work of American government like good little ant. Government don't care about you. Why you care about them?"

"I didn't come to Mexico for a civics lesson from an illiterate criminal. You going to accept your one chance to make a deal with me or keep babbling?"

"Every nation that ever been created, been result of war. America included. One group of people kill other, take land. Then when winning group in charge, they make laws to their citizens that say no can kill each other. And stupid people like you think they sacred."

"So you're saying you committed that homicide in the woods because you were somehow justified?"

"I don't know what you talking about."

"The FBI has the full cooperation of Mexico City on this case. We have a bevy of ballistics data from the crime scene. It's only a matter of time before we match you to the murder weapon."

"You no have proof to charge me with any crime now, yes?"

"We will."

"So then maybe I see you in time, detective."

"I'm not a detective."

"Same thing." Ayala stands. Blows a kiss to Jordana. Then leaves.

Clyde lights a cigarette. "Sorry you were subjected to that," he tells her.

"I'm a big girl." Her phone rings. "Yeah?" she says into it. "Yes . . . Well . . . I'll see . . . Right . . . Bye." She hangs up.

"Who was that?" Clyde asks.

"Dapino. He wants to meet with us."

FIFTEEN

Clyde sits in the driver's seat of his idling Chevy Tahoe, Jordana in the passenger's, Tommy the back. The smell of cigarettes wafts off Clyde's clothes, filling the car.

"No," he says.

"Why not?" Tommy asks.

"If I want Ayala's phone records, I'll go through the phone company. Hit them with a subpoena."

"Ayala is a career criminal. You really think he uses a number registered under his real name? He must rock a burner. To get the data from it, we need to be in possession of the actual phone."

"You're . . . fine, that's a good point. But still. This is a bad idea."

"How did your interrogation with him go?"

"That's confidential."

Tommy chuckles. "So really shitty then."

"What're you specifically proposing? How would this tactically work?"

"When I was in Ayala's boiler room, I saw where he kept his phone, back-right pocket. I can pickpocket it."

"How're you going to get close enough without him getting all suspicious?"

"He's expecting me. I have an eleven-PM meeting scheduled with him, remember? I'd show up."

"You have a meeting with him to present a surveillance video that doesn't exist."

"Yes. That's an obstacle. We'll have to get around it."

"We?"

"Believe me, the last thing I wanted to do was get you involved. But . . . our chances of success go up if we work together."

Clyde turns to Jordana and says, "This is getting even better. First I thought Dapino just wanted our blessing to do some wacko shit on his own. Now I'm hearing we're supposed to be active participants."

She folds her arms. "I actually don't hate the idea."

Tommy clenches his fist. "Boom. Agent Quick coming in hot with logic."

"You've got to be kidding me?" Clyde says to her. "Do you realize how against bureau protocol this is?"

"I know. But the search warrant for Ayala still hasn't come in yet. Even if he did have the murder weapon lying around his house, after he left the police station, I can assure you he removed it, dumped it in the ocean. Without hard evidence hanging over his head, we're not going to be able to scare him into giving up his boss. The data on his burner might be our only hope."

"Not only is this completely against FBI code, but whatever info is on Ayala's phone won't be worth crap if a judge rules it inadmissible, decides it's improperly acquired evidence."

Tommy says, "A judge won't have to hear about it. The phone is just a stepping-stone from Ayala to his boss. After you find out who he is, the FBI can investigate him, look for evidence tying him to the crime. That would be shown in court, not the stuff on the phone."

Jordana says, "If we find physical evidence on the boss, we can lean on him to give up Ayala and everyone else who was in the woods that night. This burner could effectively wipe out the entire ring."

Clyde is quiet for a while. "I'd be lying if I said this didn't make sense on a level. But still. I have a bad feeling about it. This just isn't how the FBI operates."

"When you first wanted to be an agent, was it because you were inspired to follow some instructions manual or put away criminals?" Tommy asks. "You can't do both this time." He points at the console clock. "And you need to pick one before eleven o'clock."

SIXTEEN

Tommy jogs beside Jordana through the aisle labeled "Cocina/Kitchen" in a Tijuana Super-Mart. With a hurried hand, he takes a pasta-cooking pot off a shelf and loads it into their cart.

"You've made one of these before?" she asks.

"No. But they taught us all about them when I was in the fire department. It'll work."

She glimpses her watch. "We'll have enough time to put it all together before we have to head to the meeting?"

"It'll be close." He hustles toward another aisle.

She keeps pace at his side. "Don't do anything stupid tonight."

"What's that supposed to mean?"

"You're lucky Agent Gabor agreed to your burner-phone proposition. Let's keep it at that. Don't push it."

"Push it into what?"

"Come on."

He grabs a pool-volleyball net off a shelf and dumps it into the cart. "You come on."

"Why you came down here in the first place."

"I came down here for the same reason you did. Danielle."

"I came to make an arrest. You came to commit a murder."

"When did I say that?"

"You don't have the authority to arrest anyone. The only type of justice at your disposal is murder."

"I wouldn't consider it murder. He killed my sister. It's different."

"So you're owning up to it?"

"No. Just . . . in theory."

"Well, in theory, if an FBI agent witnesses a homicide, even if the victim did in fact shoot the assailant's sister, that FBI agent would have an obligation to detain the assailant. I just want to make sure we're clear on that before we visit Ayala."

"I'm taking his phone tonight. That's it. If I happen to pay him another visit in the future, I'll make sure no FBI agents are around."

"Let the chess game play out. We'll win that way. No need for any future visits."

"So it's a double standard then?"

"What?"

"When an FBI agent kills a criminal, they're a hero. If I did it, I'm just some vigilante psycho, right?"

"FBI agents are not allowed to blow away suspects they have a grudge with. We're authorized to use force to defend ourselves or others in danger."

"And when you guys shoot someone not in defense, the bureau uses its power to alter the story to make it look legit. A win-win for you."

She stops jogging. "Apologize."

He looks at her over his shoulder. "For what?"

"I luckily haven't had to rely on my weapon. And if I ever do, it wouldn't be in cold blood. If other agents out there have done that, I promise you the bureau wouldn't stick up for them."

"Whatever. Let's go. We've got more crap to get."

"Apologize to me first."

"I don't do apologies. Most people are too sensitive. If I did, I'd waste half my life saying sorry to them, and the other half saying sorry to myself for letting them suck me into their BS."

"Gabor was right. You are an asshole."

She strides to him. He wheels the cart into another aisle, tosses in a spool of cotton yarn and a box of matches.

"All those violent lunatics you must come across, you really never had to pull the trigger once?" he asks.

"I wouldn't necessarily call them violent lunatics. Most people we apprehend are . . . misguided. Born into bad situations. After they're caught, a lot learn where they went wrong. Reform in prison."

He laughs. "Horseshit. I was in prison, Attica. Not exactly a sanctuary for reform. Almost all those guys come in bad. And stay bad."

"It's odd you'd have a social outlook that's so . . . bleak."

"Society can be bleak. Most people outside of prison are just as messed up as the ones in it. Just do a better job repressing their urges."

"Agent Gabor told me you were apparently a pretty good fireman."

"Where'd he hear that?"

"He looked into you."

"What's that supposed to mean?"

"Exactly what it sounds like."

"Well, firefighting was a long time ago."

"Just a couple years ago."

"I stopped keeping track."

"When a fireman rushes into a burning building, he doesn't ask questions about the people trapped inside. He rescues them. Assumes they deserve to be rescued just because they're . . . human beings. To do the job, you have to give humanity the benefit of the doubt."

"Like I said, I don't do the job anymore. What're you even implying?"

"I'm just wondering when you stopped giving humanity the benefit of the doubt."

"You sound like one of those well-educated people who knows nothing about the real world."

"You sound like one of those uneducated people who knows a lot about the tainted version of the world in his own head."

"So you guys also found out I never went to college? Did you look up my dental records in your system too? Jesus Christ."

She closes her eyes. "Sorry. That just came out. I didn't mean it as a knock about college."

"Don't apologize for anything. You'll thank me for the tip." He adds a roll of duct tape to the cart. A screwdriver. A saw. A few bottles of cleaning substances.

He rolls the cart toward the row of checkout registers. A familiar red-and-silver glint in the camping section catches his attention. A pick-head axe, a smaller version of the one he used in the fire department. He stops and stares at it.

"What?" she asks.

He takes the eighteen-inch axe off the wall.

"What do we need that for?" she asks.

"We had all sorts of surprises during fires. My axe got me out of a lot of them." He sets it in the cart. "Can't hurt to have one around later."

She smirks. "I thought you weren't a firefighter any-more."

He rolls his eyes.

They pay, then drive to the FBI's motel. "Yo," Tommy says, entering the room with the bags of supplies.

Clyde sits at the desk clicking the laptop mouse. "Almost done."

"Nice." Tommy sets the new cooking pot on the room's one-burner stove, fills it with water, and flips on the heat. Jordana watches at his side. He dumps the package of matches into the water.

"What's that for?" she asks.

"The match tips. We want to boil them down. Creates an explosive residue." He opens the box for the volleyball net and raps his knuckles on one of its two PVC posts. "We seal the residue into a length of PVC with the right combo of cleansers . . . voila, we've got a pipe bomb."

He saws the end of the post into a six-inch segment. Then walks to Clyde, staring at the computer screen over his shoulder. A video-editing application is open.

"That is looking fresh," Tommy says.

"Get up close to Ayala," Clyde says. "Tell him you have a copy of the surveillance video online, then open this URL on your phone. I'm about to send it."

In a few seconds Tommy feels a vibration in his pocket. He pulls out the secure phone Jordana gave him, taps the link Clyde just sent, then a play button. A white circle spins against a black background, beneath it the caption "Loading."

"How long you think you can stall him with that before he knows something is up?" Clyde asks.

"A half-minute maybe."

"Agent Quick?"

Jordana steps to them. "Yeah?"

"I'll drop you off first to get in position." Clyde closes the editing window on the computer and pulls up another one. On it is an aerial image of the business address where Tommy is supposed to meet Ayala. It appears to be a junkyard. Clyde points at an alley behind the office. "This seem okay?"

"Yeah, that's close enough," she says.

"Thought the same. So you spot up there. Then me and Dapino will drive to the front. I'll watch him from the car's tinted windows. The moment Ayala reveals himself, I'm going to text you. That's when the count starts. Thirty seconds. When the time is up, light the pipe bomb."

"Not technically," Tommy says. "I'm giving it a fuse. Ten seconds of burn. So light it twenty seconds in for a bang at thirty."

"Dapino's right," Clyde says. "Spark at twenty. Good?"

"Good," Jordana says.

"As loud as that bomb might be," Clyde says to Tommy, "Ayala's head may only turn toward the noise for a second. You going to be able to grab the phone in that tight of a window?"

"I'll make the grab."

"You miss the grab, this whole thing is shot. And if he sees you doing it, he probably shoots you."

"I'll make the grab."

"I'm zipping up in the whip either way. You get your ass in. Quick, go a block east on foot. I'll pick you up. Then the three of us get the hell out of there before Ayala has a chance to realize what went down."

Clyde hands a flask to Jordana. She has a sip and passes it back. He drinks and gives it to Tommy. He has a swig twice as long as theirs.

SEVENTEEN

Tommy gazes out the passenger window of the unmarked FBI Chevy Tahoe. The bright, busy scenery of Tijuana's red-light district transitions to the shadowy stillness of an industrial one.

Clyde pulls over at a corner, asks Jordana in the backseat, "Ready?"

She nods, then steps out with the pipe bomb, paces down the dark sidewalk.

"You really think this is a good call?" Clyde asks Tommy.

"Not if we all die."

They laugh.

"When my basketball team is down late in the game," Clyde says, "I always tell the kids you got to try anything to win. Guess this is no different."

"Hold on. You coach a basketball team?"

"Damn straight. Twelve-and-under league."

"Huh."

"Played back in the day too. All-county senior year."

"Didn't take you as a hoops guy."

"What sort of a guy did you take me as?"

"I somehow pictured FBI agents capable of only playing squash."

"I'll squash you in one-on-one. We both make it back to San Diego intact, it's on."

"How many points should I spot you due to your severe old age?"

"With age comes experience. And in my experience, most guys who talk trash do it to mask their weak-ass game."

"I've been playing prison ball the last two years. Every time you go up for a rebound, three psychopaths are trying to elbow your lights out. What do you do, strap on knee braces and take leisurely free throws once a week in some health club? We'll see who's got the weak game."

"The more trash that comes out of your mouth, the more trash your game likely is. Got anything else to add?"

"Just points. A lot of them. Tomorrow."

"We'll see."

"Yeah, we'll see all right." Tommy glimpses the console clock, 10:55 PM. "Okay, let's rock."

Clyde drives a block and turns left onto Calle Toro. A junkyard on the horizon. A squat brick office next to a fenced-in field packed with the carcasses of about a hundred automobiles. Stacks of tires. Piles of hubcaps.

Clyde idles a few dozen feet away. In his mind, Tommy snaps back into the Italian-mobster character he played earlier, then treads the pavement to the office. Knocks on the door.

It opens. A tall, muscular man in the doorway. He wears a Larry Johnson Hornets basketball jersey. Tommy recalls a similar physical description from Danielle's statement. This is likely the second shooter from the woods. In his grip is an AK-47.

"Where the hell is Carlos Ayala?" Tommy asks in his mobster accent.

The gangster says some Spanish into the building. Ayala and the pimp loom at his sides.

"Show us," Ayala says.

"You got my boss's fifty Gs?" Tommy asks.

"Show us video, I get you money from safe."

From his suit pants Tommy removes the phone. The three gangsters circle him, eyes fixed on it. Tommy clicks the play button. They all watch the spinning circle.

"Shit," Tommy says. "Bad internet connection." He keeps a seconds count in his head. Twenty down. The fuse should be lit.

Ayala's jaw tightens. "You playing games with me?"

"Goddamn international roaming on my phone. I don't know."

Thirty seconds pass. Tommy waits for the explosion.

It doesn't come.

He peeks inside. Out a window aback the building is Jordana in the alley. Four preteen boys with skateboards surround her. She waves at them as if to leave, but they stay put. She must be hesitant to light the bomb with them around.

"Come inside," Ayala says. Tommy's eyes flick to him. "I have internet in office. You go on it, you show video."

Tommy can't go in there. Too tight a space. He has a better chance taking them on over the fence, more room to work.

"Good idea," he says. "I'll show you inside." He takes a step toward the doorway. "No AC in there, huh?" He slips off his suit jacket. "That'll be better."

Tommy wraps the jacket around the head of the gangster with the AK and sprints toward the fence. He moves in a zigzag pattern, making himself a hard target for the gunfire he anticipates. He shouts toward the back alley, "Jordana, run."

Buchoo. The fence shakes as a bullet strikes it. Tommy

leaps into it, clutching the metal diamonds with his right hand, then left. He climbs it and drops to the dirt. In his periphery the three gangsters barrel toward him. Ayala and the pimp grip pistols. The tall one's head is no longer concealed with the jacket, on it an enraged expression.

He points the AK. Tommy dives over the hood of a scrap sedan. Its shell vibrates as automatic rounds pummel the other side. He peers through the gutted wheel well. The three gangsters are climbing the fence.

Tommy crawls to a heap of tires and rolls one along the ground. They turn to it. The AK goes off, dirt kicking up. Tommy runs the opposite way and hides behind a wall of hubcaps. Glances through a sliver of space.

The gangsters check for him behind the sedan. Then look around with confused expressions. They talk. And split off in different directions, Ayala north, the one in the jersey east, the pimp west toward Tommy.

Careful not to make noise, Tommy grips a hubcap. He watches the pimp search for him behind cars, watches him get closer. Once he's about ten feet away, Tommy springs out and hurls the hubcap at him. It knocks the back of his head. He crumples to the ground. Motionless.

One down.

Tommy spots Ayala. Since he doesn't have a gun, he'll have to fight him close-range. So sneaks up behind him. Ayala must hear his footsteps. He spins around. Shoots. Sparks spray from a nearby Ford Explorer.

Tommy jumps through the hollowed rear windshield. A bullet passes through it. He slides out of the backdoor opposite Ayala, maneuvers under the vehicle. Stares at his shoes. They stop beside the car, as if Ayala's looking inside for him. Tommy reaches to the rear of his waist. Pulls from it his new axe. And swipes the blade at Ayala's ankle.

A scream. Tommy scrambles out from under the car and says, "Let me give you a hand."

Ayala points his gun, but Tommy rams the axe into his head before he can pull the trigger. Blood cascades down to his eyes, the flicker of life still in them fading. Tommy yanks the blade out of Ayala's skull, the corpse falling belly down.

He snags the cellphone from Ayala's back-right pocket. Along the dirt he notices the shadow of a running body, an AK in its grip. A gunshot booms. He braces for the pain of a bullet tearing through him.

But it doesn't come.

He turns around. The gangster in the jersey is about five feet away. No longer running. Blood spills from his mouth. His big body drops to the dirt, revealing a smaller body behind it.

Jordana. Her gun in front of her. Her eyes wide.

Tommy hurries toward her, says, "Let's get out of here."

She stares at the gangster she just shot in the back for another moment, then shakes her head as if breaking out of a state of shock and joins Tommy racing toward the head-lights of Clyde's Tahoe.

He climbs the fence, lands. Waits a couple seconds for her to do the same. He notices the pimp has regained con-sciousness. He staggers around a cluster of tires. Aims his weapon at them.

"Down," Tommy yells. He wraps himself around Jordana like a shield and lowers them to the ground. A bullet flies overhead, shattering a light on the brick building.

Tommy and Jordana dart toward the Tahoe. He opens the backdoor and dives in. A moment later she does too. He hooks his foot around the door and closes it. The sound of a bullet nailing it.

"You guys good?" Clyde yells.

"Go," Tommy shouts.

The Tahoe roars away.

EIGHTEEN

Tommy throws cold water on his face in the bathroom of the FBI's Zona Norte motel room. Reflected in the mirror are Jordana packing a bag and Clyde speaking on the phone. He says into it, "It can't be logged as an official piece of evidence . . . Long story . . . Just unlock it and email me a file of all its data . . . Really appreciate it . . . Yep, see ya." He hangs up.

"Who was that?" Jordana asks.

"My old friend Gary in Computer Forensics. He owes me a favor. I'll text you his home address. Can you drop the phone off there on your way back while I deal with Dapino?"

"No problem." She glances at her watch. "The gang might be a problem if we don't get on the road soon, though."

"Let's boogie," Clyde says toward the bathroom. He picks up two bags.

The three leave the room, walk down to the street. Jordana says to Tommy, "Nice work tonight."

"Right back at you."

She paces toward the Tahoe, the men the Chevy Cruze. Tommy pops the trunk, drops in the axe, wiped of blood. Clyde loads in his bags. He gets in the passenger's seat, Tommy the driver's. They head toward the US border.

"When does your boy think he can break into the phone?" Tommy asks.

"Shooting for tomorrow morning."

"Beautiful."

"Only if he finds something useful. If there's not enough evidence on there to lead us to Ayala's boss, more homeless could get chopped down."

"Whoa. You're telling me this isn't over?"

"The shortest gap between our missing-persons reports is April nineteenth to twenty-sixth. One week. We should assume we have no longer than that to dismantle the ring before they murder again. Taking into account the four days that already passed since your sister's incident, we're potentially looking at just three more before another."

"Ayala is dead."

"The boss will just replace him. His death isn't necessarily a win. He was the best piece on our chessboard. And now he's off it. That phone is all we have. Let's hope it's fruitful."

"What is this? Some passive-aggressive bullshit targeted at me? Because I killed the son of a bitch? Jesus. He was trying to kill me. It was self-defense."

"Did I even mention you?"

"Sort of."

"Not at all. Just saying I can't make an assessment about the quality of evidence until I go over it. If there's anything I've learned after twenty-three years with the FBI, it's that."

"Twenty-three, huh? At the FDNY, they let you retire and start collecting at twenty."

"FBI lets you with your twenty too. But I'm not planning on leaving until they force me out in a few years. Fifty-seven. Our mandatory retirement."

"What're you going to do after?"

"Travel with my wife."

"Nice."

"How 'bout you? Now that you can't be a fireman anymore, what're you going to do?"

"What's that supposed to mean?"

"For work. You can't get a job in a fire department again, right? Now that you have a felony on your record for the attempted robbery."

"What ever happened to the right to privacy?"

"There's no such thing as privacy anymore. Get used to it."

"Apparently there's no such thing as accuracy either. I never attempted to rob anything. Don't always believe what you read."

"So what, you were framed?"

"Not technically. No."

"So you did it then?"

"I just told you I didn't."

"You're not making any sense."

Tommy's grip tightens on the steering wheel. "Sneaker Emporium. Ever hear of it?"

"Nope."

"Maybe it's just a New York thing. Sneaker stores."

"I got that."

"About six years ago branches started closing. Competition from online stores. Then one of them burnt down."

"You took the call?"

"Luckily me and my crew got to the scene and contained the flames before they spread. But this was no ordinary fire. The smoke. It was high. And black." A pause. "Like the sky had a shadow."

"Is black smoke really bad or something?"

"It can mean flammable fluids were involved. Can mean someone added an accelerant to make sure the fire moved faster, to make sure it was more destructive. I still remember its heat was on my face. Never felt hotter. Arson."

"There must've been an official investigation, right?"

"It ruled no arson."

"So maybe it was an accident."

"Black smoke does the same thing as any other type of smoke. It floats off. Disappears. By the next morning when the investigator showed up, it was gone. But I saw it. That was no accident."

"Other evidence?"

"The owner of Sneaker Emporium is loaded. If he was going to torch the place, he was hiring pros. Not dopes who'd leave behind jugs of empty gasoline."

"I supposed that adds up. But what does any of this have to do with attempted robbery?"

"The day after the fire, I called in sick to work. Spent the morning staking out the owner's house with binoculars. When he got in his car, I followed it. A few regular stops. Coffee. Walgreens. Lunch. Cigar shop. Then he went to the bank. And pulled a duffel bag out of his trunk. He went inside. Came back, bag looked heavier."

"Huh. You thought a cash payment for whoever lit up his building?"

"I saw who lit up the building. He met him back at the house."

"Who was it?"

"Don't know his name. Looked Russian mob. The tracksuit, the jewelry. I watched this guy knock on the front door, get let in. I checked the time. Exactly two PM. Like they had an appointment."

"So you did what? Lost your temper and barged into the house behind him?"

"Come on. Give me more credit than that. I climbed in. Second-story window in the back."

"You're nuts man."

"Wasn't nuts at all. Had the whole thing worked out. I was hiding behind a corner in the house. About to film them talking. Capture the money changing hands. That would be my proof."

"But they never spoke about the job?"

"They more than spoke about it. Laughed at getting away with it. Just as I slip my phone out of my pocket to record, the owner gets a call on his. He freaks. Runs through the house looking for me."

"Someone knew you were in there?"

"His wife. Who I later learned was sipping iced tea by their pool in the backyard. I didn't even look that direction when I snuck behind the house. She saw me climb in."

"Brutal."

"He pulled a gun on me. And kept it on me until the police showed up. I explained to the cops my side of the story. But the Russian was long gone with the cash by then. The cops told me I sounded insane."

"I would've thought the same thing."

"Thanks. Well . . . jury did too. Security-camera footage from the bank parking lot showed me following a well-known, wealthy businessman to a cash withdrawal. Prosecutor sold it as an attempted robbery. Even though I had no priors, they threw me in one of the roughest prisons in the country. I guess to make some point of me. About what happens if you take justice into your own hands."

Clyde chuckles. "A lesson you apparently learned."

Tommy chuckles too. "Thoroughly."

They ride along the Pacific Ocean, its water dark against the night like a big pool of ink.

"There's a possibility some department out there gives me a second chance," Tommy says. "But that wouldn't be for a while. I'd have to stay out of trouble for at least a couple years, prove I'm not associated with a pattern of bad behavior. Whatever. That part of my life is over. I've moved on to better things."

"You got a job already?"

"More than just a job. I own my own business. In Manhattan. We're crushing. Don't worry about me."

"Never said I was. What sort of business?"

A pause. "Sales. I have a whole team under me."

"What do you sell?"

"Not a physical product or anything. Stock-market deals. It's complicated."

"Cool."

"Really cool." A pause. "The second you looked me up, you assumed I was a piece of shit, didn't you?"

"Where's that coming from?"

"Just admit it."

"I definitely didn't assume you were going to be winning civic awards any time soon."

"I knew it. Unfair."

"What about you? You're telling me you didn't make any assumptions about me because I was an FBI agent?"

Tommy is silent for a while. "That's different."

"How?"

"Because you are an FBI agent. And I'm not actually guilty of attempted robbery."

"Well . . . the world ain't fair sometimes."

"Yeah. Yeah."

They drive a few more miles to the US line, Clyde presenting his FBI credentials to the Border Patrol agent. He explains he was in Mexico working a case with his associate behind the wheel, and clears Tommy for American entry without a passport.

"Thanks," Tommy tells Clyde.

"We celebrating or what?"

"Huh?"

"Still a lot of open questions on this investigation, but I think we accomplished enough tonight to treat ourselves to a beer or two. Agree?"

"Hell yeah. Let's jam."

NINETEEN

"Pull in here," Clyde says, pointing at the parking lot of a one-story building with a neon "Cannonball Bar & Grill" sign on it.

"This your type of joint?" Tommy asks, eyeing the other vehicles, the majority Harley-Davidsons.

"Don't think I'd fit in?"

"You cruise around on a hog off-hours?"

"They have great wings. And cold beer. Come on."

Tommy parks. Clyde undoes a button on his shirt and rolls up his sleeves. He enters the place, Tommy following him in. Saloon-style bar. Pool tables. Classic rock from the speakers.

A hostess with a lot of earrings seats them at a booth. A waitress with even more earrings comes over. Clyde orders two dozen wings for the table.

"What sort of beer you like?" he asks Tommy.

"Any with alcohol in it."

"Pitcher of Bud Light," Clyde tells her. She smiles and walks off.

Clyde rests his arm on the back of the bench. Tommy notices a barbed-wire tattoo around his forearm. He nods at it and asks, "You get a little ink to give yourself some street cred in here?"

Clyde chuckles. "Got it way before I started coming here."

"It's really original."

"Screw you. Was when I got it."

"Nineteen Twenty? Twenty-Five?"

"I'll kick your ass back to Eighteen Twenty-Five you keep flapping that mouth. What sort of tats you sporting?"

"None."

"Fireman from Queens. Really?"

"Want me to strip down?"

"Why none?"

"Came close a couple times. Then I thought . . . I don't know. Like in ten years, even twenty, what if I don't like it anymore? Now I'm stuck."

"I knew guys who got them in prison just to pass the time. Some are fine, others look ridiculous. You're lucky you didn't succumb to that."

"Guys you put away?"

"Guys I just . . . know."

"You have friends that did time?"

"I've got all types of friends."

"Is that right? Where'd you meet these friends?"

"I wasn't always an FBI agent."

"Who were you before?"

"A teenager. Like most teenagers, I did my share of dumb stuff."

"Couldn't have been that dumb. Or they never would've given you a badge."

"Or maybe I just didn't get caught."

"You're not on the clock. I'm just . . . some guy in a bar

right now. And we're just talking. Give me a little taste."

"You better not tell Quick."

"Why would I tell Quick?"

"Oh, I can think of one reason you'd tell Quick."

"What does that mean?"

"I wasn't an FBI agent my whole life. And I wasn't married my whole life either. I know how things work."

"What things?"

"The way you were looking at her when you were making the pipe bomb. You didn't think I noticed?"

"I was . . . showing her how the thing functioned. Of course I'm going to look at her. What do you expect, I do it blindfolded like Harry Houdini?"

"Nothing wrong with it. Just saying I noticed."

"I'm not going to tell her about this just for some . . . excuse to talk to her, or whatever you're accusing me of. All right? So hit me with it."

The waitress sets the pitcher of Bud Light on the table with two glasses. Clyde fills one, passes it to Tommy, then one for himself. He has a sip and says, "I sold a little herb."

"You were a drug dealer?"

"I moved a few dime bags around my high school. I wasn't some kingpin."

"Did it for the money?"

"My dad had a solid job at a power plant. We were always fine in that department. I guess I did it because Pugsy was doing it."

"Who?"

"My best friend. I was trying to . . . impress him. He was chill. Chillest kid in the neighborhood. Always had the new record or the new shoes or the new whatever like a month before everyone else did, before it was officially cool. Always had a fine girl on his arm. Anything he did had to be right, you know?"

"Was it fun? Selling with him?"

Clyde smiles. "Time of my life."

"Why'd you stop?"

"I wasn't doing it for the money. But he was. Soon enough he started moving powder. Not just at school. All over town. That's where the real bucks were. Lied to me about it. But I knew."

"Cops got him?"

"I wish. To this day, nobody knows what exactly happened. But he must've crossed someone higher up. And that was it. They mowed him down in a drive-by."

"Oh. Wow."

"I went one-eighty after that. Stopped selling. Focused on my grades. On basketball. Became an FBI agent to take down the sort of people who shot Pugsy like some dog."

"How old was he when he died?"

"Didn't die. He's one tough son of a bitch."

"He's still alive?"

"His body. But not his brain. He's in a home. About twenty miles from here. I visit him once a month."

"He can talk?"

"Mumbles a little. Nothing coherent. You look into his eyes and ninety-nine percent of the time it's just . . . blank. But that one percent, I swear . . . I'll tell a story from back in the day and I can see it. A little spark. And it's like I'm looking at sixteen-year-old Pugsy again. And I know he remembers me. For just a few seconds. Then it fades."

"You guys had some pretty good stories, huh?"

"Shit yeah."

"Tell me one."

Clyde swigs his beer. "Sophomore year. Our science teacher, Mister Leapish, had it out for Pugsy. Just straight up didn't like him. No particular reason."

"We had a couple teachers like that too."

"So Pugsy gets detention with him for like the hundredth time that year. And after it's over, he's walking out of the building. And he passes Leapish calling his girl on a payphone. Wishing her a happy birthday. Telling her he's got them a reservation at this place Beverly's, the nicest spot in town, at eight."

"All right."

"Pugsy knew a lot of people. Partly from selling drugs. Partly because . . . he just had that personality. The cousin of some acquaintance happened to work as a busboy at Beverly's."

"'Kay."

"So Pugsy gives him a fat sack of bud. On the house. Also gives him a bottle of super-strength liquid laxative."

Tommy chuckles. "That's cold."

"Whole thing goes in Leapish's glass of wine. Me and Pugsy are waiting outside Beverly's in the bushes, giggling like little kids, staring through the front window. Sure enough, Leapish rockets up from his table. Sprints for the bathroom so fast he bowls over a waiter, tray of pasta goes soaring through the air, lands all over a bunch of guests."

Tommy claps. "Good stuff. Yeah . . . good stuff."

"All right. Your turn."

"My turn?"

"A story."

Tommy drinks some beer. "My best friend in high school was this kid Josh. Still is. Plenty of material on him."

"Give me one."

"Josh has a . . . unique sense of fashion. Senior year he got into jumpsuits for some reason. You know, like a one-piece zip-up."

"Yeah, yeah, I got it."

"They were doing a lot of renovations to our school that year. There were always these crews of workers walking around. They did their thing, never interfered with the classes or anything like that, and we did our thing, never messed with their projects. Two totally separate worlds, workers and students, but existing right on top of each other, you know?"

"Sure. Was like that when they were renovating my house."

"So Josh shows up one day in this blue jumpsuit. We're eighteen, so come off like adults. He even had a little moustache going. Could've easily passed for twenty-three. He didn't do this intentionally, but the jumpsuit looked almost identical to the kind some of the workers would wear."

Clyde laughs. "I got you."

"Despite the loud outfits, Josh is an introvert. So he's in this getup. And one of the construction managers sees him. Big guy with a real gruff voice. Goes to Josh, 'Hey, where the hell have you been? The guys are waiting for you outside.'"

"He thought he was one of the workers?"

"Apparently some new guy was supposed to start that day and never showed up. So the crew didn't know what he looked like. The boss assumed it was Josh. He was too timid to talk back to him. So follows him outside."

"You got to be shitting me."

"They hook him up with a hardhat and a shovel. At this point he's too deep into it to back out. So he goes along with it. Goddamn kid puts in a full day of work. Digging ditches. And since he obviously wasn't the right guy on file, never even got paid."

Clyde bellylaughs. "Dapino, that's spicy. That's really spicy."

Soon the waitress returns with a hot platter of wings. Tommy bites into one.

"So where you crashing?" Clyde asks.

"What do you mean?"

"Sleeping. I'm assuming you're not flying back to New York tonight."

"Oh. Right." A pause. "Same place I did last night when I came out for the service. Hotel, right on the beach."

"Which one?"

"I'm blanking on the name. Something with Sea in it."

"Huh. Anyway, sometimes those places are rip-offs. See if you can get a refund. Come crash by me. We have an extra room."

"You sure?"

"In exchange I just need one thing from you."

"What's up?"

"That was a great scheme me, you, and Quick pulled off in Tijuana. But that shit's over. Once my pal in Computer Forensics unlocks the burner, this investigation goes back to running by the book."

"So what do you need from me?"

"Technically nothing. I just need you to step away. We'll find who's at the top of this thing and bring it all down."

Tommy leans forward. "I went through a lot to get that phone."

"I know you did."

"And I don't deserve to see what's on it?"

"You deserve justice for your sister. Her shooter is already dead. And we'll arrest the leader."

"I can't even get his name?"

"Why, so you can break into his house and try to slam an axe through his head? I can't even begin to list the amount of problems that would cause. Not just for the bureau. But for you. I'm doing you a favor."

"You're doing me dirty."

"We've got to play this carefully. Ideally catch him in the act when he comes up for another attack, but before he hurts anyone. You're not careful. You're like a . . . bull hopped up on Red Bull. Which served us well back in that junkyard. But won't in this phase of the investigation."

Tommy finishes his beer. "You really think he's going to surface, do this again? He must know you're looking for him. It's all over the news."

"That doesn't deter these people. You knew I wanted you away from my case. That didn't stop you from coming back with the burner-phone idea, right?"

Tommy refills his glass. Has a long sip.

TWENTY

Dr. Glen Brent's eyes are open.

His wife Cora's are closed, her hand in his as he leads her through their four-bedroom home in Carmel Valley, a wealthy nook of San Diego, her other hand resting atop her eight-months-pregnant stomach. The morning sun shines through the windows.

He stops at a door one over from the master bedroom's. "Ready?"

She grins, nods.

He opens it and says, "Okay."

She reveals her eyes. They marvel at the pink-walled nursery for their soon-to-be daughter, the result of remodeling work he wouldn't let her see until complete.

"It's amazing," she says.

Glen, forty-nine, watches his thirty-year-old wife bounce around the room, still kissed with the scent of fresh paint. She checks out the bassinet, diaper-changing table, and dresser mounted with a top-of-the-line baby monitor.

"This isn't the only change we'll need around here," he says. "Since I'm going to be a dad, I need to stock up on dad jeans. From now on, I won't entertain a pair of denims unless the waist starts at my belly button or higher."

"Don't forget the backs. Need to be totally flat. Completely hide my hubby's cute ass. That'll come in handy when Jade starts school. None of the other moms will have enough of a view to properly check you out."

"So Jade? You're done sleeping on it? You know how much I like it."

"Hey Jade, finish your homework. Hey Jade, want to go shopping with mom?"

"Hey Jade, you can start dating when you're twenty-seven."

Cora giggles. "Yeah, Jade. It fits."

She picks up the sleek baby-monitor transmitter from the dresser. "Cool. Seems like something on a space shuttle."

"Audio, plus HD video. Syncs with an app we can download to our phones. It can even record for hours and save the clips to the cloud. Nothing but the best for our little girl." He kisses her forehead, then her pregnant belly. "I have some emails I want to catch up on before I head to work."

"Okay boo."

He descends the stairs to the first floor, then navigates the meandering hallway to his study at the back of the house. He enters the blinds-drawn room. The majority of their five-year marriage he came in here only to do work for his job. He had nothing to hide from Cora.

That changed six months ago.

He locks the door. With Tor Browser on his computer, he accesses the dark web, a subset of the internet that runs on encrypted overlay networks that mask the IP addresses, and therefore identities, of visitors.

Glen goes to the dark web's leading site for black-market goods and services. With his user ID, "The_Eternal_Patriot," he logs on. And reads nine new messages from people who need his help.

TWENTY-ONE

"These are great, Mrs. Gabor," Tommy says in the breakfast nook of Clyde's kitchen, then has another bite of his pancakes.

Clyde's wife Val, a mocha-complexioned woman in her early fifties, replies, "The key is letting the batter sit for a few minutes after mixing it. Turns into a little taste factory."

"I'd punch in for work at that factory without pay."

Clyde finishes his coffee. "Time for me to punch in at the FBI factory." He stands, says to Tommy, "After I get back, one-on-one in the driveway."

"I'll make sure I have my phone handy so I can call nine-one-one when you throw out your back."

"I'll make sure I have mine propped up on a little tripod videotaping the schooling. I'll edit it after the game, lay a little music over it. Can be your souvenir from your trip to California."

Tommy gazes at Val. Makes a funny face.

Clyde kisses her on the cheek, says, "See you, babe."

"Bye Curly."

Tommy says, "Curly?"

"Bye," Clyde says, then picks up his pace out of the room as if not wanting to be around if Val explains the nickname.

Tommy asks her, "How does a guy who's almost bald get the name Curly?"

"Wasn't always almost bald. I have all the old photo albums out in the den. Making a collage. I'll show you my Curly later."

They eat for a while longer, until all the pancakes are gone. "I'll get these," Tommy says, collecting the dishes.

"No need."

"Come on. You were nice enough to let me stay here. Least I can do."

She smiles. He stacks the empty plates, sets the coffee cups on top, and carries them into the kitchen. "Just leave them in the sink," she says. "I'll do them later."

"I can stick them in the dishwasher."

"Broke."

He rests the plates and mugs on the counter, opens the dishwasher, and peeks inside. "What's wrong with it?"

She enters the kitchen. "Hasn't been draining."

"Is your drain hose connected to your garbage disposal?"

She laughs. "No idea."

"Hose is probably clogged. I'll have a look." He gets on his knees, opens the cabinet beneath the sink, and eyeballs the piping.

"You don't have to do that, Tommy. I've been meaning to call a repairman. Will today."

"They come to a nice house in a nice neighborhood, they'll start ringing up the bill. I'll knock it out. Simple."

"Is this the sort of work you do?"

A pause. "No . . . nothing like that. Just . . . have a knack for it."

"Thank you. Really. If you want more coffee, there's still half a pot."

"Cool. Do you guys have a pantry with household supplies, basic tools, that sort of thing?"

"Hallway. Second door on your left."

He gives her a thumbs-up. She leaves the room. He turns on the garbage disposal. Listens for any irregularity. Then grabs a wrench and bottle of Drano from the pantry. A bit later, the dishwasher is fixed. He cleans his hands, pours a fresh cup of coffee, and finds Val in the den.

She sits at a table topped with a piece of poster board surrounded by glue and glitter. "What's this for?" he asks.

"Our thirtieth anniversary is next week."

"Congrats." A moment. "Is that the right word you say to someone for an anniversary? Is it congrats or another one?"

"Nowadays, with all the split-ups, I guess congrats is more apt than ever. We rented out a room in the back of our favorite restaurant the Saturday after next, having some friends and family for a little get-together. Figure I'll put this up inside."

Tommy glimpses the collage photos, Val and Clyde in various settings over the years, the Caribbean, Disneyworld, a ski resort, seven or eight others. A son with them in some. About Tommy's age.

"Curly," she says.

"Yes."

"One sec." She grabs the oldest-looking album, flips through it. And points at a picture of her and Clyde in their early twenties with friends at a nightclub. Clyde poses in a flashy suit and sunglasses. His hair is done into a Jerry curl.

"There you go," Tommy says. "All that hair. Oh, man. What happened?"

"You'll like this. The Jerry curl was already out of style for about five years when this picture was taken. His pals all have hi-tops, see? I guess Clyde was too busy studying back then to notice."

"Look at him. Look at how cool he's trying to come off. All with an outdated haircut. Thank you for this."

Tommy feels a vibration on his leg. He takes out his

phone. A text from Josh:

You alive T? I'm worried. Hit me back.

Tommy was so wiped last night, he passed out as soon as his body touched a bed. And still hasn't returned Josh's four missed calls.

"Excuse me," he tells Val. "I've got a call to make."

"Sure. Any luck in the kitchen?"

"You're good to go."

"You fixed it? Already?"

He grins.

"Clyde needs to bring you around more often," she says.

He climbs the stairs, turns into the guest bedroom, and calls Josh.

"He lives," Josh says. "Or is this a Mexican gangster who confiscated his phone?"

"Other way around. I got his phone."

"How did it go down?"

"It was . . . insane. I'll tell you all about it when I get back to New York."

"When's that?"

Tommy closes the door. "I told Clyde I was going to fly out tomorrow morning. But—"

"Who's Clyde?"

"One of the FBI agents. I'm at his crib. They plan to run the rest of the investigation by standard procedure. If so, it's doomed. I need—"

"Sounds like the plan worked last night. Sounds like this guy Clyde is pretty competent."

"So . . . what's your point?"

"So . . . what's the problem?"

"Last night's plan was anything but standard."

"And they went along with it. Like I said."

"Fine. You were right about that."

"And I bet they actually care about catching Danielle's killers. Was I right about that too?"

"Why're you acting like a prick?"

"You're lucky you got out of Mexico alive. And by the

tone of your voice, I'm sensing you're still not going to drop this vigilante thing."

"Clyde and Jordana are legit. You were right. Okay? But they're not the issue. Now that they're back in the office, they're rejoining the ... bureaucratic machine. Organizational bias against victims like Danielle is just as real now as it was before Mexico. The system will dismiss her ... the same way it's dismissed ... you know ... so many other good people."

"You mean, the same way you feel it's dismissed you?"

"This isn't about me." Tommy gazes out the window, an older man gardening in one next-door backyard, a fit woman doing yoga in the other.

"'Kay," Josh says. "It's not about you at all."

"I've got to go."

"To do what?"

"Find out who's behind all this." Tommy hangs up. "Jackass."

TWENTY-TWO

At the San Diego Veterans Affairs Hospital, Dr. Glen Brent hovers above a patient whose appendix just burst. With little time to perform an appendectomy before the infectious condition peritonitis turns lethal.

He says, "Knife." Nurse Peggy Wiggins, a freckle-faced, curly-red-haired woman of about forty, his compatriot through years of operations, hands him the instrument.

Her eyes, a trace of flirtation in them, meet his. He is quite certain she is in love with him. Probably just a wink from him and they could be having sex within the hour at a nearby motel. He imagines she'd smell like apples naked. Which turns him on for some reason. But he'd never cheat on Cora.

He moves his gaze back down to the patient, inserting the tip of the blade into the man's lower-right abdomen, a worm of blood wriggling out.

"Another operation that could've been avoided," Glen tells her. "If he just saw a doctor on a regular basis. Any MD could've diagnosed and treated the appendicitis before rupture."

"I checked his chart. Hasn't seen a general practitioner in years."

"Fricking VA makes it near impossible for a vet to book even a routine checkup."

"And most aren't well-off surgeons like you, can't afford private treatment. We're all they've got. Shame."

"Not our fault. It's those shortsighted, self-serving buffoons in Washington. They spent billions on wars after Nine Eleven, yet didn't consider the healthcare burden after wounded participants hobbled home."

He maneuvers his rubber-sheathed index finger into the patient's incision, feeling for the base of the appendix. He cuts it off the large intestine, extracts it from the body, and cleans out the abdominal cavity with a saline solution.

The stabilized vet is wheeled to recovery. Glen peels off his scrubs, exits the operating room, and walks through the corridor, younger hospital workers greeting the passing senior-level surgeon with respectful nods. He moves through the hectic crowd with agility despite his prosthetic right foot, the result of a Desert Storm injury.

He enters his office. A wall full of diplomas, military distinctions, and civic awards. He locks the door, and unlocks the drawer where he stashes the burner phone he's been communicating on the last six months.

He calls an associate. When he tried the number the last few days, it wasn't answered. He left a voicemail yesterday, still not returned. Now the number doesn't even ring, as if the phone is off. He hangs up.

Glen understands why his associate might want some distance from him, but ignoring him, denying him a chance to communicate, is unacceptable behavior. He collects his wallet and keys. And sets out for a surprise meeting in Tijuana.

TWENTY-THREE

"Hey," Tommy says from the Gabors' doorway into the den.

Val looks up from her collage. "Yeah?"

"I was trying to find flights to New York on my phone, but on the small screen it's difficult to compare all the different times and prices. I noticed in the room upstairs with all the basketball stuff there was a computer. Guessing it's Clyde's. You think he'd mind if I used it?"

"That old desktop, no. Go for it."

"Happen to know the password?"

"Lakers. Like the LA Lakers. Capital L. Then five, two, nine."

"Cool. Thank you." He returns upstairs and enters a study, on one wall a shelf filled with trophies from the San Diego Youth Basketball Association, on the opposite wall a whiteboard with hand-drawn plays.

Tommy sits at a desk, covered in Post-it notes with reminders Clyde's left for himself. He keys in the password. By this morning Clyde's friend Gary in Computer Forensics should be emailing him a file of all the burner phone's content. If Tommy could access Clyde's inbox, he could open the message and see the data.

He navigates to the web browser's list of recent visits, selects Gmail. He eyeballs today's received messages in Clyde's inbox. One with a subject line about an electric bill, another a college reunion, a few more. Nothing from anyone named Gary.

Tommy folds his arms. He peeks at the time in the corner of the computer screen, already past ten AM. Gary likely sent Clyde the contents. Just not to this personal Gmail address, rather his FBI one.

Tommy searches the computer for an FBI email application, but finds none. He figures if Clyde ever needs to work from home, he brings back a laptop from the office, doesn't rely on the old desktop.

"Shit," Tommy says. He spins in the swivel chair, facing the whiteboard of basketball plays. And considers how to approach this challenge.

He gets up and enters the guest bedroom. He opens the window, gazes down at the mid-sixties man gardening next door.

"Hi there," Tommy calls to him.

The neighbor, using his canvas-gloved hand as a visor, peers up at him. "Hi. Need something?"

"I'm a friend of the Gabors. In town for a couple days. Just wanted to tell you I noticed your garden. A real beaut."

"Oh. Well. Thank you, young man."

"No problem. I'm Tommy by the way. You?"

"Peter."

"Keep up the good work, Peter. See ya."

"Have a nice day."

Tommy closes the window. Step one complete. Now on to step two.

He goes downstairs, asks Val, "How's the collage coming?"

"Getting there. What do you like better for the words at the top, thirty years of cheer or anniversary glee?"

"Eh. Don't love either, not gonna lie. How about a heart with Clyde, a little plus sign, and Val in it? Like they carve into trees."

"Ooh, that can work."

"Speaking of Clyde, he just texted me."

"Everything okay?"

"Yeah, totally. A couple of the agents have some questions for me about my sister's past. He wants me to come in. I forgot to ask him where he sits. He's not writing me back, probably in a meeting. Did you ever visit him in the office?"

"Fourth floor. Toward the corner. It would be . . . the southwest one. Not all the way in it, but near it, in one of the cubicle thingies."

He smiles. "Thanks."

On to step three.

TWENTY-FOUR

Glen cruises through Tijuana in his Mercedes. An audiobook plays from the speakers. *Shield of Armatron*, the seventh installment of a fantasy series featuring the brave and noble Prince Troy. Each book is about a different evil force trying to destroy his country. This one involves a demon who casts a famine spell on Prince Troy's people. Glen is up to the part where the prince and his worthy allies transport themselves to the demon's realm to confront him.

Glen turns onto a pothole-dented street. Idles in front of his associate's brown-roofed house. Waits until the chapter is done. Then shuts off his engine and paces to the door. An image in the window grabs his attention.

He peeks into the space between the curtains. He doesn't see his associate. Rather, three other Latinos who dress like him, probably in Los Hombres del Vacio too. On his knees in front of them is a fourth man about thirty years older. He is crying.

Glen, fluent in Spanish, hears them talking in the language. He steps closer to the window. "Please, don't do this," the one on the floor says.

One of the gangsters pulls a girl, about nineteen, off a chair. He holds a razor blade inches from her face. And tells the man on the floor, "This is what happens when you place bets you can't pay back, you broke-ass bitch."

"She wasn't a part of this."

"This isn't about her. It's about you. This is good for you, old man. Every time you look at her face after I'm done with her, you'll be reminded to never make another bet you can't honor."

"I'm sorry. Please, do it to me. Not my daughter. You can't—"

"If the bets went the other way and you made money, you'd likely spend some of it on your daughter, wouldn't you? Maybe some new shoes. A new phone. Show her what a big man you are. Am I right?"

"I . . . maybe. I never thought—"

"Are you a bad father? You'd keep the winnings all to yourself you greedy dickhead?" The other two gangsters laugh.

The father says, "No. I'd buy her something nice."

"That's what I thought. So if she could be involved in the upside, she could be involved in the downside, no?"

The father cries for a while. Then yells, "You are despicable. All of you. Just because you bribe the cops and get away with this stuff for now, doesn't mean you will forever. You're all going to hell."

"Hell doesn't exist." The gangster with the razor locks an arm around the girl's neck. "What should I do first? Play tic-tac-toe against myself on her forehead or cut off her lips?"

Glen has seen enough. He marches to the door and bangs on it. In a few seconds the gangbanger with the razor opens it. "Who're you?" he asks in Spanish.

"An associate of Carlos Ayala," Glen replies in the same language. "What's going on in there?"

"Carlos Ayala . . . doesn't live here anymore. Are you trying to mess with me?"

Glen sticks his head through the doorway, asks the girl, "Are you all right?"

The gangster shoves his face back outside. "Get out of here."

"You should let her go."

"Suck my cock." He slams the door.

Muscular, six-foot-two Glen stops it with his shoulder. Rams his way into the house. He hears the click of pistols. Sees the two other gangbangers aiming at him. Since firearms aren't permitted from the US into Mexico, Glen came down unarmed, and raises his hands in indication.

"You got some balls," the one with the razor says.

Glen hears the front door slam shut. "I didn't come here for any trouble. I came to give Carlos Ayala a big bag of money, double what he usually gets for a job. But this . . . what you're about to do to her. I want you to reconsider. It's wrong."

"There is no wrong in the world," the one with the blade says. "Or right. The world is just filled with people trying to get what they want. And other people trying to stop them. Sometimes they do. Sometimes they don't. That's all there is."

"Please . . . reconsider."

"Or what?"

Glen eyeballs the gunmen's sideways aim of their weapons, ragtag form likely picked up from the streets. They may have him outnumbered, but surely don't have him out-skilled.

He kicks the one behind him. Hears his body knock into the wall. Glen drops to his back, thrusts himself toward him, and clasps his wrist. He snaps it, the crack of the bone audible, and snatches his pistol.

The other gunman re-aims at him. Before he can fire, Glen sweeps his legs, toppling him. Then drives the heel of his shoe into his chin.

"Get out of here," Glen screams to the girl. She dashes toward the door.

The one with the blade peers at him with panic in his face. Glen blasts a bullet between his eyes. He falls into the chair. Dead. Glen hands the girl the gun. "Take this for protection."

"Thank you, mister." She opens the door. Darts outside. Glen runs out behind her.

A bullet whizzes past his head, hitting his Mercedes. He scopes his six o'clock. The gangster whose legs he swept is back on his feet, blood oozing from his mouth. He storms outside.

Glen sprints across the street. Cuts around the corner of a house into an alley, a fence to his left, a line of adobe homes his right.

A gunshot. A chalky puff in the air as the bullet whacks a house. He picks up a metal trashcan and hurls it backward at the chasing gangbanger, loose garbage spilling onto Glen, a chunk of pork hitting his lips.

He reaches the edge of the alley. Makes a right onto the sidewalk. The lone pedestrian in view, a boy in a backpack, gawks at the man covered in trash. Glen hustles toward an active cross street about a hundred feet ahead. His left shoulder twists. Then heats up from the core, as if a hot coal were packed inside. A splatter of blood on his polo shirt's sleeve. He's been shot.

He pelts toward an Isuzu Trooper at a stop sign. He blocks the vehicle's path and yells at its driver in Spanish, "Get out."

The driver lifts his forearms over his face and says in the same language, "Don't hurt me. I'll give you my wallet. Whatever you want."

Glen pulls on the door handle. Locked. He elbows the driver-side window. The glass stays intact. He hunches over and removes his prosthetic foot. Hears a bullet zing over his head. Shatters the Isuzu's window with the foot's metal connective rod.

The prosthetic tucked under one arm, he stuffs his other through a star-shaped space in the window, opens the door, and heaves the driver onto the pavement.

Glen jumps in his seat. A bullet crashes into the trunk hatch. He pounds the gas. Turns a corner at about fifty miles per hour, the SUV almost tipping. And zips out the gangster's sight.

TWENTY-FIVE

Tommy's Chevy Cruze pulls in front of a firehouse in Clyde's neighborhood. With a fresh, white facade and large lawn of palm trees, it's a departure from the old brick building on the tight city street where Tommy worked in Queens. Yet also has similarities. The same gleam on the polished fire trucks. The same American flag out front. The same relaxed readiness of the men walking around.

Tommy wanders through the garage door, says to the first passing fireman, "Excuse me."

"What's up?"

"I did the job in New York for a few years."

The fireman grins, extends his hand. "Drew."

"Tommy." He shakes it. "When I'm on vacation, I like picking up gear from local ladder companies. You guys sell shirts and stuff?"

"Yeah man. What're you, a large?"

"That should fly."

"Red or blue?"

"Blue."

The fireman disappears through a doorway. Returns with a blue City of San Diego Fire-Rescue Department tee shirt, a price tag of twenty-five dollars.

"Sweet," Tommy says. He pays in cash. "Be good, Drew."

The fireman waves.

Tommy returns to his car, removes his shirt, and slips into his new one, tucking it into his jeans. He slides his phone from his pocket, downloads an app for web-based phone calls, and dials Clyde's cell, the app assigning a local number to the caller.

"Agent Gabor," Clyde says. "Who is this?"

Tommy puts on the voice of Clyde's neighbor and says, "Sorry to bother you at work. It's Peter. Next door. I was working on my garden and noticed something in your lawn. It's getting worse every couple minutes. Had to let you know."

"What's getting worse?"

"It's like a green goo. Smoke coming off it."

"A smoking green goo?"

"I guess that's how I'd describe it. I've never really seen anything quite like it."

"Jesus. How much is there?"

"Oh, hmm. Maybe a bathtub's worth."

"A sewage leak?"

"Hard to tell. I don't want to go near it of course. Seems toxic. I'm getting another call. I need to go. You should—"

"Wait. What's—"

"Sorry, this is important. My doctor. You should really come home and check it out yourself. Bye Clyde."

Tommy hangs up. Then makes another call from a local number. A receptionist says, "FBI San Diego field office. How can I assist you?"

Tommy, mimicking Clyde's voice, says, "This is Agent Gabor. I'm having issues with the wires connected to my computer. They've been sparking up for some reason. The fire department is sending a guy over to check things out. Let him right up to four when he gets here. About ten, fifteen minutes."

The receptionist confirms. Tommy drives five or so miles to the FBI office, a contemporary compound with plenty of glass and right angles. He grabs the clipboard he took from Clyde's study, the sheet of basketball plays that were on it replaced with a fire-inspection checklist he printed from the internet.

He walks into the building. On the wall of the high-ceilinged lobby is a large FBI seal, the words "Fidelity," "Bravery," and "Integrity" at its center. He signs in at the front desk with a fake name, weaves his way among a bustle of bodies to an elevator, and presses the "4" button.

He steps out onto Clyde's level, filled with dozens of cubicles, and paces toward the southwest corner. On the computer screens in his periphery are all sorts of charts and lists. He figures his name is on ones just like these. *Thomas Dapino, felon* forever ingrained in America's official record.

His feet slow as he scans the placards on cubicles. *Special Agent Clyde Gabor*, empty desk. A woman with heavy blue eye shadow who sits next to Clyde asks, "Can I help you?"

"Hey there. Routine inspection for electrical hazards. An agent named . . ." He pretends to read something on his clipboard. "Clyde Gabor made the report. I was told he sits here. Is that accurate?"

"Yes. But he had some emergency at home, had to run out. He should hopefully be back in a bit."

The two agents across Clyde's desk in the four-person cubicle pod are behind a divider. They should be fine. But the woman with the blue eye shadow has too clear a view. She needs to leave.

"It's better he's away," Tommy says. "I need to run a couple tests. For safety reasons, when I do, he shouldn't be near any wires. Due to proximity, it seems your workstation could be affected as well. Would you mind taking a quick break? Get a cup of coffee or something."

"Oh. Jeez. How long?"

"Fifteen minutes max, ma'am."

"Ma'am?" She grins. "I don't look that old, do I?"

"Not a day over . . . thirty?"

The woman, at least forty-five, blushes. Then walks away. Tommy crawls under Clyde's desk. *Lakers529* was his home-computer password, Tommy assuming it's his work one too. He enters it on the keyboard. And receives a message back saying, "Sorry, wrong password."

He clenches his fist. A high-security institution like the FBI may require password refreshes every few months, *Lakers529* possibly Clyde's once, now replaced with something else. If so, keeping mental track of all those passwords would be confusing. Tommy recalls the Post-its in Clyde's study.

He slides open the top drawer of the filing cabinet. Binders, notebooks, folders. Nothing indicative of a password. Similar items in the cabinet's second drawer. But on the third's inner wall, a Post-it. He peels it off, reads a sequence of pen-drawn letters, numbers, and symbols. And inputs them into the password field. The screen unlocks.

"Hell yes," he whispers to himself.

With Clyde's mouse, he clicks on the email-app window, eyeballs the inbox. At 3:12 AM a message came in with no subject from a sender named Gary Flim. Tommy opens it. No content in the body. Attached are three files, one titled "VM," the other "SMS," the third, "Log." Tommy forwards the message to his email address, arranges the windows on Clyde's desktop as they were, and relocks the screen.

He walks to the elevators. Rides to the first floor. The lobby is denser with employees than it was earlier, probably due to the start of lunch hour. He works his way to the exit. When he's about a dozen feet away, he hears, "Tommy?"

He stops, glances over his shoulder toward the female voice. Standing in the crowd, a "Happy Greens" to-go bag in her hand, is Jordana. He smiles. "Jordana. Hey."

"Agent Gabor said you were going back to New York. I was . . . well, I was hoping to say goodbye. Glad I ran into you. What . . . what're you doing here?"

"Clyde forgot something at the house. Just doing him a favor, dropping it off."

Her gaze angles to the City of San Diego Fire-Rescue Department logo on his chest, then the clipboard in his grip. He presses it to his hip to hide the inspection checklist. Her eyes narrow in suspicion.

"That doesn't sound like him," she says. "Not very forgetful. What'd he leave behind?"

"Oh, just . . . vitamins."

"He made you drive all the way over here to bring him vitamins?"

"It was my idea. I saw his baggy of pills left behind on the kitchen counter. He's letting me crash by him and all. Figured I owed him one."

"I didn't realize he was such a health nut."

"According to his wife, the vitamin thing is a new habit. Wouldn't want him to break it while he was just getting started. Well . . . glad I ran into you too. Good luck with the rest of the case. Bye."

"All right. Bye."

He continues to the glass door. It opens from the other side. A woman holding a Starbucks cup. Tommy glances at her face. Clyde's cubicle mate with the blue eye shadow.

"Oh, hi," she says. "Did you figure out what was wrong?"

"Easy fix. You guys are all set."

"Wow. You really . . . took care of business up there."

Jordana paces over, says to the woman, "Hey Patricia."

"Quick."

"You know him?"

"I . . . just met him before. Why . . . do you know him?"

"Well, I . . . where do you know him from?"

"If he's your boyfriend or something, I'm not trying—"

"No. He's not my boyfriend."

"He's a fire inspector. Was working on Agent Gabor's desk."

Jordana turns to Tommy, concern in her expression, then back to the woman. "Can you give us a minute?"

"Of course." She merges with the lobby crowd.

Jordana says to him, "I didn't know the fire department recently branched out into vitamin delivery."

He considers lies. None would work.

She says, "Whatever this is, is a bad idea. Please ... step away, let us do our job."

"I want you to do your job. I just want to ... help. Same as I did in Mexico. What's wrong with that?"

"A lot. I have to tell Gabor about this. Whatever the hell it is. He's my partner." She taps her phone, says into it, "Dapino is ... Ah, you knew ... Okay ... Lobby ... Yeah." She ends the call.

His eyes shift to the window.

"You can leave before he gets here," she says. "But that won't make this go away."

He cracks his neck.

A couple minutes pass. Then he hears from behind, "My Goddamn wife?"

Tommy faces a livid Clyde marching toward him. Startled employees clear a path. "You spent the morning bullshitting her? And my neighbor? Who do you think you are?"

"Mrs. Gabor is a ... she's great. I didn't mean any disrespect. I just needed to know where you sat."

"Why?"

"Did you really think I was going to just ... quit?"

"There's nothing for you to even quit. This isn't a team you're on. Me and Quick, we're a team. And you ... you need to go back to New York."

"I deserved to see what was on that phone. You know I did."

"You don't deserve anything. You're lucky I didn't have you charged for interfering with a federal investigation."

Tommy laughs. "I'm the best thing that happened to this investigation."

Clyde looks around. People watch. He quiets his voice, says, "Not here. Let's talk about this at my house later. Can you—"

"Why not here? Don't want me to embarrass you in front of your coworkers?"

"Keep your voice down. Let's at least go outside."

"Nah. I'm fine here."

Clyde grasps his forearm. "Outside, now."

Tommy rips his hand away. "Don't touch me."

"Let's just go outside where—"

Tommy says loud enough for the observers to hear, "Where we can talk about everything I did last night? How you sat in the car while I got my hands dirty in the junkyard? How I risked my life to help your failing case? How you want to pretend it never happened? Is that what you want to talk about outside?"

Clyde's eyes jump to the faces of the surrounding employees, then settle back on Tommy. "You stupid son of a bitch."

TWENTY-SIX

Tommy, Clyde, and Jordana sit in a row of chairs in an office on the top floor of the FBI building. Etched on the frosted glass of the closed door is "Helga Wichita – Special Agent in Charge."

Wichita, a late-forties woman in similar business attire as Jordana, but a much larger size, paces at the head of the room. She must be into bodybuilding, with each step her quadriceps bulging like supermarket turkeys under her skirt.

"Okay," she says into her phone. Her eyes zero in on Clyde's. "He's here right now . . . You bet I will . . . Thanks . . . You too."

She hangs up, sits at her desk. Behind her are half a dozen plaques showcasing newspaper pages with mug shots of criminals and headlines about their capture, hanging high on the wall like a hunter's prized busts.

"That was the FBI's liaison in Mexico City," she says. "What the hell happened in Tijuana?"

"We worked with his team to identify the suspect," Clyde says. "Then we interrogated him. Exactly as planned."

"Then what?"

"Unfortunately, the suspect didn't provide much in the interrogation. But I'm confident we can get around that. Give me until the end of the day, I'll piece something together."

"The federales found your suspect dead last night. Skull cracked open. Not long after you talked to him. From what they gathered, potentially some mix-up with the Italian mafia."

Clyde fakes a surprised expression. "I . . . we . . . know nothing about that. The man is . . . was . . . a gangster. A feud with another organized-crime syndicate isn't surprising I suppose."

"One based in Mexico, sure. But one based three thousand miles away in New York . . . come on."

"What're you suggesting?"

She nods at Tommy. "Your new friend here is from New York, isn't he?"

"He's not my friend. And he's not in the Italian mafia. Look him up in—"

"I already did. He may not be in the mob, but he's still a felon. And he's involved in some type of dirty work here. Did you hire him as a contractor? Couldn't handle Mexico without outside help?"

"I have no business arrangement with him. We—"

"That's not what the agents who heard you two screaming at each other downstairs seem to think. The FBI has thirty-five thousand employees. I could've sent reinforcements if you asked. What would motivate you to call on some ex-con?"

"He's not just some ex-con. He's one of the victims' brothers."

"Fine. I still don't see how that changes anything. I sent

you to Mexico to do a job on behalf of the federal government. And you outsourced a chunk of it to someone the federal government wouldn't go anywhere near."

"He went down to Tijuana on his own. With his own agenda. We just happened to cross paths."

"And then the lead suspect just happened to get his head split like a coconut, huh?"

"That was unrelated—"

"Save it." She peers at Jordana. "If Agent Gabor didn't partner with this wannabe vigilante, I'm assuming you did. You were the only two—"

"She had nothing to do with any of this," Clyde says. "I'm the lead agent on the case, ma'am. If anything didn't unfold according to . . . proper procedure, I take full responsibility."

"This load of responsibility is heavy. And it reeks of shit. Glad you're dumping it on your own shoulders. Sounds like you deserve it."

"Let me know how I can make this right."

"You can't. Not only did this felon do whatever the hell he did in Mexico yesterday, but stormed into the office today. Tampered with your workstation according to Patricia Volmes. Which houses a computer packed with sensitive information. Then made a scene in my lobby. He embarrassed the FBI. He embarrassed me. And more than anyone, he embarrassed you."

"I apologize."

"I don't care. You're suspended, Gabor. Effective immediately."

Clyde stands. "Miss Wichita, that would be detrimental to the case. We've made progress. Removing me would set us back and—"

Wichita stands. "Effective immediately. Badge and gun."

A loud exhale from Clyde's nostrils. He glares at Tommy, sets his badge and gun on the desk.

"Quick," Wichita says. "You're the new lead. Is that something you can handle?"

A pause. "Yes ma'am."

Wichita points at Tommy. "And you. If I see you near this building again, if I see you near this investigation again, if I see you near me again, I'm going to throw you in a federal prison so despicable Attica is going to seem like Barbados."

Clyde stomps out. Slams the door. Tommy follows him into the hallway. "Clyde, I didn't mean for any of this to happen. I was just—"

"Shut up." Though Clyde is in a work suit, inside a work building, Tommy doesn't see him as Clyde the FBI agent right now, but Clyde the person. The one from Cannonball Bar & Grill, from home. Pugsy's best friend, Val's husband.

Clyde turns around. His shoes clack on the marble floor as he distances down the hallway. He vanishes into an elevator.

"What were you thinking?" Jordana asks.

"The burner data. I had a right to see—"

"Maybe you did. Maybe you didn't. Either way, this wasn't the way to get it. Did you even consider the consequences for Gabor and me? If he didn't take the fall like the class-act guy he is, I would've been in just as much trouble."

"I didn't have bad intentions. For either of you."

"I believe that. You just weren't thinking about us at all. You were only thinking about yourself. Which is just as bad as having bad intentions."

"Whatever. I've got to go."

"Where?"

"It's probably best if I kept you out of this. Don't want to get you on the naughty list like I did to him."

"You're not done yet?"

"I've endured a lot worse in life than an angry speech. None of it's stopped me. Neither will this."

"Wichita can swing around a lot more than anger. She has serious pull, at the highest levels of the federal government. And now she has a grudge against you. If she sees you poking around, she'll nail you for what we didn't. Interfering with a federal investigation. You will end up back in prison."

"I'm a felon. Maybe I belong in prison. But I'm finishing this first."

"You don't belong in prison. Let me . . . help you."

"With what?"

She looks around, a few employees conversing nearby, then leads Tommy into a conference room, the sun shimmering through its big window. She closes the door. "I probably should be talking you out of this. But I know you wouldn't listen. If you're going to pursue the leader, let me at least keep you off the FBI's radar."

"How?"

"Simple. Honesty."

"What do you mean?"

"Inform me of all your moves. Before you make them. If I feel any of them are going to bump up against the FBI's investigation, I'll warn you. Sound good?"

"Thanks."

"And in return, you need to promise me you'll listen if I tell you to back away from something. Can you do that?"

"Yeah, I can do that."

"Can I trust you?"

"Yeah, you can trust me."

"Good." A pause. "I have a feeling your invitation to stay at the Gabors' is now rescinded."

He chuckles. "I'd say so."

"I have a sofa. You can stay by me."

"You sure?"

"It's cool."

"Why're you being so nice to me after I dicked over your partner?"

"Let's get something straight. I am pissed you dicked over my partner. But . . . you lost your sister. And as reckless as some of your behavior is, I guess I can see the place it's coming from. And . . . it's a good one."

A pause. He opens the door. "See you after work."

"A vitamin drop-off? You could've done better than that."

"You got me off guard, I guess."

"It's my job."

A slight smile from him. "Yeah. I know." He leaves the conference room.

TWENTY-SEVEN

Tommy is at the same computer in the same library he was yesterday researching Los Hombres del Vacio, the midday sun shining down on him through the domed-glass ceiling. In prison he spent a lot of time in the library reading the sort of books he was supposed to in high school but was too distracted to open. He likes libraries. They give him a sense of belonging, though he isn't certain to what.

The email he forwarded himself from Clyde's computer is open on the web browser. He creates a second tab, logs into Facebook, and messages Josh:

Yo kid.

Josh replies:

Wut's good.

Tommy:

Just spent two hours typing every text the gangster sent or received the last week into a translation website to see them in English. All dog shit.

Josh:

Why?

Tommy:

Mostly just him sending weird messages 2 chicks about how big his cock is. Nothing to or from someone who hired him. Nothing at all about Danielle's murder.

Josh:

Crap.

Tommy:

There's a voicemail file too. Gonna see what's up w that.

Tommy opens the "VM" file attached to the email. Twelve voicemails were recovered on Ayala's phone. Eleven are from foreign numbers. But one is from a US one, with San Diego's 609 area code. Tommy puts in his headphones and plays the file.

"It's me," a male voice says, Tommy's posture straightening. "Again. I know there's a lot of heat right now. I get you want to lay low. But I have people I made promises to. I need more . . . supply. Call me back. You have no right to keep ignoring me. I've paid you a lot of money so far. You owe me this call."

"Huh," Tommy says to himself.

He opens the email's last attachment, "Log," a log of Ayala's recent calls. The 609 number in several entries. He checks their timestamps, a call from it received the night of Danielle's shooting, less than an hour before.

Tommy messages Josh:

I think I got this piece of garbage. "I've paid you a lot of money so far." In a VM. Something a boss would say to an employee.

Josh sends Tommy a link. He clicks it. A reverse-lookup website. Tommy inputs the 609 number. It's unregistered. No owner address, no name. His posture slackens.

He messages Josh:

Thx. But no dice. Looks like the boss uses a burner too.

Josh:

What now?

Tommy:

I don't know. Gotta think.

Josh:

Don't do anything stupid.

Tommy:

You're the second person who's hit me with that today.

Josh:

Thank the other guy for me.

Tommy:

Not a guy. Girl.

Josh:

??

Tommy:

Jordana, the FBI agent.

Josh:

I like her already. Hot?

Tommy:

Why do u always go right there?

Josh:

What's her last name? I'm gonna scope her on IG.

Tommy:

Ur out of ur mind man. She's not on IG. Or anything else. Kinda odd tbh.

Josh:

Liar. U just don't want me to check her out because u like her urself.

Tommy:

She's giving me a place to crash. That's it.

Josh:

You're sleeping at her pad??

Tommy:

Not in her bed u idiot. The couch. It's not like that.

Josh:

Again, is she hot?

Tommy:

She's gorgeous. But it's not like that.

Josh:

Ur ridiculous bruh.
Tommy:
I gotta go. Ltr.
Tommy logs out of Facebook. He replays the voicemail from the 609 number, focusing on the tone of each word, trying to imagine the sort of man this is.

TWENTY-EIGHT

Glen watches a Spanish-language game show on television. After he raced away from Los Hombres del Vacio in the Isuzu Trooper, he kept moving until outside Tijuana, parked behind an abandoned missionary building in a slum, and knocked on the first door he saw. He exchanged all the cash in his wallet, a hundred thirty-eight US dollars, to the occupants of this house for hiding.

The mid-thirties married couple sits beside him on a ratty couch eating soup. A contestant on the game show states a wrong answer to a question from the host, who whacks a big red button, dropping the contestant's friend into a dunk tank. The husband and wife laugh. Glen does not.

His burner phone vibrates in his pocket. He says into it, "Yeah?"

"I'm pulling up," Bo Archer, his army buddy from Desert Storm, says.

"Great. Thanks again."

Glen ends the call and stands. In Spanish, he thanks the couple for their hospitality and says goodbye. He walks to the front window and peels back the curtain. The chrome grille of Bo's GMC Sierra pickup glints in the sun.

He parks and out steps his big boot. Extending above in cargo shorts and a skull-and-bones tee shirt is Bo's bull-dog-like, five-ten, two-hundred-thirty-pound body. He hits the ground and maneuvers on his back under his truck. He stays there a few seconds, then slides out and stands with a hand in his pocket. Inside is likely a gun he smuggled over the border despite the heavy prison sentence.

Bo conducts a three-sixty sweep of the area, gives a thumbs-up. Glen trots outside and climbs into the passenger seat. They start driving.

"What's going on, my man?" Glen asks.

"Same shit."

"Work all right?"

"Same shit."

"They got to fire that boss of yours."

"Wait till you hear what the little prick did today. Some guy buys a big-screen TV from the website. Shows up at the store to pick it up. Policy is I've got to check his ID before I load the box into his car."

"Of course."

"Got to take a Xerox of it too. You know, to keep on file with the order."

"Right."

"So I do it. Get the TV in his car. The bald shmuck didn't tip me, but that's beside the point. And I come back into the store. And my boss, with that stupid head of his, he's eyeing down the Xerox I just took. Like some . . . like some pain-in-the-ass teacher judging a homework assignment."

"Was the copy unclear?"

"Clear as the ocean."

"What's that supposed to mean?"

"It was clear. What?"

"Oh. Because with the ocean, sometimes it's really clear and in other places it's not. Wasn't sure what you meant."

"Clear. All right. So this pussy ... I swear I want to bite off his nose, just lean forward and clamp down on it with my teeth and shake my head as he screams ... he tells me the customer's driver's license is expired. So I go, so what? He's like, well, it's not a valid document, you shouldn't have done that. And I go, was it valid when he originally showed up to the DMV and got it? You know?"

"Fair question."

"Right? We're just cross-referencing to make sure the names match so I can give him the damn TV. I don't care about some expiration date. Not a valid document? Kiss my ass."

"What'd you do?"

"This twat went to some crappy college for two years and what, he thinks he's better than me? But I didn't say shit. Walked away. Hit the Chili's in my mall after my shift. Put a thrashing on a slab of ribs. Calmed my nerves."

"Glad."

"Yeah. I'm fine. Good to see you, brother."

"You too."

Bo surveys the towel bandage protruding out from Glen's sleeve and says, "Show me what you're working with."

"The couple leant me a pair of tweezers. I got the bullet out. Still a little raw though." He reveals the hole in his shoulder.

"Just a scratch. I'll stitch you up at the warehouse."

Glen peers out the window at the slum's ramshackle houses, the scattered trash in the streets, and the rag-ged-clothed people walking about. "Makes you feel lucky," he says. "Seeing all this. Doesn't it? To be an American."

"Greatest nation in history. Didn't get that way by chance. Got that way because people like us fought for it to be that way. Don't ever forget that."

"You know I'll never forget that."

They merge onto a northbound highway. In the rearview mirror, Glen views the distancing Mexican hills. He says, "We'll need another way to kill junkies."

"Amen."

Glen thinks back to when he and Bo first began their secret initiative six months ago. They pretended to be drug dealers and lured San Diego addicts on their own. However, the two middle-aged White men often didn't pass for dope pushers, plus ran into frequent turf squabbles with San Diego's real dealers. So they formed a paid alliance with Los Hombres del Vacio to gain credibility on the street. Which is now gone.

"We'll come up with something," Glen says.

"We always do. Just glad you got out of there."

"Down a duffel bag of cash and a Mercedes."

"You've got plenty of cash. For the car, just say it was stolen in San Diego. Nab the insurance."

"Not to mention, the gang wants me dead."

"I knew these bastards weren't saints. But to do . . . that . . . to an innocent girl. Over a gambling debt. Next-level twisted. You did the right thing helping her out, brother."

"Let's hope they don't find out where I live. No more than thirty-something miles to the front door of my house from here."

"We never gave Ayala our names. How could he find out?"

Glen shuts off his burner phone, tosses it out the window. "Yours too. You've called Ayala from it, he knows your number. If they somehow track your signal, they'll use that to get to me. We'll buy new pre-paid phones when we get back to the US."

Bo snaps his burner in two pieces, chucks them out the window.

Silence for a bit. Then Glen says, "How could I be so Goddamn dumb?"

"What?"

"My Mercedes. The plates."

Bo grunts.

"That's my regular car," Glen says. "The one I drive to work. It's registered to my real name. A modest bribe to a DMV employee could get them my address. It's not just me I have to worry about there. Cora."

"I got your back. You'll be fine."

"Maybe she won't."

"You going to warn her?"

"About what? That a Mexican gang may show up at our home looking to kill me? She'll ask too many questions. Ones I won't be able to lie my way out of without telling her . . . everything."

"You can't do that."

"No kidding."

"So what're you going to do?"

Glen is quiet as he considers the question. Then punches the glove box.

TWENTY-NINE

Tommy knocks on the door labeled "16E" in Prescott Plaza, the Downtown high-rise Jordana lives. She opens it, Tommy seeing her for the first time in a non-work outfit. White tee shirt, yellow shorts, sneakers. He takes off his sunglasses, asks, "Did you listen to the voicemail from the US number?"

"Multiple times. I reviewed it with a team of narcotics experts at the office. We—"

"Isn't any data from the stolen phone supposed to be a secret?"

"I had to tell them a lie."

"Look at you."

"A white lie. The FBI still doesn't know we stole the phone. I said a federale CI got me the voicemail recording. And I could potentially blow his cover if I went into details."

"Smooth."

"Thank you."

She waves him in. Nice apartment. On a wall a heart-shaped sculpture lit in purple neon, the wall across all glass, outside a view of the city and its bay.

"So what's the FBI's expert opinion then?" he asks.

"That line the leader said about needing more supply, supply must be narcotics. Standard lingo according to the team. The way they see it, the two Caucasians with the box truck are buying drugs in bulk from the Mexicans, then using drug-addicted vagrants as dealers in California, enlisting them to sell to others in their encampments. Probably compensating them with the product. And it seems killing them if they become unreliable."

"They're wrong."

"What? Why?"

"Supply. It doesn't mean drugs. It means organs."

"No reason to infer anything about organs."

"My sister struggled with substance abuse most of her life. But she would never sell the stuff. If the FBI's theory were true, she was killed because she was a poor-performing street dealer. No way. They murdered her and the others for their organs."

Her eyes angle upward. "Kill the homeless for their organs and sell them to rich people without donors. It's plausible as a concept. But nothing ties that motive to this case. Organs haven't come up once the whole investigation. Where drugs do at almost every turn."

"Yes, these guys are baiting addicts with the mention of drugs. But aren't actually selling any. Danielle mentioned that in her statement. She and the four she was with never received the smack they were promised. Seems to me that was just a ploy to get them out to the woods. Where they could be killed without witnesses around."

"That's a stretch."

"She also said they shot everyone in the head. A hard target to hit, especially at night. Why avoid firing at the body?" He points at his stomach. "To not damage supply."

"Reasonable. But still a stretch. You—"

"The victims were all on drugs, but notice how none appeared sickly in recent photos? Youthful, mostly twenties and thirties, nobody strikingly underweight. Organs viable still."

"Still, too reliant on context. You need specifics."

"I have specifics."

She raises an eyebrow.

"Danielle said she saw coolers in the box truck," he says. "Remember?"

"Yes."

"Like me, I'm guessing you didn't pay much attention to that comment when you first heard it. Hot August night, makes sense these men would bring along some cold waters, sodas, whatever. Right?"

"Sure."

"But she used the plural. She said coolers. I reread her statement to make sure. There were only two men in that box truck. I don't care how hot it is, two guys aren't going through multiple coolers of beverages on a single trip."

"Agreed, they're not. Maybe the coolers were just . . . stored in there. Weren't used for any function that night."

"Why store empty coolers in the back of a vehicle versus in a garage like everyone else?"

"I . . . look, I'm not sure. There's still a lot of gray—"

"Danielle said Ayala and the other Mexican passed a dead body to the White guys on the truck. They were about to do the same with her. Then likely the others if the teenagers on the quads didn't roll up. If this was just some drug hit, why load up the bodies?"

"Maybe . . . to hide them, hide proof of the crime."

"They were already in the middle of the woods. Could've buried them there. No, they were going to cut them open, take out their organs, put them on ice in those coolers."

"I don't know."

"That one missing-persons witness you guys let me read about in Tijuana, the one from Chula Vista, said she bugged out when she saw big knives on the truck. But the suspects don't murder with knives. They do with guns. Maybe the knives she saw weren't for hurting her when she was alive, but removing her organs once she was dead. Surgical knives."

"It's . . . possible."

"It's probable. Drive up to homeless encampments talking up some super hit of heroin to healthier-looking people. Bring any takers out to the woods. Shoot them in the head, cut out their organs, put them on ice for sale to the highest black-market bidder."

She walks to her mini-bar, pours herself a glass of red wine. Then points at the bottle as if to ask if he wants some.

"Yeah," he says. "Thanks." He eyes the ten or so bottles on her mounted wine rack. Almost all have the same label, "Velatti." Though he's not much of a wine drinker, he's heard of the company.

"What'd you rob a Velatti truck?" he asks.

Grinning, she hands him his glass. "Don't have to. I get it for free."

"How'd you manage that?"

"I was born Jordana Velatti. My family . . . well, owns the company."

"Come on."

She nods at a photo on her mantle of men, women, and children posing in a lush vineyard in matching fleeces with the Velatti logo. "That's me on the end. I was . . . eleven I think. That's my grandfather in the middle. He started the company from nothing after migrating from Italy. My dad, the one behind me, took it over after he passed away."

He has a sip. "So you're like a billionaire?"

"It's a family business. Not my personal company. I don't—"

"You must have a big share of it in your name though?"

"It's . . . I don't know. You like your wine?"

"You next in line to run it?"

"No. No. I'm happy where I'm at."

"Chasing criminals?"

"What's wrong with that? Didn't you come here to do the same thing?"

"Nothing's wrong with that." He points at the family photo. "That just seems like a better lifestyle."

"Napa is a short plane ride away. I still get to see my family a lot."

"Can you be an FBI agent up there?"

"Sure. But I like it down here."

"It's nice here. But—"

"Your wine. You like it or what?"

"Yeah. Yeah, it's bomb."

"Good."

"Jordana Velatti."

"Jordana Quick."

He recollects that Google search he did on her in Tijuana, how no results came up for Jordana Quick beside her Quantico graduation. Maybe the last-name change was recent. He peeks at her left hand for a ring. Nothing.

She chuckles as if aware of what he's doing. "I didn't change it to Quick because I got married. My mother's maiden name. With a job like mine, it's difficult to find a boyfriend, let alone a husband."

"Why's that?"

"The hours, obviously." She has a long sip. "But more than that too. I think it freaks a lot of guys out. The stuff I have to do. The people I have to go after. They don't come out and say that. But I suspect it."

"So why'd you change your last name then?"

"If you're around criminals all day like me, you don't want them to know your family has resources. Makes you a kidnapping target."

"Do FBI agents get kidnapped a lot by people they're investigating?"

"I wouldn't say so. But still, better to play it safe."

"You don't seem like the type that plays things safe."

She gives him a tilted-head look that's part agreement, part skepticism. Though he doesn't want to probe, he assumes kidnap avoidance wasn't the real motivation for her last-name change. Since her career choice is such a departure from her family's business, he guesses she went with a different name to define her own legacy in her own field instead of facing constant associations with a famous name on a wine label.

He says, "I told you before I'd be honest with you about what I'm up to. Hopefully giving you my organ-trafficking theory is proof of that. It'd be nice if you could be honest with me too. About the case from the FBI's perspective. Doesn't mean I'm looking to insert myself into your investigation. Just want to know if you're getting . . . close."

"I gave the tech team the US burner number. They're going to dig into that."

"Can they track him from the signal? The FBI does creepy stuff like that all the time, right?"

She gives him a sarcastic look. "I already spoke to the pre-paid calling company that sold the leader's burner. Unfortunately the phone isn't giving off a signal anymore. Not for the last few hours at least. He must've shut it off for some reason. Which makes detecting his current location impossible."

"Even if you can't trace him in real time, I'm sure you can get access to the phone's records. There's got to be a ton to learn about him in those."

"That's my hope. Like the majority of pre-paid firms, his rents network space from a national carrier instead of building and operating its own cellphone towers. I talked to an FBI contact at the national telecom corporation that provided his service. They're compiling a data file for us."

"What do you expect to get back?"

"All his texts, numbers of incoming and outgoing calls, and locations of the cell towers his burner's pinged. That location data, even if days, weeks, or months old, can lead us to his identity."

"How?"

"If we look at the towers his number pinged while it was still on, a pattern will emerge. We expect the highest activity in two geographic areas, one corresponding to where he lives, the other where he works. We'll search the areas' residential and employment databases for all White, middle-aged males. Not many names should show up in both places. Those names would belong to men who live and work in the burner's high-activity zones. A good chance somebody in that subset is the phone's owner."

"How soon until the FBI can do that search?"

"I put a rush on the telecom company for the raw data. Then we need our Intelligence analysts to go through it and cross-reference everything. Not easy, but our people are the best. I'm guessing we'll have a narrow list of suspect names sometime tonight."

"Sometime tonight. That's good. I like that." He holds up his glass.

She clinks it with hers. "Nobody can hide from the FBI forever. If we want you, we have the power to find you."

THIRTY

Glen takes a piss in one of his home's two downstairs bathrooms. He hits the rim of the bowl, urine spraying off it onto the floor.

"Shoot," he says.

He clenches his pelvic muscles, stopping the piss, and pulls up his pants.

"Stupid," he says. "You're so stupid sometimes."

He sinks to his knees and cleans the mess with water, hand soap, and wads of toilet paper. A small puddle remains. He takes a deep breath, dabs it with his fingertips, and licks them.

"You deserved that," he says to himself, keeping his voice low so Cora doesn't hear from the den.

He flushes the toilet, then walks to her, joining her on the couch. "Hey cutie," he says.

"How's your shoulder feeling?"

"Still a little sore."

She makes a sad face, then goes back to her laptop. She's working on a new post for the fashion blog she runs.

"What's this one about?" he asks.

"Maternity chic."

He pats her thigh, then puts in his headphones and continues his Prince Troy audiobook from his phone. The next chapter opens on the prince and his allies finding disguises in the demon's realm. One of the men admits he's scared, tells the others he wants to go back home. But Prince Troy delivers a stirring speech explaining how they're in a battle of good versus evil and their purpose in life is clear, to fight and win. The man stays.

Cora taps his arm.

He pauses the story. "Yeah?"

"I was wondering . . . why didn't you call me?"

He removes his headphones. "When?"

"After the accident."

"It was just so . . . hectic. Dealing with the other driver, the Mercedes, then the police. By the time the tow truck took me to the auto body, and I had a minute of quiet, my phone was dead. I usually charge it in my car. Which I of course didn't have access to."

"Then what? Your army friend came to the auto body and took you here?"

"Bo."

"What?"

"My army friend. His name is Bo. You met him at our wedding."

"Right. So . . . how did you call him for a ride if your phone was dead?"

"A landline. At the repair shop."

"You have his number memorized? You don't even see him that often."

A moment. "They let me use their computer. I have all my contacts backed up in the cloud."

"Since when?"

"Recently." He kisses her on the forehead. "Can we talk about all this tomorrow? I just need to relax after my day, cutie."

"Yeah, okay. Sure."

"Speaking of relaxing, I had a great idea before. The hospital gave me the rest of the week off while I heal from the accident. Let's take advantage of it, drive the Aston Martin up the coast to a resort, pamper ourselves for a few days. How about that one in Dana Point we always say is so nice when we pass it on the PCH?"

"I don't really feel like being in a hotel right now. I always sleep better in my own bed." She pats her pregnant stomach. "And Jade and I need the rest." She moves her attention back to her computer.

"No problem." He forces a smile.

The next few days, he wanted her out of the house in case Los Hombres del Vacio made a move on him at this address. But she is just as stubborn as sweet and if she says she doesn't want to sleep in a hotel, she won't.

He puts his headphones back on and continues his fantasy story.

THIRTY-ONE

Tommy and Jordana drink wine on her deck. High above San Diego, a tangerine-colored sunset hugging the city. He notices a pair of inch-long lines parallel to each other on the skin of her right knee. They're faint, only detectable up close, scars maybe a decade old. He believes he knows their cause. Cutting. His ex-girlfriend in high school did it. She'd nick herself on purpose with a blade. The way she explained it, the rush of pain would bring some sort of comfort.

"My favorite part of the apartment," she says. "Out here. This time of the day. The sky."

He gazes downward at the cars and pedestrians funneling between buildings. "I used to like looking up at the sky. Don't do it anymore."

"Why not?"

"I still see black smoke. The kind I saw when fighting an

arson fire. If I stare at the sky long enough, the image of it flashes in my mind. So I don't look anymore."

"What was it like being a firefighter? Going into a burning building?"

"When you're in a burning building, you need to just . . . do. Your unconscious takes over. It moves you through the rooms. You have to trust it. If you think about the flames, you'll get burnt."

"FBI agents go into a similar zone closing in on criminals. You cross a point and . . . just let instinct take over."

"Your family must be proud of you."

"For what?"

"You're the heiress of a wine empire. You don't have to work a day in your life. But you chose one of the hardest gigs on the planet. And are pretty good at it if I may say."

"Oh . . . well . . . thanks. That wine empire only exists because America empowered my grandfather to build it. He came here with just a couple bucks in his pocket. Worked hard. Took some chances. And . . . had success. Being an FBI agent is my way of giving back I guess. To a country that was so good to my family."

"I wouldn't call that sort of work giving back. Come on. Not you personally, but the FBI as a whole, does some messed-up stuff. It's not like it's a charity."

"A lot of charities are scams."

"Yeah?"

"Google it. The FBI isn't perfect either. I'm aware."

"Think it'll ever improve?"

"And become perfect? No. Is anything perfect? Is anyone perfect? What does that word even mean?"

"I don't know."

"Me neither. But I do know the FBI is the best resistance we have against our own downfall. Without us enforcing laws, America isn't America anymore. A lot of people out there want to ruin all this." She sweeps her hand over the San Diego skyline. "The scariest part is, in their own heads, they think they're right."

A pause. "How many charities are phony?"

"I can probably pull a report for you at the office if you really want to know."

"Nah. Forget it."

She grabs the bottle of wine from the table and tops off their glasses. "Your family must be proud of you too. For being a fireman for all those years."

"Oh. Yeah. Definitely."

"You guys close?"

"Very."

"Your parents live in Queens too?"

"They moved to the suburbs a couple years ago. Westchester. Wanted more space. More land. Built a big house. My dad designed it himself."

"He's an architect?"

"One of the top ones in Manhattan."

"I've always been into architecture." She grabs her phone. "What's his company's website? I'm sure they have a portfolio up."

"They're really private. Not online. All the business is from word of mouth. They don't do advertising, nothing like that."

"I see."

"A California girl."

"What?"

"That's you. California girl."

"New York boy."

"Yeah. New York boy."

She stares into his eyes, holds her gaze a couple seconds longer than she ever has. She may be inviting him to kiss her. He wants to. But something stops him.

He turns his head, pretends to point at something on the street. "Look at that."

"What?"

"Some guy. He was like juggling or something."

"I don't see."

"He just turned into an alley."

He swigs half his wine. And thinks about how his mother hurt his father. If he kissed Jordana, then became close to her, he assumes she'd hurt him one day too.

"It might be a few more hours until the analysts get back to me with the suspect list," she says. "Until then, think it'll be good to get out, unwind a little. Want to do something with me?"

He smiles. "Okay."

THIRTY-TWO

Tommy, in virtual-reality goggles, spins the wheel of a street-racing arcade game, his red car on the projection in front of him hitting a sharp turn. Before he and Jordana came to the arcade, he showered, changed into a collared shirt, and put on cologne.

"You're about to get smoked," she says from the plastic driver's seat next to his.

Her pink car goes into turbo mode, zooming past his. It crosses the finish line first, "WINNER" blinking above it.

"How'd you get an extra turbo?" he asks, removing his goggles.

"Secret," she says, removing hers.

"Not fair. This is my first time playing. I don't know the secrets."

"That's called the advantage of experience."

"How often you come here?"

"Maybe once a month. Great place to blow off steam."

"I haven't been to a spot like this since . . . man, since I was maybe ten." He glances at the rows of high-tech simulation games. "Different then. *Addam's Family* pinball. *Mortal Kombat* machine. Simple. None of this crazy computer stuff."

"They have a room of old-school games in the back."

He nods at his goggles. "Kind of scary how advanced all this is getting. Do you see computers being able to think soon, like in movies?"

"They already think. AI. As for the debate of whether or not they'll become conscious, like how humans are, no way."

"Why not?"

"We don't even understand where our own consciousness comes from. So how can we expect to design the same thing in a computer? That's just as silly as someone giving out a recipe for a dish they never cooked themselves."

"I read this journal article in prison that said if computer scientists can just create enough like electrical connections, like circuits, billions of them same as there are billions of cells in the brain, then consciousness would just sort of pop up, like it just would be born on its own, without a recipe."

"Nah."

"Sounds reasonable enough, no?"

"Scientists can be full of themselves. So certain. But they contradict themselves just like everyone else. There's a universe, no a multiverse. Smoking is good for you, smoking is bad for you. Just because their minds are smarter than most other humans', doesn't mean they can create a human mind."

"Hmm. Yeah. Maybe not. I don't know."

"No person is God."

"You believe in God?"

"Not the kind from the Bible. Robe, beard, that whole thing. But in a higher power . . . yeah. You?"

"Got to be some sort of higher power, right?"

"If you had one question to ask it, what would it be?"

A pause. "How do I unlock the secret turbo in *Fury Street Racing* so I have a Goddamn chance at an even match against Jordana Quick?"

She giggles. Then cups her ear with her hand. "God's silence."

"While I wait for my answer, let's check out that old-school section."

She leads him across a floor of teenagers and through a doorway with a sign over it styled like Blockbuster Video's logo. They play Skee-Ball. While talking about their favorite childhood TV shows, the likelihood of aliens existing, over-rated black-and-white movies, whether or not moustaches are cool, and Trent Reznor's transition to film scores.

Their Skee-Ball playing leaves them with heaps of tickets. They take them to a prize counter, trading them for a stuffed zebra, then progress to the establishment's restaurant area and sit at the bar.

"What're you drinking?" Tommy asks. "It's on me."

"We'll split it."

"No way. You're letting me crash."

"I'll do one, just one. Margarita."

He orders it, plus a beer for himself.

"That is frickin' adorable," a female voice says.

They turn to it. A late-twenties woman with glasses and pigtails sits a couple stools over, pointing at the zebra. She presents a stuffed owl about the same size, says, "We went with this. We named him Hoot."

The mid-thirties man next to her nods at Tommy. He nods back.

"Cute," Jordana says. "We didn't name ours yet." She turns to Tommy. "What do you think?"

"How 'bout Zeb?"

She chuckles, nods.

"Adorable," the tipsy, pig-tailed woman says. "How long you two been dating?"

"Oh," Jordana says. "No. We're not dating. We ... work

together I guess you could say."

"Get out. You totally look like a couple."

"You guys ... dating?"

The woman flashes a wedding ring. "Nope. Marrying. Is that even a word?"

"It's a word," her husband says. "But not in that context."

"Yeah. Right, right." She turns back to Jordana. "This place is so stupid. But I love it."

"Ha. Same."

"We live around the corner. We come a lot after we have sex. Especially when it's really good."

"Ah. Okay."

"We get a drink. Then take a stroll on the beach." She grins. "Join us. We're going right after this."

"Thanks, but—"

"Come on."

Jordana glimpses Tommy. He shrugs as if to say, *Why not?*

"We're down," Jordana tells her.

"Yay."

They finish their drinks and walk three blocks to the beach, the married couple's arms around each other's backs. The sun has set, the sand appearing dark purple in the night. They wander a path, a breeze carrying over the scent of the sea.

Jordana talks to the wife about some new type of rentable scooter available in parts of San Diego, Tommy to the husband about shark attacks. Tommy was at first skeptical of him, felt he might be full of himself, but decided he likes him. He seems like the type of guy who could be his friend.

"I have an idea," the wife says, slipping off her shoes.

"What?" Jordana asks.

"It'll be fun." She trots onto the sand.

The other three join her. She asks Tommy and Jordana, "You ever do a fight in the pool, with those noodles, girl on guy's shoulders? Same thing but with Hoot and ... Zeb."

"How drunk are you, honey?" her husband asks.

"Four out of ten."

He makes a doubtful face.

"Six out of ten," she says.

"I'll buy that." He turns to Tommy and Jordana. "What do you think?"

Tommy peeks at her. She shrugs as if to say, *Why not?* Then climbs on his shoulders.

The wife gets on her husband's, says, "First couple to tip over loses. You're not a couple, whatever, but you know what I mean. Ready?"

"Ready," Jordana says.

The men take a couple steps toward each other. The women start whacking each other with the stuffed animals. Laughter.

"What sort of an owl is the size of a zebra?" Jordana says. "That thing is a mutant." She wobbles. "No." She falls off Tommy's shoulders. He catches her.

"We win," the wife shouts. "Yes."

Jordana smiles. Then turns to her, says, "Let's go again."

"Bring it on, girl."

Tommy and Jordana take the next round. They do two more, each team winning one. Then catch their breath on the sand. The four have a conversation about beach volley-ball. It morphs into one about how much real gold is used in Olympic medals. According to Google, they are all wrong.

They walk into the ice-cream shop across the street. Red curtains, wicker tables, photos on the wall of old-time surfers.

"What're you getting?" Jordana asks Tommy.

"They have banana. Most places never have banana." He smiles at the attendant, points at the tub of ice cream through the glass case. "Large cup, please."

The four sit at a table by the window and eat their ice cream with plastic spoons. For the first time since his attempted-robbery arrest, Tommy feels like a normal person.

"Excuse me guys," Jordana says. "I'm getting a call." She pulls her vibrating phone from her pocket, scans the screen, and steps outside.

Tommy follows her. "Intelligence?"

"We're about to get our list of suspects."

THIRTY-THREE

Glen rips a piece of duct tape off a roll. On a ladder in his den, he sticks the corner of a strip of cardboard onto a tall window. The Prince Troy audiobook plays through his headphones. The demon's army is stronger than the prince and his allies expected. But they're about to retrieve the Shield of Armatron, which could protect them. Only those with pure goodness in their hearts can unleash the powers of the shield. Glen believes Prince Troy is one.

"Glen?" Cora says.

He pauses the story, takes out his headphones. "Hi cutie."

In a robe, she peers at the pile of torn cardboard on the floor beside him. "What're you doing?"

"I heard there've been a few burglaries in the neighborhood," he lies. "Trying to stay safe is all."

"I didn't hear that."

"Yeah. Some people were talking about it at Whole Foods."

"The window looks so . . . ugly like that. How is cardboard keeping us safe?"

"Probably a few tweakers running around. Anything to get that next high. What we don't want is them snooping through a window, seeing one of our paintings, a piece of your jewelry, anything else of value, then trying to get inside to take it. I closed all the curtains and blinds. Make sure you keep them that way. For any window without a cover, I figured I'd put up cardboard. It's just temporary. Until the cops catch them."

"We have an alarm system. And cameras."

"I know. I know. I guess after having such a close call today with the accident, safety is on the brain. I never, ever want to let anything happen to you and Jade. If a little cardboard could help, call me paranoid all you'd like. I'm still doing it." He yanks the duct tape, a *curuck* noise echoing through the room.

"All right. I guess as long as it's temporary."

"One other thing, now that you're down here."

"What is it?"

"Bo has really been having a hard time with his girlfriend. We spoke for a while in the car before. But he still has a bunch to run by me. Wants to come over later. We won't leave my study. You won't even hear us. Is that all right?"

She holds her stare on him for a while. "That's fine."

"Appreciate it."

She paces out of the room. He has an urge to run over and tell her everything. That he's not blocking the view of burglars, but murderers. That the gang is after him because he rescued a teenage girl from an atrocity in Mexico. That he was in Mexico in the hopes of continuing his conducting of life-saving transplants.

But he stays on the ladder. Cora, like the rest of America, would never forgive him even if she understood him.

THIRTY-FOUR

Tommy watches Jordana's face during her call with the Intelligence analyst. Her complexion's turned pale. "I don't know," she says into the phone. "You did all you could . . . Okay . . . Bye." She hangs up, paces along the sidewalk.

"How many names are on the list?"

"What the hell am I doing? I'm the lead agent on this case and I'm what . . . drinking margaritas and eating ice cream instead of making progress? What's the matter with me?"

"You were just waiting for them to get back to you. Everyone needs a break sometimes. So?"

"Huh?"

"What'd the analyst say?"

She sits on the curb. Rubs her forehead. "Zero."

"What?"

"You asked me how many names were on the list. He told me zero."

"How is that possible?"

"This is my first case as lead. Everyone is waiting for the twenty-six-year-old rich girl to screw it up. And this is the hand I get dealt. All we went through in Mexico to get that phone. Led to nothing. I have nothing to work with."

"Maybe the analyst botched it. Get . . . a second opinion."

"It's not his fault. Anything we were hoping to learn from the data just isn't there."

"Maybe the data is incomplete. Ask the phone company for . . . more."

"Not their fault either. They sent over the complete record for the leader's burner. He only used it to make calls to two other numbers. The first is Ayala's. The second is another US burner. Probably belongs to the other White male your sister saw on the box truck. If he even called a single regular, registered phone, we'd have a contact's name, someone to interview. But no."

"What about texts?"

"He received zero in the phone's six-month existence. Sent zero."

"Everyone texts. That has to be wrong."

"No. It has to be by design. He must've known the phone company keeps records of all texts, even for burner devices, must've known we could get our hands on them if we wanted. So he planned ahead. Avoided them entirely. Which means he's not only savvy. But disciplined."

"What about voicemails? He left one on Ayala's phone. He obviously didn't avoid them."

"Sure. He probably does have voicemails on his phone. And they'd probably teach us a lot. But telecom firms don't store copies. Audio files take up a lot of digital space, would be too expensive for carriers to duplicate every one in their data centers. VMs only live on phones themselves. We were able to listen to Ayala's because we had his physical device. But we don't have the leader's."

"You seemed optimistic about the cell-tower location data before. Did that come back?"

"Was nearly as useless as everything else. The phone company identified a region of San Diego where the burner sent the bulk of its cell-tower pings. The issue is it was the only high-activity region. We were hoping for two, one for work, one for home, so we could cross-reference the information. There were other pings, but they were too scattered for a pattern. He likely planned for this too. Concentrated almost all his phone business to a single place to keep himself anonymous if we ever got his usage file."

"But he's not anonymous. You said they identified a region. I get one isn't as good as two. But it's way better than none. Pull up the names of any middle-aged White men who work or live there and see if any registered a white box truck with the DMV."

"Yes, the team is doing that."

"Great."

"Not really. Based on the sort of forward thinking he exhibited with his phone, I doubt he registered his truck under his own name."

Tommy sits next to her. Quiet for a while. Then he says, "I'll go door to door in the region, question every White guy between forty and fifty. Ask if they killed my sister. When I come across the one who did, I'll know. I'll see it in his eyes."

"Come on, Tommy. You sound desperate."

"Maybe. But desperate sounds better than hopeless. That's what you sound like right now. Like you gave up."

"I'm not giving up. I'm just thinking practically. I have to stay practical if I'm going to find a guy like this. The high-activity area the telecom company identified is the part of San Diego where the VA Hospital is. That place is the size of a small country. It employs thousands. Many if not most of them middle-aged White men. Going up to each, looking into their eyes, and hoping for a hunch isn't the answer. I need to do better than that."

"So he works at a hospital?"

"Likely."

"He could have surgical experience, maybe even be a doctor?"

"Sure."

"My organ-trafficking theory. It's got to be right."

"Fine, you were right. And I was wrong. Congratulations."

"Jesus. What's with the sarcasm? I'm just trying to . . . talk you through this."

She closes her eyes. "Sorry." Then opens them. "It's just . . . this is all a lot. And it's all my responsibility now. I can't even call Gabor for help."

A pause. "Well . . . you have me."

"Thanks. Really, thanks." She folds her arms, looks toward the ocean. "According to the timeline, just one more day before they kill again. If I don't figure something out by tomorrow, this is going to turn into a nightmare."

"San Diego police are keeping a close watch on the city's homeless encampments for a white box truck. They may need more time before attempting another attack."

"Not with a leader like this. I studied criminals like him in Quantico. He's a planner. He'll stay on schedule."

"Of the eight related missing-persons cases, only two were a week apart. There were longer gaps between the others. His next move's spacing may be more like theirs."

"You mean the eight missing-persons cases we know about. Most residents in tent cities are zonked out on drugs or booze. There could've been plenty more incidents of homeless people disappearing the last six months that nobody even noticed, that were never reported. If we knew about all of them, based on the suspect's attention to planning, I wouldn't be surprised if they all fell a week apart, give or take maybe a day."

"Why?"

"Anything shorter would've drawn too much attention, too many disappearances in just one city. And anything longer wouldn't be characteristic of the suspect's diligent profile. If he decided a week was a sufficient amount of time once, he wouldn't allow himself longer in the future. It'd feel to him like cheating."

Tommy tries to assemble in his mind an image of this man she's describing. He sees a body, but no detail in the face, just a red blur.

"The one thing that did change from attack to attack is his victim count," she says. "But not for the better. The first four disappearances involved just one person. In the next three, two. The eighth, three. In the last, Danielle's, five. Meaning he's getting better at this. Getting comfortable. And the next attack he has planned should dwarf all the rest."

"Why?"

"In the voicemail he left Ayala, remember that line about promises? People I made promises to."

"Yeah."

"Who do you think those people are?"

"Sick people who need organs."

"Yes. But likely not just any sick people. The word promise implies a personal connection, like this is about more than money. Since he was interrupted with Danielle's group, he didn't get any of those organs. Meaning the recipients they were earmarked for didn't get them either. In his next attack, he has to make up for last week's loss of supply, plus account for this week's recipients. For him to keep his commitment to all these people, we're looking at something massive in the next attack. A double-digit body count."

THIRTY-FIVE

Glen leads Bo into his study and locks the door. Bo says, "You might want to sit down for this shit."

Glen descends into his desk chair. "Hit me with it."

"You convinced me junkies really don't want to live, that they're filling themselves with poison because they have a death wish on some level. While sick vets want the opposite. They'd give anything just to live a little longer. Which is—"

"A life in exchange for another life, one its owner doesn't want anymore traded for one its owner is clinging onto."

"Right. We'll still help the troops. But we can't use drug addicts anymore to do it. It's not just the loss of Los Hombres del Vacio preventing it. But the ramped-up presence of cops by homeless encampments."

"Where're we going to get the organs then?"

"We relied on the gangsters to lure targets out of tent cities so we could take care of them in isolated areas. What if we went for targets who didn't require any luring?"

"People who would willingly drive to their own death? Makes no sense. How do you bypass a lure?"

"I'm warning you, we're going to have to open our minds here. But if we do, we can save the vets we gave our word to. Isn't that all that should matter?"

"I suppose. But—"

"Plus, you won't have to go out of pocket for the sixty-five-hundred-dollar-per-body hit fees Los Hombres del Vacio were getting. And we won't have ask the vets to cover any of those costs."

"So what's the catch?"

"When I drive to work, I pass a bunch of farms in Imperial County. Plots of quiet land, isolated for miles on all sides, nowhere near police or possible witnesses. A lot of farmworkers sleep on the properties. No need to be lured to another location for handling. We can—"

"You expect us to kill innocent farmworkers? No way. No Goddamn way."

"We've been killing innocent junkies, haven't we?"

"Because they have a death wish. Farmworkers don't. They're some of the hardest working people in the country. They don't deserve to die."

"So soldiers deserve to die instead?"

Glen puts his elbow on his desk and sets his forehead in his hand. Silence for a while.

Bo nods at a portrait of Ulysses S. Grant hanging beside a shelf of medical textbooks. "When Grant won the Civil War, did everyone his army kill deserve to die? Of course not. A lot of victims were innocent civilians. Women and children. Fellow Americans. But they had to die for him to achieve his goal. And isn't the country better off because he did?"

"Yes. But he was at war. It's—"

"So are we, dammit. We're soldiers. At war for the lives of other soldiers left behind by their own government. I know this isn't easy. War is about making hard decisions for a cause bigger than yourself."

Glen sighs. Then logs into the dark-web site for black-market trade. A stack of over twenty unanswered messages in his inbox. Three from a woman named Susan Birch. A veteran of the War in Afghanistan with severe cirrhosis who filed a transplant application with him over two months ago. Last week he assured her he'd have a liver for her by now. He reads her latest message:

My doctor told my husband and me this morning we should start thinking about what we want to say to the kids. He suggested we stop putting any spin on it. Gather them into a room and tell them mommy is going away. Not just like she does when she visits grandma. But going away forever. Since they're so young, and might not be able to comprehend my goodbye now, he also suggested I write each of them a letter. Ones they shouldn't open until they're fifteen.

I started mine to Dylan, my oldest, about an hour ago. But had to stop because my nose gushed blood all over the paper. I am down to 89 lbs. I don't know how much longer I can go. You are my only hope sir. Is it money? Is that why you're not writing me back anymore? The cost seems so low. Do you want more? My husband and I talked. We can sell things. We can get you $14,250. Is that enough? –Sue

He asks Bo, "How would it even work?"

"I did some research tonight. Darrington Farm. It's perfect." He shows Glen a photo of a one-story building on his phone. "This is what we move on. A dozen farmworkers are bunking in this barrack."

Glen takes the phone, scrolls through additional pictures of the farm, capturing the barrack, woods, and service roads from a variety of angles. "What sort of security does Darrington Farm have?"

"No armed guards or anything like that. Too much land for them to cover. I noticed cameras though. Mounted high on poles near the barracks. Nothing a couple masks over our heads tomorrow night couldn't get around. I doubt anyone is actively monitoring that security feed. After the workers don't show up for their shift the next morning and someone checks on them, sees the mess we leave behind, I'm sure they'll review the tape. But we'll be long gone by then."

Glen stares at the face of Ulysses S. Grant for a while. "All right. I'll do it."

THIRTY-SIX

Tommy and Jordana sit on her couch, her laptop open on her knees. The neon from the glass heart on the wall mixes a purple glow into the darkness of the apartment. On her screen is an informational website about organ donation.

"Like I thought," she says. "The federal government manages the national transplant waiting list."

"Which must make it obscenely inefficient."

"It's not the government's fault. There're just not enough donors. Says here a new person is added to the list every ten minutes, outpacing the rate of new organ givers. Every day twenty Americans die as a result. So sad."

"What is the government's fault is mismanagement at the VA. Where this guy works. A few years ago, the problems were national news."

"There's definitely room for organizational improvement at the VA. So what?"

"Check out their transplant program. I bet it's a mess."

She does another Google search. Clicks one of the results, a news article with the title, "VA Delays Turn Deadly." She scans the page. "You're actually right. Various organ-deteriorating medical conditions are rampant among vets. Due to excessive waits at the VA between stages of the transplant process, many patients wither away before their surgeries."

"Those patients are more than statistics to this guy. He's experienced this shit firsthand. But was powerless to change anything inside the bloated government bureaucracy."

She performs another search, clicks a result. "Over a hundred grand for a liver or kidney on the black market. Way more for a heart or lung. The average soldier doesn't have that sort of cash."

"So he created a black market within a black market. If he kills people, he can cut out their organs for free. Sell them to soldiers for way less than a hundred K without going broke. Like you said before, this is about more than money to him. He wants to help these people. And he's sidestepping the bureaucracy to do it."

"He sort of sounds like you."

"What?"

"I didn't mean it to be offensive. Sidestepping—"

"He murdered my sister. I'm nothing like him."

"You're not a murderer. Of course. I just . . . it was silly. Forget I said it. You good?"

"I'm fine. It's getting late. Think I want to go to bed."

"Tommy, I really didn't mean—"

"I said it's fine. I'm just tired."

She stands. "You need an extra pillow or anything?"

"No."

"All right. Good night."

"Good night."

She steps into her bedroom with the laptop. Closes the door. Tommy lies on the couch. Unable to fall asleep.

THIRTY-SEVEN

Glen's arm reaches to the side of the bed where Cora sleeps to pull her in for a good-morning kiss. But his hand drops to the mattress. She isn't here. Odd. She never wakes up before him.

He rips the covers off himself, attaches the prosthetic foot he keeps bedside, a sliver of sun squeezing its way between the closed curtains onto him.

"Cora," he says toward the master bathroom, its door open a bit.

No reply.

He peeks inside. Nothing but marble, porcelain, and glass.

"Cora," he yells louder, toward the hallway.

Again, no response.

He snatches his phone off his night table. No calls or messages from her. He clicks her contact, "Cutie," and calls her.

No answer.

A second attempt. Same result.

He exits the bedroom, the head atop his nude body scanning the second story for signs of his wife.

"Cora," he shouts, louder yet, his voice echoing through the big house.

Nothing.

She's probably outside by the pool, can't hear him. He crosses into the guest bedroom, sticks his hand between the slats of its blinds, widening them for a view of the backyard. No movement down there except for a raft drifting about the water. No Cora on any lounge chair.

Maybe an emergency compelled her to leave the house. Though she hasn't experienced morning sickness since her first trimester, it could've returned today. She could've driven to Whole Foods for some of that ginger supplement she'd take for the nausea.

He descends the stairs to the first floor, veers into a room with a piano they refer to as the music room, and pulls open the curtains for a view of the driveway. Her Porsche is gone. She's probably at Whole Foods. Relaxation sets in.

But it's torn away when he notices one of the planters in the driveway is toppled, soil spilt all over the pavement, flowers strewn among it.

He rushes into his study, logs into the website of the security-system company. He finds the recording of the camera above the front door. Speed-rewinding through it, he notices motion around seven AM.

Cora's arm and leg flail. Then the planter falls. About ten seconds after, a door and wheel of her Porsche come into view. The vehicle backs out of the driveway, disappears from sight.

A gangster must've been lurking in the bushes, waiting for him to leave the house this morning. Instead, Cora must've come out first, the gangster deciding to abduct her as part of Glen's payback.

He rewatches the video. Since she's at the edge of the

frame, he can only see some of her and none her attacker. But he can imagine it all. He interrupted them with that girl in Tijuana. For his punishment, they'll possibly do to Cora what they planned for her. Maybe mail him photos.

His knees weaken. He clutches the piano to keep himself from falling. He stays drooped over the big, dark instrument for about a minute, remembering all those times he played it while singing to her.

An overwhelming hotness courses through his body. It impels him through the hallway into the kitchen. He clutches the Williams Sonoma blender and hurls it into a wall. He grasps a glass canister where Cora keeps her green-tea bags and smashes it on the floor, fragments swarming in all directions across the kitchen, some spilling over the dip into the den. He kicks the microwave with his prosthetic foot, bashing through the door, then heaves its tray into the den, the TV screen spider-webbing as the objects connect.

He glares at his reflection in the broken screen. "You're a pathetic man." He picks up a piece of jagged glass. And pounds it into his thigh. His screams fill the empty home.

THIRTY-EIGHT

Tommy's legs pump through a set of crunches on Jordana's rug. In prison, he grew accustomed to working out in his cell. He can do plenty in a tight space without gym equipment. He stands, his reflection staring back at him in the dark television screen, veins running down the muscles of his forearms. His hands lower onto the sofa and he begins a set of dips.

Jordana emerges from her bedroom in a work outfit. "Morning."

"Morning."

"You sleep okay?"

He slept for just a couple hours. That comment she made about his similarity to the leader stewed in his head, kept him awake.

"Yeah," he says. "Slept fine."

"Good. I've got a coffee maker in the kitchen. You can help yourself."

"All right. Thanks."

"I've got to head to the office. I'll see you after—"

"The idea of the leader isn't as generic as you think. You know a lot more about him than his skin color, gender, and age."

"Like?"

He picks up his phone from the coffee table, clicks a few buttons. The leader's voicemail to Ayala radiates from the speaker. "His voice," Tommy says. "You know the sound of his voice."

"That's true. But—"

"If the FBI played this at the VA, his coworkers could tell you who he is."

"Maybe. But even if that was a success, we'd blow the only advantage we have."

"Which is?"

"Comfort. He knows the FBI is still just after an idea of him. If we had his name, we would've questioned him by now. We want him to continue feeling comfortable. Want him to surface on schedule tonight to kill again. Then capture him in the act."

"He wouldn't know you had his name. Like you said, thousands of people work at the VA. You don't need to play the voicemail for all of them. Just select twenty at random. The probability he'd be one is super low. Then you can put surveillance on—"

"Imagine if you were in that twenty. A team of FBI agents tells you one of your coworkers is a mass murderer. Gossip would fly around the hospital. Within minutes the leader would hear we're looking for him. And go on the run. We likely couldn't get an arrest warrant by the time he fled the country."

"Fine. Whatever. Don't do it."

"I'm not."

"Only trying to help."

"I know. But that wouldn't help."

"Nice to know. Have a good day."

"Yeah. You too."

She leaves the apartment. He cranks out a set of push-ups, then goes into the kitchen, notices the coffee maker. He scoops some grounds from a canister, brews a pot. The machine hums. He peers at the rack of Velatti wines. Then the "Stanford University Alumni" magnet on the refrigerator.

THIRTY-NINE

Tommy walks through the San Diego VA Hospital. He batted the dust from the Tijuana junkyard off his suit pants, washed his dress shirt in Jordana's laundry machine, and now wears the clean outfit.

His eyes scan the names and titles on office doors. He knocks on one labeled "Brandy Cho – Senior Human Resources Administrator."

"Come in," a female voice says.

He enters. Staring at him from a desk is an Asian lady in her early forties. "Can I help you?" she asks.

He places a box of convenience-store chocolates on her desk. "Hi. I'm Dean Ruserri. From PuroGrip Surgical Instruments. I need just a minute of your time."

She eyes the chocolates, then his grinning face. "A minute is all I have. But I'm not sure if I'm who you're looking for. What's PuroGrip Surgical Instruments? I never heard of them."

"We're only a few years old, but growing. Like crazy. All because we view the surgical instrument differently than anyone else. An operation can be one of the most important events in someone's life. If it doesn't go perfectly, it can mean their life. So when it comes to the medical instruments slicing and stitching and all the rest, we should demand perfection. Not generalities."

"Yeah. I suppose. But what . . . is it?"

"We do to a pair of forceps what a tailor does to a pair of pants. We create bespoke surgical tools, none the same, each custom-fitted to a surgeon's hand, going off the width of the fingers, the rise of the heel, the flex of the knuckles, and eleven more data points. A comfortable hand is a steady hand. And a steady hand can save a life."

"Huh. Cool concept."

"I didn't come up with it. Our CEO did. I'm just an account executive. Which leads me to why I'm here today. The representative who was covering the San Diego VA account recently left the firm to pursue his passion, hang gliding. Though we wish him all the best, he soared out of the office rather abruptly, pardon the pun, which created a bit of confusion at PuroGrip. He's virtually impossible to get in touch with, living on a mountaintop somewhere in South America. I've been tasked with taking over his accounts."

"Okay. Where do I fit in?"

"The last couple days I've been going through all his unanswered company emails and voicemails and reaching out to clients he . . . left in the wind. One message was from a San Diego VA phone number, left by a man who unfortunately didn't provide a name or extension. Since you're in HR, I presume you speak to a lot of employees, would be familiar with their voices. And could hopefully tell me who left the voicemail once I play it for you. Sound good?"

"No guarantees. But I can try."

"Fantastic."

From his pocket he removes his phone and opens a snippet of the original message file he edited. He plays it.

The voice says, "I need more . . . supply."

She kicks her head back. "Eeh."

"Once a hand gets used to a PuroGrip, it's difficult to go back to generic instrumentation. Patient safety is on the line, here. Please, think as hard as you can, Miss Cho."

"Play it again."

He does.

Her brow creases. "Once more," she says. He lets her hear it a third time. "It's not a super-distinct voice. And a lot of people pass through this office."

"Anything could help."

"Three . . . no, five men . . . come to mind. Who that voice could belong to." She scribbles on a piece of VA stationery, rips it off, and hands it to him.

He reads the five names. "Much appreciated. Do you happen to know where in the hospital these guys work? I'd be happy to introduce myself."

"Let me see." She types on her computer for about two minutes. "Four are here now. And one . . . it says he's out sick." She taps a few more keys. The drone of a printer behind her. She collects five sheets, gives them to Tommy. "This is the info on who's who, their schedules today, plus their office locations. Anything else?"

"That's all, Miss Cho. Thank you again."

He leaves the office and visits the first man on the list, a radiologist. Tommy asks him if he'd like to hear about a new and exciting product. When the doctor says no, Tommy decides his voice isn't quite a match, tells him to have a nice day, and visits the second name on the list. Same result, similar to the suspect's voice but not exact. He concludes the same with the third and fourth names.

One remains, the man out sick. Cho didn't provide his cell number or home address. Tommy jogs through the hospital, out to the parking lot, and climbs into his car. He pulls from the glove box the FBI phone Jordana gave him in Mexico, finds her number, and calls.

She says, "Hey."

"Hey."

"You all right? You seemed a little . . . pissed at me this morning."

"You're good. I need a favor."

"I'm swamped, Tommy. The telecom report on the second US burner number came back. Same deal as the first. It's been completely off since yesterday. No texts sent or received, calls only to and from Ayala and the first US burner. Cell-tower activity was concentrated near a busy shopping mall in Imperial County, no second high-usage zone to cross-reference against. I'm leading a brainstorm for new ideas. And I've got to get back to the team. Maybe we—"

"You guys may not need a new idea."

"What?"

"I might know who the leader is."

A pause. "Where are you right now?"

"It's fine. Everything is fine. He has no clue I'm looking for him. All I need is his address. If I speak to him for just a few seconds, I'll know if it's him or not."

"Do you remember the promise you made to me when I let you stay at my apartment?"

"Yes. And—"

"You were supposed to run everything you did by me. And you did not run this by me. You broke the promise."

"I did run this by you."

"What?"

"A version of it. Then I came up with a better version. And it worked."

"You didn't answer my question. Where are you right now?"

"The VA."

"What's the matter with you? Did you not listen to a word—"

"I didn't mention anything about a crime. There's no hospital gossip. I didn't cross paths with the FBI investigation. Your boss doesn't know what's going on. You're not in any trouble. Everything is fine, Jordana. Please, I just need—"

"It's not fine. You lied to me."

"We can . . . debate that later. For now, let me capitalize on this opportunity. Take his name from me, look up his address in the FBI database. All I want is to go there and verify if it's him. If it is, I'll call you ASAP. Keep my eyes on him from a distance until you show up, then you take over from there. I'll let you finish this, let you get credit for the arrest."

"I thought I could trust you."

"Give me shit for that later. If the HR rep talks to him for whatever reason and brings me up, he could get suspicious and hit the road. Time is an issue. Please, give—"

"I thought everything was fine? Why would he get suspicious?"

"He won't . . . it's . . . I'll explain later. Okay? Please. Before this slips away."

Silence on the other line for a while. "What's the God-damn name?"

"Glen Brent."

FORTY

The American flag on Glen Brent's lawn waves in the breeze. Tommy pulls up to the address, 873 Laredo Drive. He puts on his sunglasses, grabs his FBI phone to text Jordana from after hearing the voice. He walks onto the driveway, spots a mess of dirt and flowers near a tipped pot. Weird.

He rings the bell. No answer. He rings it again. A flash of motion in the window. Tommy takes in the image of a middle-aged naked man for an instant before the curtains reclose. Also weird.

"Doctor Brent?" Tommy asks, stepping up to the glass.

The curtains stay closed. Tommy makes his way to the house's side hoping for a peek in. He finds three windows, two covered with blinds, the third cardboard and duct tape. Again, weird.

He opens the latch on a gate leading to a manicured yard with a pool, a raft gliding across the water. The rear windows are like the rest, shrouded by curtain, blind, or cardboard. The whoosh of a sliding-glass door. In the doorway is the man Tommy caught for a split-second out front.

A red robe hangs over his broad-shouldered frame, defined pectorals showing in the gap. He's a bit taller than Tommy, with at least fifteen pounds of muscle on him. He's shoeless, one foot a prosthetic.

"What're you doing on my property?" he asks.

That's the voice from Ayala's phone.

Glen Brent is the leader.

Tommy's central nervous system lights up. That's him. Just twenty feet away. Tommy wants to bull-rush him. But holds back. He broke one promise to Jordana today and won't a second.

"Missed you at the front door," Tommy says. "So checked back here. Probably shouldn't have intruded. I'll go."

Brent descends the three deck stairs, at the edge of each a garden gnome about a foot high, one's hands over its ears, the next its mouth, the third its eyes, *hear no evil, speak no evil, see no evil.*

Brent walks across the grass to him, asks, "And who might you be?"

"Just introducing myself to people in the neighborhood. I'm with a new-age diet organization in town. We prepare meal plans strictly involving the consumption of live fish. But now that I'm getting a look at you, doesn't seem a fella in the shape you're in needs any sort of a weight-loss regimen. I'll get out of your hair."

Tommy paces toward the gate.

Brent cuts him off.

FORTY-ONE

Glen is convinced he knows who this punk is. Late twenties, early thirties. Sneaking around his property. Clearly with a sham story. Los Hombres del Vacio must've sent him. He likely abducted Cora. And now is back for him.

"So you're signing up new members for your organization?" Glen asks.

"Yes sir. But we specialize in the morbidly obese. Obviously that's not you. So—"

"No, no. I want to hear more. I have a friend who's morbidly obese. Maybe your system can help him."

"Just tell him to look us up online. We're called Fishy Business."

"Cute. I commend you for starting this program. I—"

"Well, I didn't start it. Just work for it. But I'll be happy to pass the feedback to the founder when I get back to headquarters." He checks the time on his phone. "Where I am due in ten minutes. Shucks. I should really—"

"If you are only supposed to speak to overweight individuals, some mistake must've been made with your leads list. You should look into the error. Could help you avoid oversights like this in the future. Only two people live here, myself and my wife. Neither of us has a body mass index on the spectrum of obesity. Where do you source weight data on your prospects?"

"No, we do nothing like that. We don't have a file of people's weights. I'm just going door to door, speaking to everyone in your neighborhood. You weren't specifically targeted. Neither was your wife."

"Then how come you know my name?"

Silence for a few seconds.

The punk says, "Not sure what you mean, sir."

"In front a couple minutes ago, you called out my name. Doctor Brent. Why do you know my name if you're just canvassing the neighborhood?"

The punk's lip flinches. "Well, back at headquarters we have directories of who lives where. Public info. Outreach reps like me read it before going into the field."

"And you can memorize who resides in each home? Neat."

"My boss sometimes asks me if I ever wear a little hat and do tricks at the circus. You know, a memory like an—"

"Elephant. Of course. If you're that good, I'd love to see you show off." Glen points at the house next door. "What's the name of the family who lives there?"

"The . . . they're . . . huh. I didn't have enough coffee this morning. I'm drawing a blank. This is pretty embarrassing. I'll take it as my cue to leave. Have a good rest of the day, sir." He steps toward the gate.

Glen steps in front of him. "Why did you remember my name, then? What's so special about me?"

They stare into each other's eyes for a few seconds. The punk throws a punch. Glen ducks it, then unleashes one of his favorite moves from military training, stabbing him in the throat with the ends of his fingers.

The punk gasps, clutches his neck. Glen whips a right hook at him. But the punk blocks it and elbows him in the forehead. Glen grunts, kicks him in the stomach. The punk hunches forward. Glen knees him in the chin, drops him on all fours.

"I'll kill you," the punk screams.

Glen darts to the deck steps, grasps the gnome with its hands over its eyes. The punk staggers to his feet, sprints at him. Glen whacks him atop the head with the gnome. The punk falls to a knee. Glen hits him on the head harder, the force knocking his sunglasses off. He plummets face first to the grass.

His eyes are closed. Glen grabs him under the armpits, tows his body into the pool shed. He rummages through a crate of supplies for bungee cords. Then wraps the punk's wrists and ankles in sturdy military knots.

Glen hoists the body over his shoulder and carries it through the sliding-glass doorway into the house. The punk mumbles something, blood from a cut on his head trickling down his face.

"Shut up," Glen says.

"It's you. I'm not you. I'm nothing like you."

"Shut up I said."

Glen heaves him into a wall. His head slams the hardwood floor, a thump echoing through the house. His eyes are closed again. Glen trots upstairs to his bedroom, changes into khakis and a polo shirt, and fishes through the black doctor's bag in the closet. He loads a vial of sedative into a syringe, goes back downstairs.

The punk has risen to his feet. Ankles clasped together, he hops along the floor. "You're dead," he yells. And delivers a sloppy head-butt. Misses.

Glen laughs. Pushes him over, then sticks him in the arm with the needle. He holds his body to the hardwood, waits while the drug saps its vigor. When the punk loses consciousness, Glen collects his burner phone, a gun, and a few other items.

He carries the punk into the garage, situates him in the

passenger's seat of his Aston Martin DB11. He climbs into the driver's, stashes his gun in the glove box, and backs out.

He calls Bo with his burner.

"What's good, brother?" Bo asks.

"The gang got Cora."

"Shit. I thought you took off work to stay there and watch her?"

"I did. They . . . I'll explain later."

"She's dead?"

He takes a deep breath. "It's possible. Or just kidnapped."

"Son of a bitch."

"Meet me at the warehouse. I got the guy who did it."

"Dead or alive?"

"Alive. If Cora is alive too, he's going to tell us where she is."

"Why?"

"Because I'm going to make him. They same way you get information in a war. You inflict more and more pain until your enemy talks."

FORTY-TWO

Jordana paces in the FBI case room dedicated to the investigation. A middle-aged male agent with pockmarked cheeks says, "I tracked down archived listings from the three biggest private-transaction auto-sale websites. Filtered them to ones about white box trucks in the greater San Diego area."

"If he didn't register the vehicle under his real name, what would make you think he used his real name on some website?"

Jordana glimpses her phone. Over a half-hour passed since Tommy went to that doctor's house to verify his voice. And he still hasn't contacted her with the result.

The male agent says, "No way he used his real name. But the seller of the truck likely did. Had no reason not to. I can call them all, ask if they remember anything about the person they sold their trucks to. Maybe they chitchatted about work. Something about being a doctor came out. And the seller gives us a defining facial feature on the buyer."

"It's a stretch. And will be a slog. People rarely answer calls anymore from numbers they don't recognize. But . . . we're out of other ideas. So yeah, go for it."

"Great. As for a phone script, I could—"

"Excuse me." She pretends to receive a text, read it on her screen. "Dammit."

"Everything okay?"

"No actually. They're doing work at my apartment building. A pipe just burst."

"Oh no."

"I have to . . . check on my unit. I'll be back in the office soon. Fully available on my phone until then. Email me the script you have in mind."

She steps out of the room. Goes down to her bureau-issued Chevy Blazer in the garage. And drives toward 873 Laredo Drive.

"Shit," she screams, slapping the wheel. If the doctor who lives there is the voice's owner, she sent Tommy to the home of one of the most dangerous men in America without backup.

She is angry he lied to her, but still wants to help him. He is different than all those other guys, the ones she meets on dating apps, the ones her friends' boyfriends set her up with. The lawyers, the finance bros, the tech executives. They all bore her. Tommy doesn't. She tells herself she isn't falling for him. Then realizes she's lying.

Overwhelmed, she craves a release. And feels an urge she hasn't since high school. When striving to get into Stanford, she told her dad not to donate any money to the school so she could do it on her own, and would cut herself when the coursework grew too demanding. She takes a deep breath and repels the impulse.

She coasts to a stop in front of a house with an American flag in the lawn. She steps out of her car, peeks into Tommy's. Not there. She rings the doorbell. No answer. She glances around the corner of the home. The latch on the backyard gate is open.

The side windows are veiled like the ones in front, one with cardboard. She pushes the gate, steps into the backyard, and sweeps her gaze over the acre or so of land. No Tommy, no anyone.

But something is in the grass. She walks to it. A gnome, its hands over its eyes. A smear of blood on it. A smaller object glints nearby. She crouches. And stares at Tommy's sunglasses.

Her heartbeat picks up. She unsheathes her gun, holds it in front of her. The sliding-glass door at the rear of the house is open. She approaches with cautious steps. And peers inside. Shivers of glass on the kitchen floor, the guts of a blender on top of them, a demolished microwave jutting out of a cabinet.

She holds her ear to the doorway listening for indications of people. Voices, a TV, anything. A half-minute passes. Nothing.

She sticks her head in the house. "Tommy."

No reply.

She paces on the deck, calls him. He doesn't pick up. She tries again, same result.

"Goddammit," she says.

Then rubs her forehead and dials the only other person who might be able to help her.

Clyde says, "What's up, Quick?"

"I've got good news and bad."

"Oh man. All right."

"The good, I think we might finally have a name for the leader. The bad, I think he has Tommy."

"How'd you find out who he was?"

"We didn't."

"I thought you just said—"

"The FBI didn't. Tommy . . . maybe did."

"How?"

"I'm not entirely sure. It doesn't matter. He's in trouble.

He needs our help."

"I'm not involved in this anymore."

"You're the only person I could call. Nobody at the bureau would understand."

"I'm the last person who'd understand. You think I want to help Dapino, after what he did to me?"

"He can be a jerk. I know. He lied to you. And today he lied to me. Does he deserve to die because of it?"

A pause. "Where is he?"

"I don't know."

"Where's the suspect?"

"I don't know."

"What're you even proposing we do then?"

"I . . . don't know."

"Quick."

"What?"

"Take a deep breath."

She does. "Just . . . meet me. Let's figure this out."

"I'm off the case. If I intervene, I could get fired. I can't just—"

"This isn't about the case."

"What?"

"It is . . . but . . . right now . . . it's about . . . look, what Tommy did to you was wrong. But I think he's had a hard life. He has issues."

"No shit. Tried to convince me he had a room at some seaside resort. On the way back from Mexico, I saw a tooth-brush and toothpaste in his car. Pretty sure he's staying in it."

"He's told me similar things. He's . . . I don't know . . . sort of lost. But he's not a bad person."

Clyde laughs. "So it's mutual."

"What is?"

"You like him."

"I don't think he's a bad person. He—"

"No, no. More than that. Something's going on between you two."

"No it isn't."

"So you're not into him then?"

A moment. "No."

"I've seen this, Quick. Especially with young agents. You have a lot of promise. Don't let some handsome face cloud your professional judgment. In the FBI, one slip could ruin your career."

"I . . . thanks for the advice. But . . . can we not talk about this now? An innocent guy's life is on the line, if it's not already gone. I'm just asking you to help me find him. Can you help me?"

FORTY-THREE

Tommy wakes up. A pain in his head. It throbs against the stainless-steel table he's lying on. He tries to roll off. A clang. He's stopped. His arms are chained to the table. His legs too.

Twenty feet or so above him lights and an industrial fan hang among rafters. He supposes he's in a warehouse. Two vehicles are parked by the garage door, a fancy sports car and a pickup truck.

To his right is a multi-knobbed contraption of pumps and valves he pegs as an anesthesia machine, recalling something similar years ago in Queens during his tonsil removal. To his left is a block of shelving. On the bottom level are four boxes with "UW Cold Storage Solution" printed on their sides. On the top two are red-and-white coolers. Straining his eyes, he reads pen-scrawled writing on strips of masking tape stuck to them. "Kidney – O Positive." "Liver –

O Negative." "Pancreas – A Positive."

These must be what Danielle saw in the box truck. He screams, "Help. Someone, help."

Footsteps behind him. Brent paces into view. "Nobody can hear you."

Tommy concludes he's right, no windows on the big cinderblock walls. He glares at Brent. "You're no doctor. You're a disease."

"So, saving a girl's face from a razor makes me a disease. But doing the maiming is what ... healthy behavior?"

"What're you talking about?"

"Where is my wife?"

"What? I have no idea."

"Make this easy on yourself."

More footsteps. Standing at Brent's side is a stocky man with a coarse, reddish-blond beard. Tommy assumes the second White suspect.

"Is she even alive?" Brent asks.

"I never met the woman. I wouldn't—"

"What did you do to her?"

"Nothing."

"What did your associates do to her?"

"What associates?"

"Do you really think I bought that act about you working for a diet program?"

"That was bullshit. Fine. But I know nothing about your wife. That's the truth."

"If you lied to me about one thing, you very well could lie to me about another."

"You know what's a bigger lie? That nice house of yours. The nice job. Nice clothes. Just a disguise to hide who you really are."

"You work for a gang that participated right alongside me."

"You think I work for Los Hombres del Vacio?"

"So you're admitting you know who they are?"

"I ... no ... it ... let me out of here you crazy son of a bitch."

Brent disappears behind him, returns with a scalpel. "A good doctor knows how to use this to cause the least amount of damage to a patient. In order to avoid damage, you must of course be aware of what causes it. Thus, a good doctor knows how to use this to cause the most possible damage as well. The most agony. If of course motivated." A pause. "I ask again. Where is my wife?"

"If I was in a gang, I'd have a tattoo, right? You ever hear of a gangster without one? Look under my shirt."

With the scalpel, Brent shreds the sleeves of Tommy's dress shirt. Then rips open the buttons. He and his partner peer at arms and a torso lacking tattoos.

"See," Tommy says.

"Maybe you have an allergy to ink. This proves nothing."

"I'm not even Mexican. I'm an Italian guy from Queens. Look in my wallet. Front-right pocket."

Brent pulls out the wallet, headphones tangled around it. He slides out the New York driver's license. Studies it for a couple seconds. "Dapino," he says, looking at his partner.

"That sounds kind of familiar, brother. Right?"

"I'm sure you've been watching news coverage of your murder," Tommy says. "One of your victims was a Dapino. They mentioned her name. Did you realize that, the people you butchered, they have names? They have names. And they have families. Danielle Dapino. She was my sister. You killed her. And I'm going to make you pay."

The partner says, "How? You going to squeal really loud when Glen starts on you? Hurt our ears?"

He chuckles. Brent doesn't join him. He slips the driver's license in his pocket, tosses the wallet and headphones over his shoulder, and asks Tommy, "How'd you find me?"

"Go screw yourself."

"Hate me all you want. But I did your sister a favor. If she came to those woods, she was addicted to heroin and fentanyl. Can you imagine being enslaved to substances like that, the miserable existence? She was looking for a way out. It was going to happen soon enough. I just sped things up for her."

"You're giving the organs to soldiers, right?"

"Hell yes we are," the partner says. "You got a problem with that?"

"Not with helping soldiers. But how you're going about it, yeah. I have a big problem with it."

"Were you in the service?" Brent asks.

"No."

"Well we were. We get it. And you never will."

"I get it all right. You made the blanket assumption that all sick soldiers deserve to live, while anyone sick with substance-abuse problems deserves to die. You must know a lot of homeless people are veterans. Ones with PTSD who turned to drugs. How do you reconcile that?"

"Well . . . we . . . most vets—"

"You can't reconcile it. Because you shouldn't make decisions about who should live and who should die off of some Goddamn category you put them in."

"I doubt we killed a fellow vet. But if we did . . . then . . . well, it was collateral damage. A few are hurt to save many. That's a reality of war. Which you wouldn't understand because you were never in one."

"No I wasn't. And I don't have PTSD. But I was a fireman. And I knew other firemen who had it. And I'm sure you both do."

"You don't know me. You don't know us."

"I don't. But I know PTSD. Know the extremes it pushes people to. Extremes just like this crazy shit you two got into."

"Shut up." Brent slaps him across the face.

"What're you, like fifty? So you fought in what, Desert Storm? What happened to you there?"

Brent slaps him again.

Tommy says, "Or maybe it's not something that happened to you, but something you did to someone else. Is that what made you crack? I saw guilt tear firefighters apart, good men. Something they could've done to save a victim, but were too scared to. Couldn't face themselves. What were you too scared of in Iraq?"

Brent grabs his throat. "You want to see scared?" He steps to the base of the table. "Are you familiar with the tibia? It's commonly referred to as the shinbone. I've always found it a particularly interesting part of the body. Its second largest bone. Yet, unlike other sizable ones, the tibia hardly has any flesh on top of it. That's why banging your shin hurts so much. Not a lot of cushion to absorb the pain. It's as if it shoots right into your nerves."

Brent lifts the cuff of Tommy's right pant leg, exposing his shin. "Who else knows about me?"

"I'm not telling you shit."

"An understandable position. But one I'm confident I can change. First I'm going to set my blade a half-inch below your right knee. Then swipe downward, scraping the epidermis off. I'll keep going until I see the white of your shinbone. Then I'll switch implements. Move from a cutting device to something blunt. Possibly the tire iron in the trunk of my Aston Martin. My motion will change. Instead of scraping, I'll bang. Onto your skinned shin. Until the bone cracks."

"I don't scare like you do."

"Once the bone breaks, I'll let you have a minute to scream. When you're done, if you're able to muster up the air to speak, you'll likely tell me everything I want to know. If you don't, I'll repeat the process on your left tibia. If you still don't talk, I'll simply move to another section of your anatomy. And we can keep going. And going. Or . . . we can bypass all that complication. What do you say?"

"I say you're never getting away with this. Even if you kill me."

Brent chuckles. "Okay then."

Tommy closes his eyes, awaiting the first of the pain. A boom echoes through the warehouse. He hears Jordana shout, "FBI." Tommy, opening his eyes, whisks his attention toward the voice. Jordana, in an "FBI"-imprinted bulletproof vest, runs into the warehouse. Clyde, in the same vest, stands in the doorway clutching a battering ram.

"Glen Brent," Jordana yells, pointing her gun at him. "Put your hands where I can see them."

FORTY-FOUR

Brent raises his hands over his head. "You too," Clyde says to the other suspect, aiming his weapon at him.

The partner lifts his bulky hands. The fingers of his right move as if dispatching a military signal. Brent nods.

"Both of you get down on your knees," Jordana says.

They remain standing, Brent's left hand signaling to his partner.

"Now dammit," Clyde shouts. With slow steps, the agents cross the warehouse toward them.

"Go," Brent yells. He sprints to his right. His partner dashes left behind the block of shelving, uproots a gun from his waist. The agents scramble for cover behind a metal trash bin.

Brent rolls under the stainless-steel table. Tommy feels it going vertical. The chain links dig into the flesh of his wrists. Brent seems to be employing Tommy as a human shield.

"Stay calm Dapino," Clyde says.

A scraping noise as Brent drags the table toward the sports car.

"Out from behind there," Jordana says.

He ignores her. The authority in her and Clyde's expressions when they barged in here is gone, replaced with antsiness. Their eyes jump between Brent and his partner, training a gun on them.

Brent reaches the Aston Martin, shoves the table forward. Tommy crashes onto the concrete, banging his cheekbone. "Son of a bitch," he says, pain crackling through his skull.

The stainless-steel slab pinning him down, Tommy watches Brent open a car door and reach in. He points a pistol at the agents, says, "We're flanking you. You will not survive in this position if we open fire. We do not want to kill you. We just want to leave. Slide your guns toward the center of the floor, let us simply drive away. Nobody will get hurt."

Jordana pulls a radio off her waist, says into it, "I need backup. Dunbar Warehouses, Building C. All available units. Two suspects are armed and—"

Puchaw. A gunshot from Brent's partner smashes into the trash bin. Clyde shoots at him, missing, hitting a cooler.

Brent's weapon blasts. Clyde flails, drops to the floor.

"No," Jordana shrieks.

He isn't moving.

She shoots at Brent, shattering an Aston Martin side mirror. Brent climbs inside. The engine starts. The car hurtles toward the agents. Jordana pulls Clyde's body out of its path. It slams into the trashcan, sending it careening toward her. She dives out of the way.

The car backs up toward Brent's partner. He opens the passenger door and hops in. The garage lifts.

Jordana unloads at the car, striking the side, but neither suspect. The vehicle zooms out of sight. The tires screech. Then the sound of the engine softens as if distancing from the warehouse.

"I need an ambulance," Jordana shouts into her radio. "Agent down. I repeat, agent down." She scurries to Clyde, a crimson puddle around his head. She kneels, pressing her hands on the back of his neck as if to control the loss of blood.

It does not seem to help. The puddle soon triples in size.

FORTY-FIVE

Glen zips along a road in his Aston Martin. "Goddamn son of a bitch," he screams. "Shit, shit, shit."

"You hit, brother?" Bo asks.

"No. You?"

"I'm good. We're both good. We got out of there, right?"

Glen takes a deep breath. "You're right."

"How did the feds find us at the warehouse?"

"Must've been Dapino. He has to be working with them. The one agent, the man, called out his name."

"You said Dapino was out cold before you left your house. When did he have a chance to tell them he was there?"

"Got to be his phone. I heard it vibrating in his pocket on the drive over. He was sedated and his hands were tied, wasn't going to answer it, so I just . . . disregarded it. Could've been the feds. Who almost certainly have access to his signal. They likely tracked him via GPS."

"Dammit. That shit-talking prick. I was looking forward to killing him before they showed up."

"If I come across him again, he's finished."

"Where you driving?"

"Just . . . away from Dunbar."

"We got to get off the road in this thing. The feds probably already have APB out."

"You don't think I know that?"

Bo points at an intersection a couple hundred feet ahead. "There's a Shop-N-Save grocery store a few blocks to the right of the light. Let's park it there."

"Then what?"

"We'll take a new car from the lot."

"You know how to hotwire one? Don't you need tools?"

"We don't have time for that. We'll have to . . . be more direct. Be quiet too. Get your head straight. We can't hack this up."

Glen slaps himself across the face. "I'm good."

"The girl said your name. Cops are probably already surrounding your house. My truck is still back there. They'll figure out who I am from the plates any second."

"We'll need a place to hide. Somewhere safe."

"Remember my friend Hawks?"

"The guy you did mercenary work with after Desert Storm?"

"He lives about an hour from here. Lost a couple buddies who couldn't afford the right medical care after the war. He'd be sympathetic to our cause. He should let us duck out at his place and regroup."

"That's huge."

"Plus he's an absolute psycho. Will do anything for the right price. If we need an extra body on the run, he's our dog."

Glen turns at the intersection, pulls into the lot, and kills his engine. He gazes at the fifty or so other parked vehicles. Then the automatic doors beneath the red-and-yellow Shop-N-Save sign.

Two beefy guys in San Diego State tee shirts come out, a case of beer in each hand. A half-minute later a late-thirties woman pushes out a shopping cart, a girl no older than eight at her side. A few seconds after, a scrawny, mid-twenties man in a plaid shirt and glasses leaves with a canvas shopping tote over his shoulder.

"He's perfect," Bo says. "Follow my lead."

They step out of the car. Tail him to a Toyota Prius. He opens the hatch and lays his tote in the trunk. Bo nudges the barrel of his gun into his lower back, says in his ear, "If you scream, I shoot."

A whimper. "My wallet is in my front pocket. Take it."

"I don't want your wallet. I want your keys. Give them to my friend." Glen holds out a cupped hand. A set of keys plops into it.

"There. Can I go?"

"No. Get in."

Bo opens the backdoor, gets in with him. Glen turns on the quiet electric engine, exits the lot.

"Oh my God, oh my God," the shopper mumbles. "Where're you taking me?"

"We need your car to get out of the area," Glen says. "Once we do, we'll let you go."

"What're you, like bank robbers or something?"

"No."

Bo says, "In the meantime, to prevent yourself from doing anything stupid like calling the police, give me your phone."

In the rearview mirror, Glen watches the shopper passes Bo his phone.

"You promise you'll let me go?" the guy asks.

"I promise," Glen says.

FORTY-SIX

A pair of double doors at Mira Mesa Hospital zings open as EMTs push through Clyde's stretcher. "Stay with us, come on, come on," Tommy says over a paramedic's shoulder, he and Jordana pacing the gurney.

Clyde's shirt is off, his neck swathed in a special pressure-application bandage that would look like a scarf if it didn't extend across his chest under his armpit. Little creatures of blood squeeze their way from under the bandage.

An Indian man in scrubs, gloves, and a mask strides to the stretcher. "Has he undergone hypovolemic shock?" he asks the paramedics.

They answer in medical jargon Tommy can't make sense of, one addressing him as "Doctor Khurana." Backpedaling down the hallway, the doctor flashes a light in Clyde's eyes.

The EMTs hook the gurney through another set of doors, Tommy following. "This is as far as you can go," a paramedic says, clasping his shredded dress-shirt sleeve. Tommy glares at him.

"Let the man do his job," Jordana says to Tommy.

He looses a pent-up breath, follows her back into the main hallway. He stands at its center, the stream of foot traffic bending around him. She disappears into the crowd.

He kicks the first door he sees, a thud radiating through the hall. A man in a lab coat steps up to him, asks, "What do you think you're doing?"

"Get out of my face, asshole." Tommy roams the corridor for a while. Finds Jordana in a waiting room, its ceiling low, at least a foot shorter than the one in the hall.

She doesn't make eye contact with him. He sits a few chairs from her. Sets his elbows on his knees, hangs his head in his hands, closes his eyes. He wants to put on music, drown out the reality of the waiting room, but his headphones are gone.

Jordana says into her phone, "Agent Quick."

During the next fifteen minutes or so, he listens to her field two more calls about the manhunt for Brent and his partner, whose last name is apparently Archer. A recognizable voice flows through the waiting room. Tommy turns to it, noticing Clyde's wife Val talking to a receptionist. Her feet are still in slippers, as if she didn't even want to spare a minute to put on proper shoes after hearing the news about her husband's emergency surgery.

Her gaze stops on Tommy. It's cold. She must know about his role in Clyde's suspension. He walks to her. "Hi Mrs. Gabor."

"What did they say? What are they saying? The doctors."

"The EMTs told me the bullet luckily missed his jugular and trachea. They gave him fluids to help with the blood loss. But they . . . well, they said part of his spinal cord was hit."

"Lord." She presses her palm over half her face and looks up at the fluorescent lights. Her mouth moves, but he can't make out the wispy words. He guesses she's praying.

He sits back in his chair. His foot taps the linoleum floor. Another twenty minutes go by. A figure appears from a doorway. Dr. Khurana, his scrubs dotted with blood. He looks at Tommy and Jordana, then nods at an empty corner of the room.

They meet him there with Val. Their gazes stick to him. He says or does nothing for about five seconds. Then shakes his head, three quick, horizontal motions. "We did all we could."

Val's body smacks onto the floor. She yells. Cries. Yells while crying. "No. I can't."

Tommy lifts her to her feet. On the linoleum is a sprinkle of the glitter from her anniversary collage. She must've been working on it when she got the call.

"Give me drugs," she screams. "Numb me."

People stare at her. Jordana stares at Tommy. Her complexion is red with anger.

Soon Helga Wichita, the Special Agent in Charge of the FBI's San Diego office, stomps into the room. She asks Jordana, "What the hell were you doing at that warehouse?"

She hesitates to answer.

Tommy says, "Don't blame Jordana. Blame me. Brent . . . lured me there. I called Clyde for help, and he called Jordana. She didn't even know what she was walking into."

Wichita points her finger in his face. "You son of a bitch. First you get the man suspended. And instead of walking away like I told you to, you get him killed." He wipes specks of her spit from his cheek.

"This was your fault?" Val shouts. She slaps him over the ear. Hits him again. He raises his arms over his face. Her fist bangs the top of his head.

"Please ma'am," Dr. Khurana says. He steps in front of her.

Tommy looks around the room. Jordana, Wichita, and Val scowl at him. "I'm sorry," he says to all three. "I'm so sorry." And leaves.

FORTY-SEVEN

Glen drives the stolen Prius through a desolate region of San Diego County's Mountain Empire. A red ball of sun burns in the sky above sandy hills checkered with cacti. He glances into the rearview mirror at the abducted supermarket shopper, says, "I don't think the chance of a cop driving by is too high out here. Should be safe to drop you off."

"Thank you sir."

"We're keeping the car. You'll have to hitchhike back. Could be a while before anyone picks you up. Your bag from the grocery store. Anything good in it?"

"I guess. Why?"

"You should put something in your stomach now. It's only getting hotter outside. Whatever you bought could lose its flavor sitting in the sun. What's your favorite food in there?"

A pause. "The apples probably."

"Green or red?"

"Green."

"I like green apples too." Glen smiles. "Reach into the bag and enjoy a green apple." Glen watches him grab one, have a bite. "How is it? Juicy?"

He swallows. "It's good."

"Don't stop there. Finish."

Glen eases off the gas, slows to a stop on the side of the long rural road. He turns around, watches his abductee chomp away at the apple. "All done," the guy says. "Am I getting out here?"

"This seems like it'll do."

A boom fills the car. After it subsides, the only audible sound is a croak from the abductee's mouth. His eyes go to his chest. Where a bullet hole oozes blood. Then to Glen's hand, clutching a pistol. Bo watches him die without a trace of surprise in his expression.

Glen hooks the Prius off the road onto the desert terrain. He drives about three miles. They dump the body behind a couple bushes, then get back in the car, return to the road.

Soon they pull up to the property of Hawks, Bo's mercenary friend. A weathered one-story home on about ten acres.

Bo knocks on the front door. A man about their age in a black eye patch, smoking a cigar, opens it.

"The FBI is after us and we just killed a guy," Bo says. "Need a place to hang for a little."

Hawks takes a drag of his cigar, blows out the smoke, and motions them inside with his head. He leads them into the den, a mounted buck head on the wall. He sits in an armchair, Bo and Glen on a couch. They tell him about their transplants initiative and today's debacles.

"You boys are patriots," Hawks says.

"Thank you brother," Bo replies.

"I've got a guy in Nevada. Ran a couple paramilitary ops with him after Afghanistan. Good with data, systems, documents. Shit like that. He can find you whatever you need to get off the grid, out of the country. Phony passports. Identities. I'll get him on the horn."

Glen says, "Not yet."

"Feds work fast. You need to disappear. What's stopping you?"

"One more job tonight. One more round of surgeries tomorrow. Then we're done. We leave America for good." He glances at Bo and lifts his eyebrows, as if to ask if this arrangement works for him.

Bo nods *yes*.

"Risky," Hawks says. "But I suppose anything worthwhile in this country can only be accomplished by someone with a taste for risk."

Glen pulls Thomas Dapino's driver's license from his pocket, shows it to Hawks, and says, "I'd appreciate if your friend in Nevada could get started on this. He's who found me. I want to know everything about him."

Hawks snaps a photo of the ID with his phone. "Anything else you boys need?"

"Supplies," Glen says. "With our faces all over police computers, we obviously can't walk into a Walmart. If you could pick some stuff up we'd need for tonight, it'd be pivotal. I'll give you a list. Let me know the bill when you get back. I'll compensate you every cent with bitcoin, plus a service fee ... say twenty percent on top."

"I appreciate your cause. But I'm also aiding and abetting two federal fugitives. Let's make it thirty."

Glen extends his hand. Hawks shakes it. While Glen composes a supplies list, Bo turns on the television. He flips through channels, stops on a news one. On the screen a photograph of Glen smiling among coworkers at a VA-sponsored charity event, next to it one of Bo from his army days, across the bottom "MURDEROUS MANHUNT." A newswoman provides a voiceover summary of last week's shooting in the woods.

The network cuts to a clip of the female FBI agent from

the warehouse, reporters with microphones following her in a parking lot asking for a comment. She says, "They killed my partner. They're armed, extremely dangerous. If anyone sees either of these men, do not approach. Go to a safe location and immediately call nine-one-one. Excuse me." She gets into a car.

"That's who's after you?" Hawks asks.

"We should've killed her too," Bo says.

"Oh no. A glorious specimen like that? No, no."

"What?"

"In war, when you come across a beautiful enemy woman, you don't kill her." He licks his lips. "Not at first at least."

"You've got gear to pick up. Let's—"

"Did you get up close to her in the warehouse?"

"Sort of. Why?"

"What did she smell like?"

"Come on dude."

"You wouldn't have intercourse with her?"

A pause. "Of course I'd bang her. But that's—"

"I rest my case. I'll see you boys soon." Hawks grabs his wallet and keys, steps outside.

Glen and Bo keep watching the news coverage. The channel cuts to live footage of a correspondent on a porch with a boyish-faced, mid-thirties man Glen recognizes.

The correspondent says, "I'm in Duluth, Minnesota with military veteran Clint Erickson. Who just contacted the network with a shocking claim. In May, he says he flew to San Diego for an organ transplant at the hands of Glen Brent. According to him, Brent and his accomplice, Beaufort 'Bo' Archer, may be killing homeless people for their organs. And then implanting them inside sick veterans. Mister Erickson, what can you tell us about your experience?"

"I was really ill last winter. And didn't have a donor. Then a miracle came. A guy I deployed with told me about this man who does transplants for US vets for just a few thousand bucks. It seemed too good to be true. So I did some research online. And it checked out. Real veterans were applying for this program, flying to California, and coming home with a new chance at life. I was so overwhelmed it was, that it was . . . you know . . . that it was going to happen for me . . . that I didn't ask questions I should've."

"About where the organs came from?"

"I just assumed the donors consented. That it was a sort of charity. So I applied. And a few weeks later received a message telling me to get to San Diego in the next twenty-four hours for an operation. I did. Where I met a man who never gave me a name. But like he promised, gave me the surgery I needed. I thought he was a hero. Until I saw his face again on the news. Now I know where the organs really came from."

"If Doctor Brent happens to be watching this, do you have anything you'd like to say to him?"

Client looks into the camera. "You have no right. No right to do what you did. You aren't performing a good for us soldiers. You're cursing us. Now I have to live the rest of my life knowing part of a murdered person is inside me. I would've rather let my disease run its course. I would've rather died an honorable soldier's death. Now every breath I take is in disgrace. Because of you. You took my honor from me. And you took the honor from all the other vets you thought you were helping."

"Wow, a powerful statement . . . "

The interview continues, but Glen no longer listens. He feels as if a hammer is smashing spikes beneath the toenails of his missing right foot. He screams.

"What?" Bo asks.

"Phantom pain."

"Uh . . . what should I do?"

"Nothing." Glen writhes. "Let me feel it. I need to feel it." He bites the couch cushion. A growl.

In about a minute the pain subsides. He pants.

"Better?" Bo asks.

"I don't know."

"Don't let this crap get to you. You're above it." Bo turns off the TV. "You're the bravest guy I know. When Erickson is celebrating his sixtieth birthday someday with his wife and kids, he's going to thank you. Thank you for giving him his life back. Giving him decades he never would've had. He may not say it publicly. But he will to himself. We're giving these people the best gift in the world. Others will be appreciative, vets like Hawks who see things the way we do."

"I hope you're right."

"One last trip into the jungle. Let's make it count."

"There won't be a trip unless we get all the supplies we need. Hawks can buy the basics. But not the specialized medical equipment I'd need to perform transplants. All ours is back at the warehouse. Now a crime scene."

Bo strokes his beard. "What the hell do we do about that?"

"I have an idea. But it's borderline insane."

"At this point, we may need a dash of insane on our side."

FORTY-EIGHT

Tommy wanders inside the first restaurant he sees that looks like it'd have a bar. Some chain with a dumb name, its decor an Applebee's rip-off. A group of three sits at the bar, two men and a woman around Tommy's age in business attire, probably on lunch break from one of the corporate low-rises he walked past from the hospital. Ten or so patrons scattered about the dining room, four of them noisy kids with a fortyish lady.

Eyeballs sway toward Tommy, still in his torn shirt, most of his abdomen exposed. He sinks onto a stool. The bartender, a mid-twenties woman with pudgy cheeks, steps to him.

"Shot of Jack," he says. "Double."

"Sir . . . we have a dress code."

"Okay."

"I'd be happy to serve you if you changed, came back."

"You've never seen ripped jeans before? It's a ripped shirt. Fashion statement. Same shit."

"Your whole . . . chest and stomach are out."

A few of his buttons are missing. He attaches the remaining ones. "All right?"

Gaps of flesh show between the fabric. "I suppose. Yeah. What did you want again, Jim Beam?"

"No. Jack. Double." He sets his elbow on the bar, his head in his hand. He overhears one of the males in the corporate trio telling a story. A brag about some big ski jump he did on vacation last winter in Utah.

The bartender places a wide-rimmed shot glass full of brown booze in front of Tommy. He dumps it down his throat. "One more."

"One as in a single? Or another double?"

"Double."

She refills the glass. He slugs it back.

"Oh . . . jeez," she says.

"What?"

"You. You're bleeding."

A couple crimson drops on the bar top. He leans over it, glimpses himself in a Miller Lite mirror. A line of blood runs from his hairline down the side of his face. Val hitting him at the hospital must've opened up the cut on his head from Brent's garden gnome.

He chuckles. "Guess I am."

"You need to clean yourself up." She peels a bunch of napkins from a stack, sticks them in front of him with a plastic cup of water.

He dips a napkin in the cup, wipes his face. Then checks out his reflection. Wipes some more. He notices the corporate guy with the ski-jump story is looking at him with a smirk.

Tommy crushes the napkin into a ball, drops it on the floor. "See something funny?"

"No, not at all." The smirk remains.

Tommy marches to him. "Say one more thing to me. And

I will end you. You understand? I will end you."

Tommy clenches his teeth, waits. The smirk disappears.

"Sir, you need to go," the bartender says. She points at the door.

"I'll go back to my stool."

"No. You'll go back outside. Or I'm calling the cops."

"One more drink."

"No. You're paying for the two you had. Thirty-six fifty. Then you're leaving."

He takes a deep breath. Slides his hand into his pocket. Remembers his wallet is back at the warehouse. "I . . . uh . . . don't have any money on me."

"Typical."

"What does that mean?"

"You know what? Forget about the bill. Just get the hell out of here."

Everyone in the restaurant, even the four kids, gape at him. "So I'm the bad guy?" he says to them all. "Is that it? I'm the bad guy?"

"Go. Now."

"I could buy this whole place if I wanted to. First thing I'd do is fire you." He storms out.

FORTY-NINE

Tommy roams the streets of San Diego's Mira Mesa neighborhood. The sun is hot. And he hasn't had a glass of water all day.

He calls Jordana. She doesn't pick up. Her recorded voice says, "This is Special Agent Jordana Quick. Please leave a message after the tone."

"I'm going back to New York. But first I need to tell you what Brent told me in the warehouse. Before you got there. It could help with your case. Call me back." He hangs up.

He walks around in the mid-nineties heat for fifteen minutes waiting for her to return his call. She doesn't. He hails a taxi. "Carmel Valley," he says, stepping in. "Eight seventy-three Laredo Drive."

The cabbie drives him to Brent's house. Yellow tape around the property. FBI evidence technicians buzzing about. "Wait here," Tommy says. "I'll pay you in a sec." He opens the door.

"That's not how this works. You need—"

"It's this or nothing." He steps out.

"This portion of the street is restricted, sir," a cop on guard says.

Tommy points at his parked rental. "Just grabbing my car and going."

"Make it fast."

Tommy gets in, rolls up to the cabbie, extends him Danielle's necklace. "It's worth way more than that ride. It's all I have."

The cabbie snatches it. Spits on the pavement. Drives off.

Tommy heads to the FBI office. He parks in the visitor lot, paces into the building. Faces in the lobby stare at him. Maybe because of his shirt. Maybe because of the scene he made in here yesterday. Maybe a combination.

He steps to reception. Asks the woman behind the desk, "Can you tell Agent Quick Tommy Dapino is here to see her?"

"One moment." She makes a call. Relays the message. Then tells him, "Agent Quick said she's busy."

"Please let her know I don't want to embarrass her. Don't have to talk inside, in front of everyone. She can meet me around back."

The receptionist passes the message. Then says to Tommy, "She'll give you one minute, she says. No longer."

"Thank you." He veers toward the back of the structure.

A door opens. Jordana in the doorway, arms crossed. "What is it?"

"I have intel. That can help you find Brent."

"Myself and my team of agents inside are fine on our own. How am I supposed to trust any information from you after you lied at my apartment?"

"What happened at your apartment was debatable."

"It wasn't."

"Maybe it wasn't. But everything I told you after that was pure truth. I tried leaving Brent's backyard. I tried letting you have the arrest. I wanted—"

"I don't care about analyzing the layers of your BS. I really don't. It doesn't matter anymore."

"It does. Brent's face was right over mine on that table in the warehouse. In his eyes was . . . obsession. If he has another attack planned tonight, despite the manhunt, he'll go through with it. You—"

"I know. We pulled his records. He was a standout soldier in Desert Storm. Silver Star for valor. Archer has an accomplished military resume too. These aren't quitters."

"So don't you want as much intel as possible to fight back?"

"Not from you."

"I screwed up today." He throws his hands in the air. "All right? Holy shit. Let's not let that ruin the rest of this investigation."

"You're not part of this investigation."

He holds up his index finger. "I found out where Carlos Ayala lived. Before the FBI did." He holds up a second finger. "I pieced together that this was all about organ trafficking. Before the FBI did." He holds up a third finger. "I found out Glen Brent was at the top of this. And led us to a warehouse filled with physical evidence linking him to the crimes. Before the FBI did. Do I not deserve to be heard at least?"

"God, fine. What?"

"Brent's wife. What do you guys know about her?"

"Cora Brent. Thirty. Eight months pregnant. She drives a silver Porsche Cayenne Turbo. Vehicle isn't at the couple's home. We have an APB out for it, nothing back yet. We assume she's on the run with her husband."

"Doubt it."

"Then where is she?"

"I don't know. But he said something really weird about her at the warehouse. About her and me actually. Her and me and Los Hombres del Vacio."

"What?"

"I told you, weird. He thought the gang orchestrated some plan to kidnap her. And hired me to carry it out."

"Why you?"

"I can't make sense of it. But I'm sure it does make sense, to him at least."

"Nothing but stellar performance reports in his VA personnel file. Had an article published in a medical journal just seven weeks ago. Brent isn't psychotic. He must've had a—"

"Good reason. His wife misled him. Did you guys find any proof at the house she knew about the organ stuff?"

"The evidence techs went through her computer. Didn't even have a password on it. No, nothing to hide. Seems like she was totally in the dark."

"Well, no way she's in the dark now. She's probably scared. Hiding. You have to find her. She's closer to him than anyone. She'd know more details about his life than anyone."

"One of my agents, Keppler, tried reaching her. Phone was off."

"What about her family? He try them?"

She huffs. Takes out her cell and clicks a few buttons. The phone rings on speaker mode.

"Hey Quick," a male voice says.

"Just a follow-up on Cora Brent. Did you get in touch with any family members?"

"Tried the parents in Newport Beach. Stewart and Deborah Hall. Got through to Stewart on his landline."

"And?"

"No luck."

"What'd he say?"

"Said he didn't know where she was, hadn't heard from her all day. Didn't seem happy I was bothering him. That was it. Then he hung up. The mother's cellphone is off. No siblings."

"All right. Thanks Keppler." She ends the call.

"Hmm," Tommy says.

"What?"

"If your son-in-law's face is all over the news for a killing spree, you haven't heard from your pregnant daughter, and an FBI agent calls you, don't you think you'd ask a couple questions? See if the feds might have any insight on where she is. If she's safe. Would you really just . . . hang up?"

"Maybe he doesn't have a great relationship with her. Are you implying he lied? Why?"

"You're an FBI agent. You're on the inside. You don't see things from the outside. A big portion of the American public is skeptical of your guys' methods. If I had to bet, Cora's dad knows exactly where she is. Just doesn't want the FBI messing with her."

"How would we mess with her?"

"Interrogate her under pressure on a stressful day like this. Try to get her to trip on her words so you could leverage them against her. The FBI is the best in the world at nasty tricks like that."

"The FBI is the best in the world at solving investigations. If you'd excuse me, I have to get back to mine." She begins closing the door.

He stops it with his hand. "You're not going to act on my info?"

"There's nothing to act on. We don't know where she is. And neither do you."

"Unbelievable. You're going to let one little white lie of mine cloud your judgment. And let the man who killed your partner kill more people."

"There's a lot more wrong with you than one little white lie. Your entire life is a lie. A dark one."

"Yeah. Okay."

"This is a pretty fascinating building architecturally, isn't it? You should ask your father for his thoughts. I'm sure they'd be intriguing."

"And you should ask your father for his last name back."

A moment. "Have a safe flight to New York, Tommy."

"I thought you were cool. But you're the same as everyone else. Just out for yourself."

"I'm out for this case."

"You were happy to let me do its necessary dirty work, weren't you?"

"I didn't force you into any of it. You inserted yourself into the case. Crashed it is more apt."

"But as soon as things get choppy, you want nothing to do with me. Meanwhile, you're just as responsible for what happened at the warehouse as me."

"That's absurd. It wouldn't have happened if you listened to me."

"You're the one who brought him there. I didn't invite him."

"I invited him to help rescue your ass."

"At the hospital I blamed it all on me so you could look good in front of your boss. I did you a favor. But I'm beginning to think you believed my lie. I'm beginning to think you actually feel you had nothing to do with this. Is it a defense mechanism to avoid the guilt in your own head?"

"So you admit you're a liar?"

"I have the clarity to admit the three of us were in this investigation together. When I made progress, it was okay for you to benefit off of me. But now that something bad happened, it's okay for you to turn your back on me? You can't have it both ways, Jordana. Stop acting like a spoiled rich girl who thinks she can."

She shakes her head. "I have a feeling you weren't always such a dick. When you'd go into those burning buildings to save those strangers. Then you went to prison. And because of your record, you couldn't be a fireman anymore. You want to talk about defense mechanisms? To protect yourself, you convinced yourself people weren't worth protecting. That everyone is out for you. Me. The whole FBI. The whole federal government for that matter. Random people you come across probably. That—"

"Nice try. You—"

"That the ugliness you saw in Attica inmates is universal. Which is why you have no qualms about lying to everyone's face. Even people who are on your side. Living like that long enough will burn you out. Isn't it starting to?"

She slams the door on him.

FIFTY

Tommy hunches forward. Puts his hands on his thighs. His breathing speeds up. The blue dumpster behind the FBI building wobbles in his field of vision. He feels his pulse rage against the side of his throat.

He sinks to a knee. Wonders if this is a reaction to the heat. But he's been hot before, in his heavy fire gear feet from flames, and never felt like this. A panic attack. Must be. Josh used to have them.

Tommy closes his eyes, takes a deep breath. Another. A few more. His eyes open. The dumpster still shakes. He needs to get away from this building. From Jordana, from the FBI. He staggers to his feet. Turns a corner and strides toward the street.

The physical activity of walking helps a bit, distracts his mind from itself. He keeps doing it, going nowhere in particular, just moving, treading the sidewalk along Via Sorrento Parkway.

A grove of trees along the road at the next intersection. He climbs a small dirt hill, steps out of the sun, under the canopy of leaves. He sits on a rock, takes out his FBI phone, and enters a number he still remembers after many years of not dialing it.

"Hello?" a female voice says.

"Hi mom."

A pause. "Tommy?"

"Yeah."

A longer pause. "Oh, Tommy. It's . . . so good to hear from you. What—"

"Hey mom, can I ask you a question? Can I ask you a question, mom?"

"Of course."

"It's just a question I need to ask. I wanted to ask it before and I didn't. But now I think I need to know."

"Your voice sounds . . . are you okay?"

"I don't know."

"Where are you?"

"I'm still in California."

"Why're you still in California?"

"I don't know."

"What is it you wanted to ask?"

He runs a hand through his hair. "Why'd you do that to dad?"

Silence.

"Mom?" he says.

"Yeah."

"He was a good dad. And he didn't deserve that. And I'm just wondering, you know, I just think I should know why you did that to him."

"There's a lot about your father you don't know."

"Like what?"

"I probably shouldn't have done what I did. Not, at least . . . with a friend of his. I only did it because there were problems between us. You were so young back then. I kept them from you."

"Problems from what?"

"Problems from . . . being people. We all have them. He certainly did. I do too. What sort of a man moves to Costa Rica with a girl about the age of his children and abandons his family? You don't just turn into that man overnight, because of one . . . incident. You were that man for a long time."

"Maybe, yeah."

"You never saw that side of him, until you saw it all at once. You just knew the good. And you were such an . . . idealistic kid. If I told you about the other side of him, it would've . . . brought your whole world down. But with people, there's usually another side."

"I guess."

"Is everything all right, Tommy?"

"I hope."

"If you ever want to talk, about this, or anything else, call me. Anytime."

"Okay. I've got to go now."

"I love you."

A moment. "I love you too. Bye mom."

"Bye."

He hangs up. And stares at the trees for a while. His heartbeat calms. Objects stop spinning. He walks out of the wooded area, heads toward his car in the parking garage.

"You get into a fight with an alligator, friend?" a vagrant in a dusty top hat asks.

Tommy glimpses his torn sleeves dotted in blood. And chuckles. "Close enough."

The vagrant offers a bottle of booze wrapped in a paper bag. "For the pain?"

"Thanks. But I'm good."

"Cool." The vagrant has a sip, extends his hand.

Tommy shakes it. "Tommy."

"Stardust."

"That's a hell of a name."

"No, friend. It's just a name. Just my name."

"Your parents give it to you?"

"I don't think anyone has a right to name you but yourself."

Tommy grins. "Makes sense."

"You have a tent around here?"

"I have an apartment. In New York. It ain't much bigger than a tent, though."

"The homes of all people are the same size, friend. The size of the world."

"I like that. It's been a pleasure, Stardust. But I've got to get going."

"Where you off to, friend?"

"I have a case to solve." Tommy starts walking.

"You a cop?"

"No. I'm a firefighter."

Fifty-One

Glen cuts into a steak. Two plates on the table across his, a bone in each, shredded meat lining the edges, all atop puddles of blood-colored juice. Bo and Hawks finished their meals in about three minutes, Glen now alone in the kitchen. The carnage in their dishes forces him to imagine Cora's mutilated body. Thomas Dapino didn't kidnap her. But someone surely did.

He loses his appetite. Scrapes the remains from all three plates into Hawks's trashcan. Korn's "Got the Life" blasts from the garage. Glen leaves the house, walks into the unattached structure. A mini arsenal of combat gear lines the shelves.

"You full, brother?" Bo asks. His shirt is off. His fist slams into a punching bag Hawks clutches.

"Oh yeah," Glen says. He looks at Hawks. "Thanks for picking up lunch. Everything else too."

"I got you."

Six new coolers rest along the wall, next to a foldable metal table and bags of other supplies. Glen will perform his final round of surgeries in here tomorrow.

"Hit it again," Hawks screams.

Bo slugs the heavy bag.

"Harder," Hawks yells. He turns up the music.

Spit oozes from Bo's mouth.

"Make that bitch bleed," Hawks shouts.

Bo strikes the bag a few more times. "Woo."

"That's it." Hawks smacks the skin of Bo's back. Then reaches into his pockets. He pours white powder on the edge of a pocketknife. "Sniff that pussy." Bo snorts the powder.

"What was that?" Glen asks.

"Want some?" Hawks asks.

"You didn't answer my question. What was it?"

"Crushed-up Advil." He chuckles. "What do you think it was, man? A little white."

Glen glares at Bo, asks, "You do cocaine?"

Bo wipes his nose. "We've got a big day, big night ahead of us. Getting amped."

"How often do you . . . engage in this?"

"Relax man," Hawks says. "He's fine."

"This doesn't concern you," Glen says.

"You're in my garage. So it kind of does."

Bo steps between them. "Ease up. Both of you. Ease up."

Glen says, "This is just . . . a surprise. After all our conversations about the drug epidemic. About junkies. About how—"

"Does he look like a junkie to you?" Hawks asks. "Is this man a bum living on the street? Does he have a needle sticking out of his arm?" Hawks does a bump of coke. The pupil of his non-patched eye is big. "You know what he looks like to me? A Goddamn American hero. And if he wants to enjoy a little toot in the privacy of his friend's home, that's his American right."

"It's actually not his right. It's against the law."

"So is murdering a barrack full of farmworkers. But you don't see me trying to stop you."

"That's different."

"How so?"

Glen hesitates.

"Don't have an answer, college boy?" Hawks asks.

"This is a dumb conversation. And I'm not having it."

"You think I'm dumb?"

"I never said that."

"You think you're smarter than me because you have more money?"

"You didn't seem to have a problem with my money when I was paying you your thirty-percent fee."

Hawks laughs. "What'd you even do in Iraq? Sit in an air-conditioned room with the other eggheads and play with a computer while real soldiers like me and Archer did the fighting?"

Glen charges at him. Bo tries to block him, but Glen shoves him out of the way. He punches Hawks in the face. "Don't ever question what I did over there," Glen shouts.

Hawks, twentyish pounds larger than Glen, nails him in the stomach.

"Stop," Bo yells. "Both of you. Stop." He bear-hugs Glen, shaking with adrenaline. Hawks dabs blood from his lip. "I fought alongside both of you," Bo says. "I know the shit both of you went through. You've both earned my respect for it. For life. Now shake hands like soldiers."

Glen and Hawks glower at each other. Glen sticks his hand out. Hawks shakes it.

"There we go," Bo says. He grips Glen's shoulders. "If we're going to steal that medical equipment, we need your head in the right place. You good?"

"I'm good." Glen points at Hawks's pocket. "I never did coke. It gets you in the zone?"

"Shit yeah."

"Give me a damn hit."

FIFTY-TWO

Tommy is parked at a CVS about ninety miles north of San Diego, in Newport Beach, where that FBI agent on Jordana's team mentioned Cora's parents lived. He has the city, but not the address. Jordana of course knows it. But he doesn't want to call her. And she wouldn't even pick up if he did.

He opens Google on his FBI phone. Searches "Address Stewart and Deborah Hall, Newport Beach CA." Learns Stewart is an insurance executive and Deborah chairs a couple charities, but finds no address online.

"Dammit," he says.

He takes his personal cellphone from the cup holder and calls Josh.

"It's all over the national news," Josh says. "Shit is nuts."

"It's nuttier than you know. Wait till I tell you the story of my day. But not now."

"Tell me, yo. I gotta hear."

"No time. I'm still . . . at it. Need to get to Brent's wife."

"I saw her pic online. Chick is fire. Even pregnant."

"Stop being weird."

"How is that weird?"

"If you're her and you hear on the news your husband is a fugitive killer, you're hiding from him, right?"

"I'd assume."

"If your parents only live a few dozen miles from you in a nice beachside town, you're probably hunkering down there, right?"

"A childhood home can offer the same feelings of comfort and safety as a womb. Sigmund Freud once said—"

"I don't need a psychoanalysis, you psycho."

"Yes. Good chance she's at her parents'."

"I'm not going to ask you to hack anything. I understand you're not a wizard."

"Can I get you to put that in writing?"

"Shut up. But I need the parents' address. Nothing on Google. But there's got to be some sort of directory with the info, right?"

"If you crapped out on Google, the address isn't online. But that doesn't mean you still can't find it."

"I need some tech advice here. Anything."

"You've given me countless demands since you got out of prison. But I think this is the first time you actually asked for advice. I'm honored."

"Am I going to regret it?"

Silence for a few seconds as if Josh was thinking. "When you Googled her parents, did you see Facebook pages for them?"

"LinkedIn. No Facebook."

"No, that won't move the chains."

"I need yardage here."

"The daughter, Cora, the picture I saw. Didn't look like a LinkedIn-type headshot. She was in casual clothes, at some smoothie shop."

"How is that relevant?"

"The news site that posted the pic must've gotten it somewhere. Probably Facebook. Which means she has an account, and it's probably public. And there're—"

"If she were going to list her address on Facebook, she'd use her current one in San Diego. She's not there. I need—"

"Yeah, bruh. I know. Nobody lists their address on Facebook anyway. Beside maybe eighty-year-olds."

"So what the hell am I doing on Facebook then?"

"News site said she was thirty. About our age. Facebook was around when we were in high school. Her too."

"So?"

"So back then she was still living at home. With her parents. Dig deep into her pics. Try to find one of her at the house. See if anything distinct is outside in the background."

"And if there is?"

"Send me the photo. I'll look at aerial footage of Newport Beach. See if I can pinpoint the part of town."

"Cool."

"Later."

Tommy hangs up. Finds Cora on Facebook and scrolls to the beginning of her photo history. He spots an outdoor shot of her smiling with a tall man in an expensive-looking sweater, must be her dad. They stand in the driveway of a Mediterranean-style house next to a Volkswagen Beetle with a bow atop, a "17" sign in it. In the background Tommy notices cliffs, the ocean below. He takes a screenshot and sends it to Josh.

Tommy's leg pumps while he waits for a response. About fifteen minutes later he receives a text:

Wambold Lane

FIFTY-THREE

Tommy turns onto Wambold Lane. Cruises along glancing at houses. Recognizes the Mediterranean one from Cora's Facebook page, parks a hundred or so feet away.

He opens his trunk. Takes off his ripped shirt, puts on a black tee shirt he brought from New York. Then, in case he gets jammed up, pulls out his axe, stashed since the trip back from Tijuana. He slips it in the rear waist of his suit pants, drapes his shirt over it, and treads the pavement toward the home.

A woman walking a tiny, fluffy dog waves at him. With a smile he waves back. He descends the sloping street toward the Halls' property, an eight-foot brick wall enclosing it on the front and sides. At its rear is a cliff dropping about fifty feet to the ocean.

An engine to his left. A black-and-white car with "Newport Beach Police Department" on the side. It pulls in front of the Halls'. Tommy stops. Watches two policemen get out, buzz an intercom at the gate. When it opens they walk to the front door.

Tommy jogs to the north wall. Leaps into it, a foot meeting the brick, and thrusts himself upward. His fingers latch onto the top.

With the upper-body strength he accumulated from years of pull-ups in the firehouse then prison, he suspends himself. Holds his eyeline steady just above the wall, obscuring as much of his body as possible.

The front door opens. A sixtyish man a head taller than the cops appears on the stoop. Stewart Hall. His mouth moves, Tommy too far to hear the words. A cop's mouth moves. Then the other's. Agitation in Stewart's expression. He screams, loud enough for Tommy to make out, "I told you the same thing over the phone. She's not here. I pay too many damn tax dollars to get harassed like this." The door closes.

The cops pace off the property. Their cruiser motors up the block, then turns off it. Tommy hoists his legs onto the wall, jumps down to the other side. In a crouch, he approaches the home, around him the sound of waves smashing into rocks.

On his drive to Newport Beach he composed a speech in his head he plans to give when he sees Cora. He replays it in his mind as he nears the house.

His feet reach the backyard pavers. He peeks through a window. His eyes cover the dining room. Long table, chandelier, encased china. No Cora. But he hears something. Her father's voice. Sees him pacing nearby on the phone.

"It doesn't end," Stewart says. "All Goddamn day. Not just the local cops. Feds."

He quiets as if listening to the person on the other line.

Stewart says, "Wives never get fair treatment in situations like this. Rick Jorrell, a former business associate of mine. Was wanted a few years ago by the FBI for tax evasion. Hundred percent he was guilty. The old prick was probably cooking his books since they were actual books, before computers. We all knew it. But the feds didn't just go after him. Ripped his wife's life apart too."

A few moments.

He says, "No way she had anything to do with it. The only financial document that airhead knew how to read was a price tag at a department store. Still, they tore through all her emails and text messages. Took her words out of context. Made it seem like she knew what was happening. Charged her as a coconspirator."

Silence for about half a minute.

He says, "What do I look like? Some chump who mans the ladle at a soup kitchen? If my whack-job son-in-law wants to kill more bums, that's his business. My business is my daughter. And I want to keep her out of prison. I don't give a shit if she can help the feds."

He's quiet for a bit.

Then says, "Cost doesn't matter. Find me the best defense attorney in California. I want to get ahead of this. All right, so long."

Stewart hangs up, disappears through a doorway. Tommy advances along the backyard pavers. Looks through a second window at a home crafts studio. Easel, canvases, paint. No Cora.

He moves to a third window. A living room. Cora isn't inside. But someone else is. Staring back at him, face no more than an inch from the fogged glass, is a Doberman Pinscher.

It kicks its head back and lets out a booming bark, its long, sharp teeth on display. The noise gets Stewart's attention. His meaty frame, about six and a half feet tall, turns a corner. His eyes meet Tommy's through the window.

Stewart opens a sliding-glass door, yells, "Rocco, get him." Tommy only has a moment before the Doberman bolts out of the house. His mind rushes to assess options.

He could hop the property wall and drive away. But he'd need to make it there first. As fast as he is, the dog is surely faster. And even if it didn't catch up to him, he'd still fail. He'd be leaving without accomplishing his goal, talking to Cora.

The Doberman's dark, muscular body rushes out of the doorway. Tommy decides to go with his second option, seeing this through.

He jumps onto the patio table. The dog does too. It snaps forward to bite his leg. Just before it does, Tommy jumps up onto the awning. His stomach lands on a beam, knocking the wind out of him. He looks back at the barking dog on the patio table.

"What're you doing here?" Stewart shouts. He runs out of the house wielding a baseball bat.

"I'm here for your daughter," Tommy says. "I just—"

"What gives you the right to trespass?"

Tommy negotiates the beam toward a second-story window. But it doesn't open. The glass is fixed in place.

Pain rattles through his left ankle. "Ahh," he yells, falling off the awning's beam onto its fabric. Stewart just hit him with the bat. In a moment a similar pain rocks through his hip. "Dammit," he shouts.

Tommy pushes himself to his knees and crawls back to the solidity of the beam. He yanks out his axe. Stewart takes another swing at his ankles. Tommy leaps, avoiding it, then lands back on the beam, almost slipping off.

He bashes the window with the axe, shards flying into the house. He bangs around the rim of the hole, widening it, then dives through. An edge cuts his bicep. His body hits the floor of the upstairs hallway among a splatter of blood.

Rising to his feet, he screams, "Cora." No response. He opens the first door he sees, glances inside. Nobody. He opens another door. No. Footsteps echo through the high-ceilinged house from downstairs. Stewart and his baseball bat are on their way up.

No one in the third room Tommy checks. Or the fourth. But this one stands out. It lacks the formal decor of the others, an adolescent feel to it. A lot of pink, a lot of posters. Seems like a teen girl's bedroom. That agent on Jordana's team said Cora had no siblings, so Tommy assumes this is her former room, likely where she stays when she visits.

He notices a desktop computer. And remembers the agent said she didn't use a password on hers in San Diego. Tommy dashes to this one. It doesn't require a password either. He opens the browser and checks the history. A few results from today. The most recent titled "Reservation Confirmation." He clicks on it, arriving at the website of a hotel called the Grand Bay Resort.

"You a reporter?" Stewart asks.

Tommy turns to him in the doorway. "No."

"An undercover cop?"

"No. I'm here to help your daughter."

"I've never seen you before. How do you know her?"

"I ... well—"

"Liar." Stewart steps to him.

"Just hear me out, we—"

"So you're what then, a thief? Think you can rob me?" He swings the bat. Tommy ducks. Stewart pulls the end of the bat out of the wall. Tommy's axe could end this right now. One shot, even to a non-vital section of the body like a knee, would incapacitate Stewart.

The guy is clearly an asshole. But doesn't deserve an axe maiming. Tommy considers a non-violent way out of this room. Notices the closet door. It's ajar, its hinges directing outward. In his firefighter schooling on building evacuation, he learned the importance of clearing obstructions from outward-swinging doors. If heavy enough, they can trap occupants inside during a fire.

Stewart brings the bat down at him. Tommy rolls to the side, the barrel thwacking the floor. Tommy keeps rolling, all the way into the closet. He moves backward on his hands and feet, leaving enough space for Stewart to enter, then grabs a sweater off a hanger.

Stewart comes in. And tries to cock the bat back for another swing. But the tight walls constrict him, the barrel striking a shelf. As the long-limbed man struggles to better position himself, Tommy chucks the sweater into his face, over his eyes.

While Stewart fumbles with this problem, Tommy crawls past his legs out of the closet. He shuts it. Then darts to Cora's bed, grasps the headboard, and shoves it against the door.

"Let me out you bastard," Stewart yells, pounding the door.

Tommy pushes the dresser behind the bed, wedging a corner against the wall. With a lot of sweat, Stewart should be able to force his way out, but should need at least a minute.

Tommy runs out of the room. Descends the staircase to leave the house. The Doberman's bark resounds. Tommy's feet stop. The dog hurtles into the foyer, turns for the steps. Tommy hurries back up to the second story, then into a bathroom. Closes the door.

Outside it he hears the Doberman's legs working their way up the steps, plus the legs of Cora's bed rumbling as Stewart struggles to free himself.

Tommy contemplates how to handle this predicament without using the axe on the man or dog. He notices a window in the bathroom facing the back of the house. He opens it. Then grabs the towel by the sink and rubs it all over his arm, bloodying it with his bicep cut. He stuffs the towel into the wastebasket and heaves it out the window.

It clangs against the backyard pavers. He hears the Doberman bark. Then run down the staircase. Tommy peeks out the window. The dog exits the house, sniffs around the wastebasket.

Tommy leaves the bathroom, trots to the steps. When he reaches the foyer, he hears a bark. Sees the Doberman peering at him from the backyard. It charges ahead, back into the house. Tommy has enough of a head start to reach the front door. He twists the deadbolt. Slips outside. Closes the slab, feels the animal jump against the other side.

Tommy sprints along the Halls' long driveway toward

the property gate. Soon he hears the jangle of the dog's collar tags behind him. It must've raced back outside, then around the house. Tommy grips the gate's iron bars and climbs. The dog's teeth clasp his pant leg. He shakes himself loose, his cuff tearing. Then plummets to the street, the Doberman's snarling snout jutting between two bars.

Tommy runs to his car. Turns on the engine and drives off the block. Once he makes it to the main road, he pulls over, catches his breath. Then enters "Grand Bay Resort" into his GPS.

FIFTY-FOUR

The stolen Prius pulls onto the property of the San Diego VA Hospital. Bo mans the wheel in a low-pulled hat and shades, his head and beard shaven. Glen sits in the passenger seat, his hair transformed blond with hydrogen peroxide and baking soda, his eyebrows waxed off. He wears scrubs and a surgical mask Hawks bought him.

"Give me another pick-me-up," Glen says.

"You've already had a decent amount."

"Do you realize what I'm about to do?"

"Of course."

"Then you know I need all the energy I can get. And clarity. Bust it out."

Bo fishes a baggy of cocaine from his pocket, taps some in Glen's palm. He snorts it all up.

"Ready?" Bo asks.

"Death before dishonor."

"Preach. I'll meet you around back."

They slap hands. Glen gets out with a camping back-pack Hawks purchased for him, and strides through the hospital entrance. He smells the VA's familiar, Windex-like scent. He's worked here for so long around so many employees, one may recognize him on body language despite his mask, new hair, and missing eyebrows. So he adjusts the way he walks, giving himself a phony limp.

He navigates the hallway amid a jumble of patients and personnel. Passes a cracked waiting-room door, overhears TV news commentators speculating on how life could've turned an upstanding citizen like Glen Brent into something so vile.

He takes an elevator up. His heart thrashes from the coke. An image flashes in his mind of two skeletons, Cora's next to the smaller one of his unborn daughter. A tear flows from his eye. He wipes it away. Then exits the elevator onto the floor where he works.

His neck muscles tense when he turns a corner and spots faces. Mabel the X-ray technician. Alfonso the physical therapist. Levi the orderly. Glen angles his head downward, accentuates his limp. And clears the three-person gauntlet.

He reaches the door to a restricted zone where the hospital stores equipment and drugs. And swipes his employee keycard through a magnetic reader, gaining access.

The room's long rows of metal shelving glint in the brightness of the fluorescent panel lights. A half-dozen doctors are dispersed throughout with carts, perusing shelves like supermarket shoppers.

Glen tucks his backpack behind a rack of medical tubing, grabs a cart, and pushes it into an aisle with no one in it. He's been in here many times, the layout imprinted in his memory, and knows where his needed items are.

He takes a roundabout path through the aisles to avoid passing other doctors. Into his cart go scissors, scalpels, and forceps. Then sutures.

No way he'll be able to snatch an anesthesia machine

from the VA, so a spinal injection must numb his final group of patients. This means syringes and lidocaine, which he stocks up on next. Then blood-testing kits. Skin markers. Rubber gloves. Various other items. And last, packets of organ-storage solution.

He wheels his cart to his backpack, unzips it, and begins stuffing the supplies inside. He glances over his shoulder to assure nobody is watching. His arm speeds up. In about twenty seconds, it's all packed. He returns to the elevator, descends to level one. He moves through the congested hallway. And soon breaks away from the crowd toward the exit door. The pat of his footsteps is the only sound in his ears.

Then he hears, "Doctor Brent?"

A pain in his gut. He knows what this is. Knows who this is. But attempts to play it off, staying in character as a doctor with any other name.

"Doctor Brent." It hits him again, like a lance through the back.

Nurse Peggy Wiggins.

At least a thousand times he's shared an operating room with this woman he believes loves him. He was so thrilled to escape the supply room undetected, he forgot to put on his limp, he realizes. Peggy, one of the few people who could identify his natural gait from dozens of feet away, apparently just did.

He steps outside. The door closes behind him. She'll second-guess herself, leave this alone. He scans the parking lot, spotting Bo in the Prius.

"Glen," she calls. Another lancing. She must've sprinted down the hallway after him. He stops moving. He has two ways to handle this and needs to choose fast.

The first option, he can continue on to the car and just drive off. He'd avoid confronting her and she'd never really know if she saw him. But she would still likely tell someone about the potential sighting. The police would soon find out he's in the area in a Prius and barricade the on-ramps to any freeways.

Leaving him with only option two.

He spins around, making eye contact with her. And nudges his mask down. "Peggy, oh my God, did you see the news on TV?"

Her freckled face is silent for a couple seconds, as if she needs a moment to absorb it's really him. Then says, "Of course." And jogs to him. "Who hasn't? I can't believe—"

"It's a huge misunderstanding. I didn't do it." He lifts the mask back up. "I came here to get some papers out of my office. Now I'm heading out of town until this blows over. I'm sure you're curious. I'll tell you what happened. Come on." He points at the Prius. "In here. I don't want someone to see me out in the lot."

Peggy's gaze has a trace of skepticism in it. Yet she still follows him. He opens the passenger door, nods at Bo as if to say, *I've got this*, then gets inside, sets the backpack on his lap, and slides over to make room for her. He extends his hand to help her in, then moves it across her body and closes the door.

"I knew you were innocent," she says. "I just knew it. Ughh."

"I was framed."

"How? By who?"

He nods at the backpack. "The evidence to exonerate me is in here. That's why I risked coming back. Once you see it, you'll understand." He places his hand on her thigh. "I always felt so close to you. Will you help me get through this? Will you take what I'm about to show you to the press?"

"Yes."

He begins opening the backpack. She watches. He clamps his hands around her throat. "Shh," he says. "Shh."

She gags. He forces her down into the space in front of the passenger seat. Her eyes seem to ask him, *Why?*

He grasps tighter. His nails cut into her flesh, her blood ringing his right pinkie. "Soldiers are dying in there," he whispers. "You see them too. Only I can help them. I'm so sorry, Peggy. But I need to help them."

Soon her squirming slows. He chokes for a while longer. Her eyeballs still, as if stopping to process information. He squeezes for another minute or so, then places his hand over her heart. Dead.

He sits up in the seat and gazes at his eyebrow-less face in the rearview mirror, covered in sweat. Then turns to Bo, says, "Go."

FIFTY-FIVE

Tommy pulls his Chevy Cruze into the lot of the Grand Bay Resort. Parks it between a Bentley and Maserati and walks through the hotel entryway to the scent of flowers in the lobby. At the counter, a blond-male attendant in a red bowtie looks him up and down, says, "You're in the wrong place."

"Excuse me?"

"Restaurant staff should come in through the service entrance around back. Did you not have your consultation with Dmitri yet?"

Tommy considers his outfit, black shoes, black slacks, black tee shirt. He looks like a busboy. "I'm not working here."

"Ah. So you're staying here?"

"No. Not that either."

The attendant eyeballs the cut on Tommy's bicep. "Then . . . why are you here?"

"My friend. She's staying here. And left a few of her things back at her house. I owed her a favor. She asked me to bring them. Here I am."

"Yes, there you are."

"Cora Brent is her name."

"Terrific."

"So?"

"So what?"

"So can you tell me what room she's in so I can bring up her stuff?"

"I don't know of a guest with that name. And even if I did, I'm not at liberty to give out information of that nature. If you're so close to this ... Cora Brent ... that she invited you up to her hotel room, I'm sure you have her phone number. Give her a call and ask."

"That's the problem. One of the things she forgot was her cell. Called me from her room phone. When I tried it back, the number didn't go to her, sent me to some automated greeting. Guessing I need an extension. Do you have that at least?"

"I'm sorry. There is nothing I can do, sir. Have a good day." Glancing past Tommy, the attendant flashes a smile and raises a hand.

A woman with a Louis Vuitton bag steps to the counter. Tommy says to her, "Ma'am, I apologize for interrupting you like this, but I need to speak to this gentleman for just a little longer."

"I am so sorry Mrs. Franklin," the attendant says. Then scowls at Tommy.

"Fine, I lied before," Tommy says. "I don't know Cora Brent personally. Her husband is the man all over the news. The surgeon who killed all those people in San Diego last—"

"Oh dear," the woman says, hand over her heart. "I heard about that. He's here, in the hotel?"

"No," Tommy says. "You're safe here ma'am." He gazes at the attendant. "But Cora might not be. I need to speak to her. For her own protection. Just give me a phone extension.

That's it. I don't even need to go near her. I just want to talk. You can listen to the whole conversation over my shoulder."

"Are you a cop?" the attendant asks.

A pause. "Not a cop."

"FBI?"

"No."

"What law-enforcement authority are you with then?"

"I'm . . . I'm not with any authority."

"Well sir. In that case, despite the rather stirring speech you delivered, I am afraid to say my opinion of who you are has reverted back to a former version. The one after busboy. A ranting vagrant who wandered in off the street. And if you don't wander out back to the street, I am going to call the real police on you."

Tommy huffs, marches outside. To get to Cora, he'll have to go around the attendant. And can't think of any strategy that's both prompt and legal. He bites his forearm and screams. A tan, well-dressed man stares, then looks away.

Tommy already axed his way into Cora's father's home and locked him in a closet. The cops are surely looking for someone with his description by now. Instead of breaking the law again, maybe he should get away from the justice already storming toward him. And leave Glen Brent's justice to the FBI.

If he fled California now, he could avert charges from Stewart Hall. Maybe Tommy's West Coast trip has come to its logical end. Maybe he should ask Josh to loan him some money, drive to the airport, and buy a ticket back to New York. Just leave the state like so many people have wanted him to do since he entered it.

Tommy gets in his car. And turns on the engine.

FIFTY-SIX

Cora sits in her room at the Grand Bay Resort. About a dozen crumpled tissues litter the rug around her chair. Her mother, who has a fading version of her good looks, sits hunched on the end of a bed biting her nails, watching TV news coverage of Glen.

The reporter says, "According to sources close to law enforcement, Brent and Archer could be responsible for at least eight unresolved missing-persons cases in San Diego . . ."

"What do you think of Allison Vandane?" Cora asks.

"What?"

"The fake name I checked us in with. I'll obviously need a new permanent one. After this. Should I just stick with Allison Vandane?"

"I don't know, darling. Let me watch this."

"We've watched enough of this." Cora turns off the

television. Then opens the bottle of valerian-root pills on the table.

"How many of those have you had?"

"I'm not counting."

"You're pregnant. You need to—"

"You don't think I thought about that? What I really want to do is dump a jug of Xanax down my throat. But I'm not. For the baby. This is an all-natural anxiety reducer."

"That makes it better for the baby?"

Cora tosses two pills in her mouth. Swallows them without water. "I don't know. I'm not a doctor."

"You'll feel better when the lawyer shows up. He'll give you pointers on how to handle an ordeal like this."

"Oh. So he specializes in pregnant ladies whose husbands go on killing sprees?"

"Honey."

"What?"

"You're a strong woman. You'll get through this."

"Maybe I am a strong woman, maybe I'm not. But I am a woman. You know who isn't yet? Far from it." She places her palms on her stomach. "She'll meet the world as the daughter of a notorious murderer."

"Change your last name like you said. Jade's too. People won't know."

"With the internet, they can always find out."

"Then why did you want to change your name?"

Cora gazes out the window, clouds blocking the late-afternoon sun over the bay. "I don't know."

Silence for a while.

"He's not a violent man," Cora's mom says. "How could he do this?"

"It was right in front of me all day. I couldn't bring myself to believe it until I saw it on TV."

"You knew about this?"

"Just . . . since this morning. But I wasn't certain."

"He told you?"

"No. But he was acting weird the last couple days."

"Being aggressive?"

"No. Nothing like that. Very calm actually, very . . . loving. I thought he was cheating on me. I was so scared that was true. Looking back, I'd give anything if it was that instead of . . . this."

"How could you confuse an affair with . . . this?"

"He came home from work with an odd wound on his shoulder. Said it was from a car accident. Then he tried to get me to leave town with him. When I refused, he taped cardboard to our windows."

"And that means he was cheating on you?"

"In the version of reality I created in my paranoid head, he wasn't in an accident. He was at another woman's place, a crazy one, breaking their affair off. She got mad and stabbed him in the shoulder with scissors, or some other sharp thing lying around. He had his army buddy, Bo Archer, the other one on TV, stash his Mercedes on his property."

"You just . . . invented all this?"

"I didn't believe his story. And I needed some explanation. In my mind, he feared this lunatic stabber woman might come to our house, so suggested we get out of town. When I said no, he covered all the windows so I wouldn't be able to see her if she was stalking him in the bushes. In my head it all fit."

"And none of it was true?"

"It was so farfetched, I needed proof to be sure. He bought a baby monitor for Jade. Last night I slipped the transmitter behind a book on the shelf in his study. Bo came over. They talked. Everything the speaker picked up recorded to the cloud. I assumed they were in there discussing his affair and his Mercedes. I was wrong." She nods at the TV. "They were talking about all that."

"About killing people?"

"Right on tape. It was so ridiculous, I assumed it was fake. Some inside joke from their army days or something."

"Did you confront him?"

"I was too shook up. Even though I didn't believe it, it

was still disturbing. The words they were using. The way they said them. How callous they were. I had to get out of the house." She points at a scab on her knee. "I was so distracted I tripped on a planter on my way to the car."

"You didn't seem yourself when you came over this morning. I had a feeling it wasn't one of your regular visits. Why didn't you tell me all this then?"

"I still couldn't make sense of it. I still don't know where his Mercedes is, still don't know why he put cardboard on the windows. And the killing stuff I still thought was just some dark joke. Then the story broke on the news. Now I know it was far from a joke."

Quiet for a bit.

"They say he may've been trying to help soldiers," Cora's mom says. "From the internet. Something like that. You think that's why he did it?"

"If so, I guess he decided the lives of random people from the internet were more important than those of his wife and daughter."

"Where do you think he is?"

"No idea. I just hope he isn't going to do this again."

"Kill more people?"

"That's what they were talking about in the conversation I recorded."

"A lot has changed since last night. Every cop in California is on the lookout for them. This won't happen again."

"I considered that. But . . . shouldn't I still tell someone what I heard, to be sure?"

"Like who?"

"The FBI."

"Dad told you to come here strictly to hide from them. Now you want to go to them? No, no. A good lawyer will prevent you from winding up in a cell like your husband. God forbid. We should both just sit tight. And not contact anyone. Especially the FBI."

Cora sighs, sits back in the chair. "When I was in like fifth grade, remember the drawing I did for school, about how I saw myself in the future?"

"You did a lot of drawings for school."

"Yeah. I, at least, always remembered this one. I knew from back then I wanted to work in fashion. Drew myself this wild outfit. And I knew I wanted to marry a doctor. When I made my husband, I put that doctor headband-light thing on the Crayon stick figure."

"Fifth grade? You didn't even start dating until you were in what, eighth?"

"It's strange, right? That young. But I knew. I think it was from watching *ER* with dad. I always thought of doctors as like ... respectable."

"Maybe."

"There was a nice house in my drawing. With a pool. And two little kids. Over the last twenty years, I was on my way to living up to that picture. First baby on the way. We planned to have a second someday. It was ... everything it was supposed to be. It was perfect. And now ... this. Now this."

"It's not your fault, honey."

"Does it matter whose fault it is?"

FIFTY-SEVEN

Nurse Peggy's eyes never closed post-death, staring up at Glen from the floor of the Prius. He shuts her eyelids, then looks out the passenger window at desert hills beneath a purplish-orange sky.

His burner phone rings, Hawks.

Glen says into it, "What's up?"

"How'd it go at the hospital?"

"A success. But we now have a third passenger. One we'll need to drop off somewhere like we did our last third passenger."

"I see." A pause. "My friend from Nevada got back to me. Pulled some info for you on that guy Thomas Dapino. Turns out he's an ex-con. Just got out of Attica."

"Huh. And now he's teamed up with the FBI."

"No official record of any relationship with the FBI."

"Whatever the case, since Bo and I have been doing . . .

what we've been doing . . . nobody got close to us. We were never questioned by a cop. An agent. Anyone. Until today. Until Dapino showed up at my house. And he's still out there."

"Is he going to be a problem tonight?"

"I'm assuming he'll try to be."

"Now that you and I have a business relationship going . . . I'd be open to extending that relationship. As Archer can attest, I'm quite good at seeing to individuals who present . . . problems. For the right fee, I'd be happy to see to this problem."

"I appreciate that. But Dapino could be anywhere right now. Plus, if he's working with the FBI, feds will be around him. He'll be a hard target for a hit. Maybe too hard."

"Then what're you going to do about him?"

"I don't know. Got to think about it."

"Big-brained surgeon like you. Sure you'll come up with something."

"Yeah. We'll see."

"A thousand bucks."

"What?"

"In bitcoin. For my friend, the data pull."

"Oh. Yeah. I'll do it when we get back to your house. Got to go."

"Bye doc."

Glen hangs up.

Bo, driving, asks, "Did you just deny his request to take out Dapino?"

"I'll deal with Dapino."

"Hawks is a professional mercenary. Not to mention, the cops ain't looking for his face. He has a lot more range than us. We're lucky to have him on our side. Let's take advantage of this asset any—"

"I don't like the guy. Okay?"

"'Cause of that shit in the garage? Who—"

"I'm over that. He just . . . gives me the creeps."

"He's a loose cannon. I told you he was. How many dudes

like that did you know in Desert Storm? A ton."

"Something about him is different."

"He's a little rougher around the edges than average. Fine. But he's a soldier at the core. Same core as the rest. I think you got different. No offense, brother. That's where the gap is."

"You're accusing me of what, not being a soldier at my core? How dare—"

"I never said that. On the outside. What you're around. Your lifestyle. It's . . . just been a long time since you were in combat."

"You too."

"I did paramilitary jobs till I was almost forty. Shoulder to shoulder with soldiers."

"I literally have my hands inside soldiers. Operating on them at the VA. To this day. Every day. Who're you around on a daily basis, housewives who can't lift their big-screen TVs into their Range Rovers?"

"That's a real dick thing to say, man. If I was as smart as you, maybe I'd have a . . . high-paying career too. I'm no genius. And I know it. But that's all right. I do what I can to make ends meet."

A few seconds of silence.

"Sorry," Glen says.

"All good." Bo turns on the radio. They drive east for a while.

"There's a county park not far from here, right?" Glen asks.

"About ten miles. Why?"

"Dapino. He's a felon. Cops wouldn't give him the benefit of the doubt."

"The benefit of the doubt for what?"

Glen smirks. "Head to the park. It should have emergency phones. Those tall pedestal ones along hiking trails, in case you get hurt or whatever and don't have cell reception. I need to make a call from one."

"To Dapino?"

"Not to him. About him."

"About what?"

"I'm going to shut him down tonight. And hopefully ruin the rest of the son of a bitch's life."

FIFTY-EIGHT

Tommy pulls back onto the property of the Grand Bay Resort. Though flying back to the safety of New York was tempting, he decided to stay in California to see this through. He just committed a crime, shoplifted items from CVS he couldn't pay for without a wallet. And now is about to commit another one.

He reaches to the stolen merchandise on the passenger seat. Opens a pack of ping-pong balls, grabs a pair of scissors, and pokes a hole in a ball with the scissors. He places it in the cup holder, takes a second from the pack, and cuts it in half. Then slices each of those halves in half and does so again and again, left with sixteen shards. He stuffs them in the hole in the first ball and wraps a piece of tinfoil around it.

The foil-encased ball goes in his pocket. As does a Bic lighter. The final stolen item, a big bottle of cold water, he chugs. Then steps out of the car. He leaves the axe behind.

The protrusion under his shirt could be suspicious. He strides to the back of the hotel.

Kneeling behind bushes, he peers through an aluminum fence at the pool. The afternoon turned to early evening, not many guests out here, just a young couple sharing a lounge chair and an older guy in the hot tub reading a newspaper.

Once the couple kisses, he hops the fence, careful not to bump it hard enough to make a noticeable noise. He darts to the rear of a cabana and peeks around the corner at the couple. As soon as they kiss again, he sprints into the hotel. He's in a hallway off the main lobby, a handful of people walking by. Too many eyeballs down here. He'll have to go up to a guest-room floor, less foot traffic.

He waits by the elevator pretending to look at something on his phone. When a guest presses the up button, Tommy follows him inside. The man scans his keycard on a sensor and hits "2" on the panel.

Tommy fakes reaching for the panel. "Ah, I'm on two also. Thanks."

They ride to the second floor and get out. The man disappears around a corner. Tommy listens to the sound of his room door opening and closing. Now alone, he removes the Bic lighter from one pocket and from the other the tinfoil-wrapped ping-pong ball. He meets the ball with the flame. The material heats up. Smoke shoots out of the half-inch tinfoil spout.

He drops the homemade smoke bomb in front of the elevator, yanks the fire alarm on the wall, and races down the hall banging on every door he passes. "Fire in the elevator shaft," he screams. "We all have to get downstairs. Fire in the elevator shaft."

The alarm blares. Concerned heads pop out of doorways. A guy shouts, "Holy shit, smoke."

Tommy isn't proud of the panic he incited. But had to do it. He descends the stairs to the first floor. Pushes open the emergency exit and dashes onto the lawn. He peers at the bodies flowing out of the doorway.

Five minutes or so pass. In the distance he hears the horn of a fire truck. A couple more minutes. A police siren.

A female about his age appears, the crowd concealing most of her. He weaves toward her. A couple feet away, he says, "Cora?"

She turns around. A pregnant stomach. The face from Facebook. "Yeah?"

"My name is Tommy. And I want to keep you safe from your husband."

Her mother is at her side, along with a man in his fifties in a shiny suit. He says, "Take a hike, chief. That's not funny."

"I'm not joking. My sister was one of his victims. Her name was Danielle Dapino. Google her. She's been in the news. We had the same nose. You can tell we're related."

The man inserts himself between Tommy and Cora, says, "I am Mrs. Brent's attorney. My client is not speaking to you or anyone else about her husband at this moment. Even if you are related to whomever you say you are."

Tommy juts his head around the lawyer, makes eye contact with her, and says, "I know you weren't involved in any of this. I'm not here to get you in any kind of trouble. Even if I wanted to, I wouldn't have the authority. I'm not an FBI agent. But I am working with them. Though you didn't start this, you have the power to end it. All you need—"

"Am I going to have to tell you again?" the lawyer asks.

"Am I going to have to make you look for your front teeth in the grass?" Tommy says, clenching his fists.

A nervous smile on the attorney.

"Let him talk," Cora says.

Tommy asks, "Did your husband contact you today?"

"He tried. Kept trying until I turned my phone off."

"Was it from a number you didn't recognize? A burner?"

"A what? No, his regular cellphone."

"Which he definitely turned off at this point. Can you get in touch with him some other way? Email him?"

"To tell him what?"

"To meet you somewhere."

"But I don't want to meet him."

"You won't. It's just a trap. You won't show up. Instead, the FBI will."

She crosses her arms. "As enraged as I am at him, that just . . .
he's still my husband. I can't betray him like that. What he did to those people was . . . I mean, whew. But to me, he was nothing but good."

"That can be a problem for you."

"How?"

"I was with him today. At his warehouse. He seemed convinced you were kidnapped by a Mexican gang."

"What?"

"I didn't get it either. Anyway, I could tell from how he talks about you that he . . . really loves you. With someone like him, that's dangerous. When he eventually learns you weren't kidnapped, he's going to search for you." A couple firefighters run through the crowd toward the hotel, one bumping into Tommy's shoulder. "He's obsessive. He won't just let you go."

"Are you saying he's going to hurt her?" her mother asks.

"No. Not physically at least. But think about the mental burden of having a high-profile fugitive in your life." He gazes at Cora. "He'll hound you to move overseas with him. To some hut in the woods of a non-extradition country. Is that where you want to raise your child?"

She cups her chin with her hand. Peers at the ground and shakes her head *no*.

"If your husband isn't stopped, he will get to you," Tommy says. "But you can prevent that. I understand if you don't want to actively participate in a trap. You don't need to contact him. Just talk to me. Any information would be helpful. Anything that might point to where he's hiding."

She's silent for a while. "I don't know where he's hiding. But I do know something else. It might be obsolete by now, though."

"Tell me."

FIFTY-NINE

Tommy holds Cora's phone to his ear, last night's recording of her husband and Archer radiating through the speaker. When it ends, he hugs her, says, "Thank you."

"You think they're actually going to do that? Tonight?"

"Yes. And because of you, the FBI is going to stop them before it happens."

"Are they going to . . . kill Glen?"

Tommy, unsure how to reply, says nothing.

"I know the news is making him out to be a monster," she says. "But he's also a man. Make sure they don't forget that. Will you do that for me?"

"They already know who he is."

She tightens her lips as if not happy with that answer. "I need to find a place to sit down." Her gaze sweeps the crowded lawn. "Huh. Did you do all this? Just to get me outside?"

He looks away for a second, then back at her. "Good luck, Cora. With everything."

"Yeah. You too."

He waves, marches through the flock of guests toward the parking lot. He calls Jordana. Her phone rings for a bit, then goes to voicemail. After the beep, he says, "It's me. I know we kind of got into it before. Can we forget about all that for a second? I found Cora. What she gave me is . . . huge. Brent and Archer have something planned tonight. And I know where and when. Call me, Jordana, call me."

He tucks the phone back in his pocket and crosses the asphalt toward his car. A voice over his shoulder says, "Excuse me, sir."

He turns to it. A Black cop stares at him, his White partner behind. "Where you headed?" the Black cop asks.

"Just to my car."

"Where you going in your car?"

"I . . . why does it matter, officer?"

"Please answer the question, sir."

"I don't see you asking the question to anyone else in the parking lot."

The cop eyeballs the cut on Tommy's bicep. "You all right?"

"Just a nick."

"From what?"

A pause. "I was helping a friend move. Edge from a coffee table."

"Ouch. When did you leave your friend's house to come here?"

"I don't remember exactly. Why?"

"You're a guest here?"

"Visiting one."

"Another friend?"

"You could say that."

"Seems like you have a lot of friends in Newport. You live here?"

"Vacation."

"From where?"

"Why?"

"From where?"

"New York."

"Got some ID?"

"I ... my license ... I don't have it on me. I misplaced it earlier."

"That sounds inconvenient."

"It is. Tried ordering a beer at the lobby bar and they wouldn't let me."

"You've got a youthful face. Take it as a compliment. How old are you exactly?"

"What does that matter, officer? I'm still not sure what all this—"

"Answer the question, sir."

"Thirty-one."

The cop glances at his partner, then turns back to Tommy, asks, "And your name?"

"Tommy."

The cop looks at his partner again, holds his gaze on him longer, then turns back to Tommy, asks, "Tommy what?"

"Dapino."

The cop grabs Tommy's wrist and puts it behind his back. "Don't move."

"What is this shit?"

Hotel guests gape at the policeman cuffing Tommy. Gripping his elbow, the cop leads him toward a cruiser. Pushes Tommy's torso over the hood and searches his pockets. Sets his cellphone and keys on the car.

"What're you arresting me for?"

No reply.

"What did I do wrong?" Tommy yells.

"Your photo, height, and age just came through the police computer system. Every cop in California has been authorized to arrest you if spotted."

"For what crime?"

"Murder."

A chill courses through Tommy's stomach. The cop pats him down for weapons. Tommy wonders how this is possible. Maybe they found out he pulled the fire alarm and some unlucky guest was trampled during the evacuation. Or maybe they found out he locked Cora's father in the closet and he slipped and snapped his neck trying to escape.

No and no. Both situations are too unlikely. And even if one were true, the accusation would be manslaughter. Not murder. Something else is going on here. And he can't wait around to find out what. Not tonight, not with mere hours to go before Brent and Archer's next slaying.

The White cop opens the cruiser's rear door. Says to the observers, "Nothing to see here, folks."

His partner guides Tommy toward the backseat. "Head down."

Tommy drops to the ground. Rolls under the car.

"Shit," the Black cop says.

Tommy's hands trapped behind his back, he uses only his legs to push himself to the left, his chest grinding against the pavement. He shimmies out from under the car on the opposite side of the officers, sprints toward the parking-lot exit.

The smack of footsteps behind him. The crackle of a police radio. He hears the Black cop say, "Suspect just left the Grand Bay Resort on foot. Turned north on Vasco Highway."

Tommy dashes along the edge of a four-lane road, bayfront homes on one side, high-end businesses the other. In the rear windshield of a parked car, he sees the reflection of the pursuing policemen. He has about fifty feet on them. But realizes backup is on the way. If he stays in their sight, he's done.

He scans the passing storefronts. After typical business hours, almost all have dark windows, seem closed. He keeps running, the motion awkward with his hands stuck behind his back. His thighs and calves burn.

A restaurant. An active valet stand out front. This place is open. Tommy cuts across the highway. The shriek of a horn. An Audi hooks around him, its driver flipping him off.

Tommy runs onto restaurant property. A trio of fifty-ish women in skimpy cocktail dresses stares at him, then behind him as if at the cops.

"Sir?" a valet says.

Tommy blows past him into the entrance. Dim lighting. Piano player at a baby grand. About three dozen well-to-do-looking citizens at tables. They gawk at the outsider in handcuffs. The soothing piano music progresses. Tommy winds between waiters, busboys, chairs.

"Stop there, Dapino," the Black cop shouts.

Tommy kicks open a service door, barrels into the kitchen. Cooks in greasy white aprons. Steaming pots and pans. Rap music.

"Yo, you good G?" a cook asks him.

"How do I get out of here?"

The cops enter.

"Dammit," Tommy says. He scuttles ahead, looking for a door. He slams into a server holding a tray. The sting of piping-hot sauce on Tommy's neck, his forearms. Their bodies fall tangled to the floor.

"You dick," the server says. He throws a lobster tail at Tommy's head.

A shattered plate beneath Tommy. A shard must've clipped his bicep cut. It's re-opened. He rises to his feet. To his right an "EXIT" sign. He rushes toward it. Boots the door open. Staggers outside.

A long strip of alleyway runs to his left and right. If he took off either way, the cops would have an easy visual on him. Ahead is a hill. At the top is the side of some large one-story facility. He'll try hiding in there.

He charges up the hill. It steepens. He has an urge to grip bushes for support, the shackles preventing him. His abdominal muscles ache. His breathing accelerates.

The surface beneath him changes from dirt to asphalt. He takes in the building. A large sign at the opposite end of the lot says, "Briar Road Middle School." He bolts to the first door he sees. Kicks it. Doesn't budge. He hooks his foot under the handle, pulls it toward him. Still, no budge.

He peeks through a window. Shadows drape a vacant hallway. August. The school must be closed for summer. He kicks the glass. Doesn't break, feels thick. He whacks it with his metal cuffs. Again. Again. His wrists throb. Again, again. The sound of a crack.

He kicks the fissure. It widens. Once more. Widens more. Once more, his foot crosses through. He hits the edges with his heel, enlarging the space. He maneuvers his head through it. Shoulders. Torso. Legs.

A sense of accomplishment flows through him. But fades when he realizes he hasn't accomplished much. He still is wanted for murder. He still has not given Jordana all the Cora intel.

A voice in his head tells him he is in danger, that he should call 9-1-1. His scattered mind needs a second to remember the people on the other end of a 9-1-1 call are the ones after him.

The cuffs. Get them off. Focus on that. Once his hands are free, his options won't be so limited. He could go down to a main road. Try to hitchhike to the FBI office, tell Jordana the intel in person.

He knees a locker. An echoing clang. "You dumb asshole," he says to himself.

He regrets not giving her all the details about tonight's attack in his voicemail. Instead he kept it vague. He wanted her to have a reason to call him back, wanted to hear her voice again, wanted a chance to make things right between them.

Something sharp. That's what he needs to focus on right now. To cut through the shackles. Maybe the school offers a shop class.

He roams the hallway, eyeballing signs on the doors. On the walls between them are motivational posters. He remembers similar ones from his middle school.

Good Things Happen to Good People

If You Can Dream It, You Can Do It
Work Hard and You Will Succeed
Kindness Is a Superpower
You Are Invincible
Smile

Blood streams down his bicep. Also his face, the cut on his head must've re-opened too. More doors, more signs. *Woodshop.*

"Hell yes," he says. He angles his back to the door, turns the knob with his hand. A high-ceilinged room with dark overhead lamps. The dull shine of metal machinery. The scent of sawdust.

On the wall a corkboard with tools hanging off. He butts his shoulder against a table, pushes it against the wall, and hops atop. Grabs a saw. He of course lacks the range of motion to cut the shackle chain with either hand. He needs some additional implement.

At the edge of the table is a vice. He sets the saw on it, twists a handle. The jaws tighten on the blade, secure it in place. He positions the handcuff chain on the saw's teeth. Drags it forward, back. Forward, back. A soft, high-pitched scraping noise.

"Ah ha," he says, his voice resounding. It's working.

He continues dragging. A louder noise overtakes the scraping.

A police siren. Then a second. The cops and their backup must've scoured the area within a reasonable radius of the restaurant. And spotted the broken window. No time to keep hacking away at the cuffs. He needs to get out of here.

He hustles to the front of the room. Peeks into the hall. No movement in any direction. The sound of a door to the right. He goes left, careful to keep his footsteps quiet. The sound of another door. To the left. He turns right. Cops, three of them, SWAT gear.

Turns left. Same sight.

"On your stomach scumbag," one shouts.

"You got the wrong guy," Tommy says. "I didn't murder—"

The cop drills him in the stomach with the butt of his rifle. Tommy topples to the floor. The police swarm him.

SIXTY

Glen peers out the Prius window at the darkening sky. The front of his scrubs top is splattered in another man's blood. "Let me ask you something," he says.

Bo, driving, doesn't reply.

"Bo?" Glen says.

"What?"

"You all right?"

"Not really."

"What's wrong?"

Bo swallows. "You didn't have to do that back there."

"You know how much that's going to help us later?"

"I get that. But the . . . way you did it. You didn't have to do it like that."

"What does it matter how I did it?"

"I don't know."

Glen nods toward the window. "We're leaving all this the

day after tomorrow. Turning into new people in Morocco. It doesn't matter anymore. None of it matters. Isn't it . . . freeing?"

"Let's just . . . let's just make sure we make it overseas."

"Why won't we make it overseas?"

"No reason. Just . . . saying."

"You still didn't answer my question."

"What question?"

"What I wanted to ask you." Glen opens the glove box. Takes out the baggie of cocaine. Pours the remainder into two lines on the back of his hand. Snorts them both. "At Hawks's house, you said I was the bravest guy you know. Remember?"

"I remember."

"Did you mean that?"

"Yeah. Of course I meant it."

"What'd I do that was so brave?"

A pause. "You manned up in Iraq."

"So did a lot of guys."

"Yeah. But not like you. You had . . . grit."

"Oh yeah?"

"Not just money?"

"What?"

"The last six months. Cost me a lot of money."

"For a good cause. What does that have to do with you fighting in Iraq when you were what, nineteen? You didn't have any money then. What're you getting at?"

"Nothing." A pause. "Dapino thinks I scare easily. Remember when he said that, in the warehouse?"

"No."

"Stop lying."

"Why would I lie about that?"

Glen points at a swath of sandy terrain along the highway. "Reminds you of over there, doesn't it?"

"Iraq?"

"Iraq."

"A little."

"I remember sitting out on a lawn chair at base. Around this time of day. Sky a similar color to how it is now. Everything around quiet like how it is now. And I asked myself why we were over there. You ever do that?"

"We all did at least once, no?"

"They told me it was for democracy in the Middle East. That the politicians in America cared so much about regular people in these foreign countries that they decided to send all that money and all those troops over there to give them democracy." A moment. "When I was young I actually believed it."

"So did I."

"What's the real reason? Why did we go over there in the Nineties and keep going?"

"I don't know."

"Neither do I."

Silence for about a minute.

"Pull over," Glen says.

"What? Why?"

"Pull over."

"We need to keep moving. Get back to Hawks's. We—"

"If you don't pull over, I'm not going to pay for your passport."

Bo takes a deep breath, eases off the gas. The Prius coasts to the side of the empty desert road. Glen opens his door.

"What the hell are you doing?" Bo asks.

"You think I'm a pussy, don't you?"

"When did I say that?"

"You didn't have to say it. I'll show you who I am. Show you right now."

"If a car passes, someone could recognize your face. Get back in—"

"I'll cover my face."

"Why're you . . . what're you trying to do?"

"You already guessed it. Waiting for a car to pass."

"For what? To steal it? We already have a car. We—"

"Just watch."

"Am I going to have to come out there and knock your head off your shoulders?"

"There he is. There's the real him. You wouldn't say that to me if you respected me. Would you say that to Hawks?"

Bo rubs his temples. "Glen . . . just get in. Let's talk in here."

A car materializes on the horizon. "Ah. Here we have it."

"Glen. Get in."

"What do you think the average reaction time is for an American driver to process an unexpected event on the road?"

"I don't know, man."

"Whatever it is, I'm sure it slows down out here. Hardly any other cars around. No sudden cautions to be ready for. Can't you see a driver just . . . relaxing? Finding a lull with the road. Almost like a dream." Glen hides behind a bush.

"What are you doing?"

Glen watches the incoming car, a small SUV. "You think the driver is in a dream?"

"I don't know. Let's talk about it in here."

The SUV nears, just a couple hundred feet away. Glen lifts the bloody scrubs top over his face and jumps out from the bush into the road. He sees nothing but the darkness he created. Braces himself for a potential flattening.

The screech of tires. Growl of an engine. A clank.

His heart rate comes down. If the SUV were to hit him, it would've done so by now. He yanks down the scrubs top. Gazes at the vehicle, nose down in a ditch. Swerve marks on the pavement.

"What the hell?" Bo shouts. "Let's get out of here. Hurry up."

Glen ignores him. Paces to the SUV. Looks through the driver's window. A fortyish man at the wheel, a boy, about twelve, in a Little League uniform next to him. The boy is crying.

Glen opens the door. The driver turns to him. His head

recoils a few inches. Maybe from the blood smeared on Glen's chest. Maybe from his missing eyebrows. Maybe something else.

"What's the matter with you?" the man asks. "Are you drunk?"

Glen says nothing. Just looks into his eyes. Then the boy's.

"You dislocated my son's shoulder," the man says.

"Was he wearing a seatbelt?"

The father reaches to the backseat. Pulls a baseball bat out of an equipment bag. Steps out of the car. "You almost get us killed, now you're being a smartass?"

"Put the bat down, please."

The father's eyes notice Bo across the street, leaning against the Prius with his arms folded. He lowers the bat, says, "Let's just . . . I just want to be on my way. I'm going to call a tow truck. We'll be fine."

"Your son doesn't look fine."

"He'll be okay. I can pop his shoulder back into place."

"Maybe I can look at it. I'm a doctor."

"It's . . . all right. You can be on your way too." He walks back to his car. Says something to his son. Then turns around, notices Glen standing in the same place. "Go. Really."

"You're lucky."

"I know. This could've been worse."

Glen steps to him. "Things would be worse if you were me. Do you know who I am?"

"Sorry . . . I don't."

"Do you watch the news?"

"Not very often. No."

"I'm on the news today."

"That's . . . that's good I guess."

"Not for something good. According to the people who run the news at least."

"Oh. Sorry about that."

"The worst part they didn't talk about on the news. The worst part is that I am a father too. Well, I was. But my little girl is dead."

Silence for a bit. "That's ... you know ... that's terrible."

"My wife too. Do you have a wife?"

A bead of sweat trickles down the man's forehead. "Yes. I have a wife."

The boy says, "Dad, it hurts. Can you do that thing you said?"

The father snaps his shoulder back into the socket. The kid screams. The father pats him on the back. "It's all over. Good job. I'll call the tow truck. Let's go home." He grabs his phone from the cup holder.

"Put that down," Glen says. He removes a gun from the waist of his scrubs pants, points it at him.

"Let's ... just chill." He raises his hands. "I don't want to ... press charges or anything. I just want to get out of here with my son."

Glen leans forward, peeks into the car at the boy. He shoots him in the face.

The father's eyes stay wide and frozen for a few seconds as if in disbelief. Then he glimpses his dead son slumped over in the seat, a caved-in red splotch where his nose used to be. He shakes his shoulders. "Owen? Owen?"

Bo runs over. Scopes the small corpse. "Jesus Christ."

The father turns to them. He opens his mouth as if to say something, then closes it. He pants.

"We're the same you and I," Glen says. "Same type of day."

"No. No, no, no."

"Or maybe it's more like your wife's. Maybe your wife and I had more of a similar day." Glen shoots the man in the heart. He crumbles to the dirt. Gasps. Glen fires another round into his forehead.

Bo shoves Glen into the side of the car, says, "You've lost your mind."

Glen smirks. "What's a mind?"

"What?"

"What is it? Something inside my brain? What's a brain? Just a clump of cells. No mind inside a clump of cells. Not that I ever saw in any medical-school textbook. I didn't lose anything. I never had anything to lose." He looks up at the sky. "I just am. Same as you. Same as them. I just am."

"What does that mean?"

Glen crosses the road to the Prius. "Let's get out of here before someone sees us."

SIXTY-ONE

Jordana stands in front of four San Diego cops under a tent set up Downtown, a makeshift command center for the FBI-SDPD task force going after Brent and Archer. "The army's combat training is even more extensive than yours or mine," she says. "If you happen to find them, do not let your guard down. If you make a wrong move, they'll put a bullet between your eyes."

"Any chatter on the APBs?" a male cop asks.

"Unfortunately nothing on Brent's Aston Martin. Or Mercedes. They could be in something else for all we know. If you see something shady with any type of vehicle, look inside, get a visual on a face. Anything else?"

"We're good. Thanks." He leads the other three officers out of the tent.

Jordana pours a cup of coffee from an urn and sits in front of a monitor showing live feeds of the public streetlight cameras in San Diego. She debates listening to the voicemail Tommy left her. His parting words before boarding his flight to New York. At best, the message is an apology for being a jerk earlier. At worst, an accusation of her being one. Either way, it could tamper with her head. And as case lead, she needs a stable one.

"Agent Quick?" a female voice says behind her.

Jordana turns to an FBI agent about ten years older than her. "Yeah?"

"A nine-one-one tip came in about a white box truck."

"You sure it wasn't another prank?"

"Caller used a business landline, not a cell. Seems legit."

Jordana's posture straightens. "We've known about the white box truck for a week. And they know we know. Why drive around in that?"

"I'm just conveying the information."

"Who made the call?"

"A gas-station attendant. About forty miles east of here."

"Saying what exactly?"

"He was watching the news earlier, following the story. TV mentioned Brent and Archer have driven around in a white box truck. Saw one pull into his gas station to fill up. He stepped out of the mini-mart and headed over to the pumps to get a better look at who was inside. Two men, late forties. They were in hats. Couldn't see their faces well. He was too scared to stare or get very close. But overheard them talking. They mentioned something about a factory in El Cajon."

Jordana's index finger fidgets with the rim of her coffee cup. "Could still be a false alarm. But it definitely doesn't sound like a prank. This gas-station attendant saw something. It's worth checking out."

"I agree."

"Call the El Cajon Police Department. Have them send a couple cruisers over to whatever factories might be in town. See if they notice anything suspicious."

"On it." She steps to Jordana. "One other thing."

"Yeah?"

"You're doing a great job as lead," she whispers.

Jordana smiles.

The agent walks off. Two others approach Jordana with questions. For the next hour, she fields even more.

Her phone vibrates, a number not saved in her contacts. "Agent Quick," she says into it.

"This is Sergeant Zimmer. With the El Cajon Police Department. You might want to get over here." Once he explains his reasoning, she goes in her Blazer, attaches the siren atop, and races up the freeway.

She drives through El Cajon toward an out-of-business pillow factory. Its parking-lot entrance is blocked off with yellow tape, a cruiser nearby, a patrolman on guard beside it.

Jordana rolls down her window and presents her FBI badge. The cop moves the tape to the side. She traverses the asphalt, the cracked windows and decrepit facade of the factory towering above the Blazer. In the distance, among huddled police officers, emerges an image that streaks coldness up the skin of her arms.

The white box truck.

She parks and steps out. A grizzled man with sergeant insignia on his uniform's sleeve walks to her. "Agent Quick?"

"Sergeant Zimmer?"

"In person you look even younger than I heard you were."

"Any sign of them?"

"Not yet. Just the truck. But it must be theirs. Splotches of blood all over the back."

"Fresh blood?"

"Dry. Probably stains from past victims."

"Anything in the vehicle that could suggest why they came here?"

"Negative."

"You search the factory?"

"Two of my best are inside as we speak. So far . . . nothing."

"So they came here, parked, and decided to what ... go out on foot? Is there a homeless encampment nearby?"

"I sent a car. According to the homeless there, no sighting of anyone with Brent or Archer's description."

"Then why come here?"

"I don't know yet. What I do know is that the nine-one-one gas-station call came in about an hour and a half ago from Pine Valley. A half-hour drive from there to here. Meaning Brent and Archer have been in town for no more than an hour. And if they're on foot, they're not covering much ground. I'd put them within a three-mile radius of the factory."

"Sounds about right."

"I have a team going door to door at businesses and residences. And we're firing up the chopper for an overhead look at the streets." He smirks. "El Cajon will be the last stop on their tour."

SIXTY-TWO

Tommy sits on a metal chair in an interrogation room in the Newport Beach jail, his head slumped toward his shoulder. The door opens. In walks a wiry man in his late thirties in a tucked-in polo shirt, a badge on his waist, a manila folder in his hand. He sits across from Tommy, no table or other barrier between them. Pulls a recording device from his pocket, flips it on, and sets it on the floor.

"I'm Detective Stince."

"And I'm not your murderer."

Stince smirks. "Who was she?"

"How should I know?"

"This is how you want to play it?"

"I have nothing to play."

"Her body is with the coroner. He's taking prints. DNA. We'll find out who she is soon."

"Good for you."

"Once we do, if we learn you knew her when she was alive, do you really want to be on record saying you have no idea who she is? You'd establish yourself as a liar. Juries don't like liars. You want to pretend I just walked in here and we can start over? Try to have a constructive conversation?"

"The only constructive conversation I can have is one with the FBI. Get me on the phone with Special Agent Jordana Quick."

"Ah yes, the FBI. Of course. Officer Huddy filled me in on everything you told him on the way over. You're working for them as a special consultant. Sounds very top secret. Very . . . James Bond."

"I get one phone call. You get arrested, you get a phone call. Give me mine."

"Why bring a lawyer into this if you're innocent? Why make things so formal? I just want to have a casual conversation. Just want to hear your side of the story."

"I don't want a lawyer. How many times do I have to tell you guys? I want Special Agent Jordana Quick from the FBI's San Diego field office. Let me talk to her first. Then I'll talk to you about this bullshit murder."

"Bullshit, huh?"

"You guys screwed up. Got the wrong person. This will go away once you recognize whatever mistake you made. I'm not worried. What I am worried about is the massacre that'll happen tonight if you don't listen to me."

Stince opens the manila folder, takes out a photo of a red-haired woman in medical scrubs lying along a trail in the woods. "What does this look like?"

"A dead person."

"Very good."

"Do you want a lot more dead people tonight?"

Stince removes a second photo from the folder. "And what does this look like?"

Tommy's throat tightens. A close-up of his New York driver's license on the dirt beside the dead lady.

"Those dress pants are pretty slick," Stince says. "Looks

like your ID slid right out of your pocket when you were strangling her."

Brent. He had Tommy's driver's license on him after taking it at the warehouse.

"This is a setup," Tommy screams.

"Haven't heard that one before."

"It's all part of the same—"

"What really happened? I'm assuming you were banging her. Let me guess, you two had been fighting. She worked at a hospital or some dentist's office or something like that. To apologize to her, you surprised her at work at the end of her shift, told her you wanted to do something spontaneous. So you took her out camping to the park. Had something nice in mind. Figured the time alone out in nature would be good for your struggling relationship. But you were wrong. It wasn't long till she made a comment you didn't like. Next—"

"I've never seen her before in my life. I—"

"Next thing you know you've got your hands around her throat. You're just squeezing to shut her up, not trying to kill her. But she got you really pissed this time. After all, you brought her out there as a nice gesture. And you squeezed a little too hard. For a little too long. She scratched at you, got your arm pretty good. But not good enough to stop it. You probably blacked out. Don't even remember most of it. And when you snapped back, she wasn't breathing."

"None of that happened. It's . . . made-up. Where's the proof?"

"What's already been proven is your attempted robbery in Queens. I know all about that. And the two years you just did in Attica. That must've hardened you up a bit, huh? Hear it's vicious over there. I can imagine the things you saw. How you had to live. Turned you aggressive, didn't it?"

"Kiss my ass."

"Oh. There's a little taste of it right there. Can't help yourself when you get that feeling, right? That burning feeling in the chest. Attica may have made you hot-tempered, Dapino. But I don't think it turned you into a cold-blooded murderer. So you got scared when the girl died. And—"

"No girl died."

"You looked at her photo, said it yourself. Dead."

"No girl died because of me."

"This one did. Then you hit the road and just drove for a while. Figured the cops might be after you. And decided you needed to find a different car. When you passed by the fire trucks at the hotel, you thought it'd be a good opportunity. Thought you could steal a car in the parking lot with all the confusion going on. Maybe pretend you worked there, in charge of clearing out a path for the trucks, and ask some gullible guest to hand you his keys. Am I close?"

"No."

"Look, things like this happen. When they do, it feels a lot better to cleanse the conscience. I don't think you're a bad person. Because of that, you'll have a long way to go to heal. Why postpone the start? Why not just tell me what happened now and we can get past tonight and on to making you whole again?"

"Does that sappy crap actually get people to confess to murder?"

Stince leans back in his chair. "I'm trying to help you here, Dapino."

"And I'm trying to help you catch the real killer. The same person trying to frame me."

"And whom might that be?"

"Glen Brent."

Stince chuckles. Then erupts into a belly laugh. "Oh, that's good. While Glen Brent is worrying about evading a statewide manhunt, he decides to take time out of his schedule to frame some guy from Queens for a murder in the middle of the woods. That's your story?"

"Yes. Now can I get my call?"

"It's my job to document your side of the story. And if you're going to tell me something ludicrous like Glen Brent framed you, that's your right, but I need to make sure I capture all the details. You give them to me, without jerking me around, and I'll give you your phone call."

"It's not yours to give. I get one by law."

"And I get to pick when. You keep playing games with me, I'll put you back in your cell. If you're really working with the FBI on some time-sensitive matter, do you want to waste the whole night there or do you want to talk to this Agent Fast?"

"Quick. Agent Quick."

"Sure. That one."

A pause. "What do you want to know?"

"For starters, why were you in the parking lot of a hotel you're not staying at, in the middle of a fire?"

Tommy could try to lie his way around the question. But Stince would call the hotel to discredit any fabrication. That preppy blond clerk would be happy to assist. As retribution, Stince would delay his conversation with Jordana. Tommy imagines the dozen farmworkers set to die tonight if he doesn't get on the phone with her soon. Then says, "There was no fire."

"Huh. You have my attention."

He tells Stince the truth about his visit to the hotel, including how and why he faked the fire.

"You realize pulling that alarm was against the law?" Stince asks. "A misdemeanor punishable by up to a year in county jail, not to mention a steep fine."

"I know."

"Whether or not the rest of your story is true, I'm definitely charging you with falsely pulling the alarm. Got your confession on tape."

"Great. And the sound of me head-butting you is also going to be on tape if you don't give me my phone call right now."

SIXTY-THREE

Jordana, pistol in hand, advances down an alley in an industrial section of El Cajon with a policeman, the setting sun stretching their shadows against buildings. The cop says into his radio, "Approaching the two seen from the helicopter. Over."

They skulk about a hundred more feet to the end of the alley. Jordana hears two voices around the corner. Her heart slamming, she turns it. And screams, "Freeze."

In front of her are two males. They're big, but no older than seventeen, holding bottles of malt liquor. One drops his. It shatters.

"We swear we'll never drink again," the other says.

She sighs. Then holsters her gun. "Go home to your parents. It's not safe out here tonight."

"Yes ma'am."

The boys run away. While the cop radios in the false

visual on Brent and Archer, Jordana's phone vibrates against her leg, an Orange County area code. She says into it, "Quick."

"Darrington Farm in Imperial County. Three AM. They're going to ambush the workers in their barrack while they're asleep."

She paces up the alley, out of earshot from the cop. "Tommy?"

"Did you listen to my voicemail before? I found Cora."

"It . . . it doesn't matter."

"Did you listen to it?"

"I . . . whatever she said is irrelevant."

"You crazy?"

"Where are you?"

"I need you to do me a favor."

"I don't have time to do you a favor. I'm running an investigation."

"And I just gave you a breakthrough piece of intel for that investigation. Brent and Archer are going—"

"Brent and Archer are in El Cajon. So am I. We have them circled."

"What's El Cajon?"

"A city. About twenty miles from San Diego."

"You're arresting them right now?"

"Not exactly. Someone saw their box truck tonight. Called in a tip over nine-one-one. We found it here."

Silence from the other line for a few seconds. "That doesn't make sense."

"A local detective took down the VIN number, referenced DMV records, and called its last documented owner. The guy said he sold it in an all-cash transaction six months ago to a man matching Glen Brent's description. This is their truck. I saw it with my own eyes."

"Based on what we know of Brent, how precise and careful he is, do you really think he'd cruise around in a vehicle associated with his killings? That thing would be a bull's-eye on wheels."

She stares at the pavement for a couple seconds. "Maybe that's why they abandoned it in a vacant parking lot. They were aware of what you just said and wanted to get off the road."

"We both saw them leave the warehouse in San Diego in an Aston Martin. If you're going to switch vehicles, why get into a second one the police know about? And why drive twenty miles to this El Cajon just to get rid of it?"

A pause. "I . . . really don't know yet. But we're on top of—"

"Who made the nine-one-one call?"

"Gas-station attendant in a town called Pine Valley."

"Holy shit."

"What?"

"A county park in Pine Valley. The murder I'm being framed for. That's where the body was spotted by a hiker—"

"The what you're being framed for?"

"I'm calling you from jail. Brent is trying to frame me for murder."

"God."

"Jordana, hear me out. I need you to—"

"Why would he frame you for murder?"

"I assume to keep me away until he carries out his final attack. Once the physical evidence comes back, I'm optimistic I can prove I'm innocent. But if I'm locked up until then, I'm off his tail. I need you to come here and get me out."

"Me?"

"You're an FBI agent. They'll listen to you. Just tell—"

"Yes, I'm the lead of an FBI investigation. Victims' lives depend on me. I can't abandon it and drive to . . . where are you, Orange County? That's like a hundred miles from here."

"Victims' lives depend on the FBI acting on my information. Get a squad to Darrington Farm."

"Completely divert the investigation from El Cajon just because you say so?"

"Yes."

"You're something, Tommy."

"If Brent wanted me off his tail tonight, I'm sure he wanted the FBI off it too. He framed me for murder in Pine Valley. Seems likely he was behind this gas-station nine-one-one call from there too. He's playing you."

"No one is . . . playing me."

"Think about it."

"I did."

"It's early enough to recover. You need—"

"Is there any evidence supporting this theory of yours?"

"Cora had him on tape talking about the farm."

"Send me the tape."

"I . . . she let me hear it on her phone. It—"

"So you have no evidence then?"

"I get you're mad at me for lying before. I get you don't like me. That's fine. This isn't about me. It's about the farmhands in that barrack. If I'm right and you let them get slaughtered tonight, you could live with that?"

She closes her eyes. Rubs her forehead. "If I told Wichita this intel came from you, not only won't she believe it, she'll skewer me for even speaking to you. It's just not . . . feasible."

"Then let's make it feasible. Come here. Get me out. We'll think up a plan. They're going to make me hang up soon. Newport Beach jail. Start driving—"

"An entire task force is operating under me. I can't just . . . leave."

"It's possible Brent got rid of the box truck last week after he heard it mentioned on the news. It was probably sitting in the vacant parking lot this whole time. And he knew the FBI would go into a tizzy once he sent them to it. If he's heading to Imperial County later, wouldn't it be advantageous for him to deflect law enforcement to El Cajon?"

"I . . . it's . . . I guess."

"A dozen dead farmworkers. See the bodies in your head, Jordana. Don't take a chance on making that a reality."

SIXTY-FOUR

From his cell, Tommy watches Jordana walk through the holding unit of the Newport Beach police station, a folder in her hand. He smiles at her. She glares at him.

"Thank you, Jordana," he says. "This is so clutch I—"

"You just better be right about the farm."

Stince emerges from a doorway. "Agent Quick. I didn't think you actually existed. I'm the detective on the case."

They shake hands. She flaps the folder a couple times. "I may have missed something in the chronology laid out in here. Hopefully you can answer a question for me."

"Certainly."

"At what time did you hear the sonic boom?"

"The what?"

"You know, the noise that booms through the atmosphere when an object breaks the speed of sound."

"I . . . ugh . . . I'm not following you there, Agent Quick."

She points at a document in the folder. "Says here a man reported the sighting of a body on a park emergency phone at five thirty-nine PM." She slides out a photo of the dead woman. "Notice the victim's hair. She's lying in the middle of the wilderness, yet barely has a speck of dust in it. Clearly the body wasn't out there long. Meaning if Mister Dapino strangled her he must've done so shortly before the call came in. Reasonable?"

"I suppose."

"But he was apprehended at the Grand Bay Resort at six twenty-seven PM. Just forty-eight minutes after the body was spotted in Pine Valley. Which is about a hundred twenty-five miles from Newport Beach. Over a two-hour drive at normal speed. So if Mister Dapino traveled from one city to the next in the time you allege, he was likely moving faster than the speed of sound."

Stince's cheeks redden. "Well . . . maybe he left for Newport earlier. The body could've been in the park longer than it seems in the picture. Up-close in person her hair could appear a lot dustier."

"If this woman and Mister Dapino got into a physical altercation, as your write-up is contesting, and he threw her to the ground, overpowered her, and choked her to death, a lot more than her hair would be a mess. No matter what time the strangling occurred. The outfit she's wearing would be covered in dirt and grass stains. She may even have bruises on her arms from banging into the little rocks on the hiking trail. But no. None of that. It's as if she were killed somewhere else and just . . . placed here."

Stince's eyes snap to the picture, then cut away from it. "If he wasn't there, why's his driver's license there?"

"I was with him earlier at Dunbar Warehouses in Mira Mesa. Glen Brent emptied his pockets there. He was in possession of Mister Dapino's ID."

"Wait up," Stince says, his brow furrowing. "He wasn't making that up? He's actually involved in the Brent case?"

"Yes. And that's coming from the lead investigator on

the Brent case. I wouldn't have driven all the way up here wasting critical time during a manhunt if it weren't relevant." She pulls her phone from her pocket. "The hiker who reported the body in the park, did you listen to a recording of his call?"

Stince nods. Jordana taps a few buttons on her screen. Out the speaker plays Brent's voicemail from Carlos Ayala's burner.

"Did his voice sound anything like this?" Jordana asks.

"Exactly like it."

"That's Glen Brent."

A moment. "Huh. I'll be damned."

"He killed that woman in the park. He killed my partner. And he will kill more people unless you let Mister Dapino out of here so we can get back to work."

SIXTY-FIVE

Jordana's Blazer drives east, Tommy in the passenger seat. He gazes at the silhouettes of passing palm trees lurching against the night.

"Your face," she says.

"What?"

"Dry blood. Your forehead. Your arm too. I have wipes in the glove box."

He opens it. Cleans his face in the rearview mirror.

"You okay?" she asks.

"Fine."

"You seem . . . shook up."

"Maybe I am a little. Been a hell of a day."

"If you're right about the farm, at least it will end on a good note."

"You got the story down?"

"Yeah."

"Call your boss."

She takes a deep breath. Taps a few buttons on her console screen. A few rings through the speaker system. Wichita says, "Where the hell are you?"

"On my way to Imperial County. I—"

"Imperial . . . I just got to El Cajon. To the best of my knowledge, you were still leading an investigation here."

"I am ma'am. Yes. But that investigation needs to move to Imperial County. Which is a three-hour drive from me. I need some reinforcements ahead—"

"Three-hour drive from where?"

"Newport Beach."

"What're you doing in Newport Beach?"

"Cora Brent. Her Porsche. A local cop spotted it in a mall parking lot. I just spoke to her. She—"

"Who cares? Her husband's car is here. He—"

"She's been secretly recording him. Has a tape of him talking about his next attack. It's not over there. It's—"

"If she was so eager to bring down her husband that she decided to play spy and get him on tape, why was she avoiding us all day?"

"I . . . you'd have to ask her yourself. All I know—"

"Sure. Put her on."

"I'm not with her anymore. Who's the Resident Agent in Charge of our satellite branch in Imperial County?"

"Brock Lopez. He rolls up to my command in the main office in San Diego. Tell Cora—"

"Lopez needs to send a team to a place called Darrington Farm. ASAP. And clear out the worker barrack. The dozen men sleeping inside are tonight's targets."

"Showing up on private property, waking up a barrack of men, and coordinating an evacuation is a hell of a request. Especially with ASAP tacked onto it. You're basing all of this off a tape recording Brent's wife gave you?"

"Correct."

"What's her number?"

"She's . . . her phone's off. Been off. Which is why I drove all the way up here to see her in person."

"And you're still up there. So why don't you drive back to her, see her again in person, and put her on with me?"

"I'm not keeping tabs on her. She ... went her own way after we spoke. I wouldn't know—"

"And I wouldn't know what on Goddamn Earth to say to Lopez."

"Darrington Farm. He just—"

"Nobody here knows where you went. You just vanished according to them. And now you're telling me to evacuate some farm, based on intel from a source that also apparently vanished. Something is ... off."

"I'm just trying to cover all our bases."

"I don't know what you're trying to do. But unless you show me something solid to support your claim, you're not going through me to do it."

"We have to—"

"I don't have to do anything. But you have to get back to the task force you're in charge of in El Cajon. You should be able to make it here in an hour and fifteen minutes. If I don't see you by then, it'll be a problem." Wichita hangs up.

Jordana slaps the steering wheel.

"Don't go," Tommy says.

"I have to. I'll drop you off at your car first."

"Call this Lopez guy yourself."

"Go around Wichita?"

"A dozen dead workers."

"What about my dead career?"

"I'm assuming stopping a massacre would help your career."

"This isn't ... it's different for me. I can't just run around how I please like you. I work in an organization. There's a hierarchy. There are rules. I'll talk to Wichita in person and convince her to get onboard with the farm."

"She doesn't strike me as someone who changes her mind often."

Jordana pulls into the parking lot of the Grand Bay

Resort, the commotion from the fire scare gone. "Are you finally done lying to me?"

"Yes."

"I walked into a mess coming up here and helping you out."

"I know. And I appreciate it. Really."

"The least you can do is be honest with me."

"Already said I would."

She hands him a twenty-dollar bill. "Get a slice of pizza or something. A cup of coffee. Don't touch anything that has to do with this investigation once I'm gone. Anything. There're already too many variables. We can't add any more. Just . . . take yourself out of the equation while I talk to Wichita. Can I trust you'll do that?"

"You can trust me." He steps out of the car.

She holds a skeptical gaze on him for a couple seconds, then drives off.

SIXTY-SIX

Wichita's wide, powerful frame stands in the headlights of Jordana's Blazer. It pulls into the parking lot of the condemned pillow factory in El Cajon.

Jordana gets out. A wind blows, a soda can and other litter tumbling across the pavement. "I might be wrong about Darrington Farm. But if there's even a chance I'm right, we have to get agents at that barrack to clear it out." She glimpses the time on her phone. "It's almost eleven thirty. Our window to safely evacuate is closing."

Wichita doesn't reply, just stares.

Jordana takes a step closer to her, says, "Have Lopez—"

"I believed you, Quick."

"Eh . . . thank you."

"Your story about Cora Brent and the recording. Sure, it sounded a bit implausible, but you never struck me as a liar."

"Because I'm not."

"Well, then I tried verifying what you told me."

"You got in touch with Cora?"

"Nope. But I knew Keppler got in touch with her father this afternoon. Figured we could again. If his daughter was back home in Newport, like you said, there'd be a shot he'd now know her whereabouts. Could connect her with me. So I called him."

"He didn't answer the phone?"

"He did answer the phone. Told me if we called him again, he was going to sue us for harassment."

"The man has been getting pestered by us, local PD, and the media all day. Of course he's going to be a little crabby at this—"

"The man was more than crabby. And he had a right to be. And not because of any inconvenient phone calls."

"What do you mean?"

"Told me he just survived a break-in. A guy smashed into his house and locked him in a closet."

"Why?"

"He's not sure. But was sure about his description. About thirty. Fit. A little over six feet tall. Olive complexion. East Coast vibe to the way he spoke. Does that sound like anyone we know?"

Jordana looks at the dark factory facade, whispers, "That prick."

"Are you working with him?"

"I know nothing about him visiting the Halls' house. Let alone breaking in."

"You didn't answer my question. Are you working with him?"

A pause. "No."

"You're lying."

"If a man snuck into the Halls' . . . no matter who he was . . . it doesn't change the fact that Cora has her husband on tape saying—"

"Ah yes, the tape that doesn't exist."

"I'm just asking you to send a team to the farm."

"No. You're asking me to buy into whatever bullshit Thomas Dapino has you on."

"I'm not—"

"You leave El Cajon without notifying anyone. Drive to Newport. Where someone with Dapino's exact description confronted Cora's father. And now you're telling me a story about Cora that isn't supported by a trace of presentable evidence."

"I'll talk to you about Tommy all you want tomorrow. Tonight, can we please just focus on this investigation? We are close, so close."

"In El Cajon. Not some random farm. Did you actually speak to Cora or did Dapino feed all this nonsense into your head?"

"If Brent and Archer show up there as scheduled, we can have a squad waiting for them. A trap. We can arrest them, finally end this."

"You're not thinking clearly."

"With all due respect, you're not."

"I'm not the one making irrational decisions like some schoolgirl with a crush. I saw the way you were looking at him in my office yesterday."

"I'm admitting I could be wrong about the farm. Just want to take precautions in case I'm right. That is perfectly rational. We can keep up the manhunt in El Cajon. And send a satellite squad to the farm. You have nothing to lose mobilizing Lopez."

"Except my reputation."

"You're his boss. I'm sure he already respects you. And has to listen to you."

"How's he going to keep respecting me when he asks what my reasoning is behind Darrington Farm, and I tell him it's not based on any evidence I can show him, but instead a theory dreamed up by some guy just released from Attica?"

"You're oversimplifying this."

"And you're no longer on this case."

"What? That's not—"

"You need some time away to shake whatever spell Dapino's got you under. Take the rest of the night off."

"No."

"That's an order."

"Who's going to lead?"

"Keppler."

"Come on. He hardly knows anything about the investigation. He's—"

"I'd rather it were you. But not . . . this version of you."

Jordana bites her lip. "The gas-station attendant in Pine Valley who dialed nine-one-one with the tip about the box truck. Did you listen to a recording of the call?"

"Read the transcript. Why?"

"Same. But there's definitely a recording too."

"So?"

"You heard the sound of Brent's voice, right? From that voicemail we have."

"Where're you going with this?"

"I bet the gas-station attendant on shift didn't make that call himself. Brent could've gone behind the counter and dialed nine-one-one from the landline. Sent us all here to throw us off."

"The delusion broadens."

"If you hear Brent's voice on that call, would you at least entertain the idea that El Cajon could be a setup? That Brent and Archer could be on their way to another town? If I'm wrong, I'll stop bothering you. I'll shut up and leave."

"That would be terrific." Wichita makes a call on her cell, talks for a bit. Then hangs up. "Dispatch is emailing me a recording from the gas station."

Arms crossed, Jordana leans against a parking-lot light pole, its bulb no longer functional. Wichita paces. In a couple minutes her phone dings. She eyes the screen. "Here we go."

Jordana pushes herself off the light pole. "Play it."

They huddle around the phone. Wichita starts the file. A male voice streams from the speaker. But it's not Brent's. More youthful, like it belongs to someone half his age.

Wichita stops the audio. "Good night, Quick."

"Wait. This doesn't necessarily prove—"

"I thought you were going to shut up and take the night off?"

"Hear me out."

"I already did."

"We can't—"

"I'm sorry you let some ex-con get to you. I thought you were stronger than that. Just leave before you make this worse for yourself."

"A dozen innocent men might die. If you're too stubborn to make a call to Lopez to prevent that, I don't care . . . I will."

A cocky laugh booms from Wichita. "I think you're an entitled rich girl who can't handle hearing no because you've always gotten what you've wanted. From countless people looking to get into your daddy's wallet or your pants. Well, I want to get into neither. If you send agents to the farm, I'll see to it you never work for the FBI again."

"This is a mistake."

"Jesus. You're still at it. I'm going to do you a solid. I'm going to protect you from yourself. Just in case you get any ideas."

"What?"

Wichita taps her phone. In a few seconds, she says into it, "Lopez. Hope Lucy and the kids are well . . . Wonderful . . . Listen, I have a young agent on my team. Jordana Quick. She's got talent. But also blind spots. She's been going on about some crackpot theory involving a place in your neck of the woods. Darrington Farm. If you, or anyone else in the Imperial office is contacted about any kind of an op there tonight, don't okay it. Call me right away. Pass the word to local police as well . . . Yep, anything at all about Darrington Farm, send them to me . . . Thanks."

Smirking, Wichita ends the call. Jordana flips her off, gets in her Blazer, and zooms away.

SIXTY-SEVEN

Tommy sits in the back corner of a Sunny Burger off a freeway. He sips a Coca-Cola, two empty burger wrappers and a box of fries on the tray in front of him. The first meal he's eaten all day.

His FBI phone vibrates on the tabletop, Jordana calling. "I've been making my way toward Imperial County," he says into it. "Just in case you needed me. Ready to meet up. What's the word?"

"Turn around."

"Huh?"

"Don't come to the farm. Don't . . . just go home. Go back to New York. For real this time."

He stands. "What did Wichita say to you?"

"Maybe she talked some sense into me. I don't know . . . everything is . . . this is all your fault."

He steps outside. "What did I do?"

"You told me you were done lying to me."

"I am. I'm getting a bite to eat. Just like you asked. Haven't touched the case."

"Breaking into the suspect's father-in-law's house and locking him in a closet isn't an action you'd consider touching the case?"

He runs a hand through his hair. "That was . . . before. And I never lied about it. I admitted to you the thing I did with the fake fire at the hotel. You never asked me how I knew Cora was there. So I never told you. Figured the less you knew the better."

"Omitting a key piece of information is no different than lying. You sent me into my meeting with Wichita looking like a fool."

"Screw Wichita."

"No. She screwed me. I'm off the investigation. You got me suspended same as you did Gabor. What's next? You going to get me killed same as you got him killed? I just need to . . . get away from you."

"Jordana?"

"What?"

"You don't sound like yourself."

"I haven't sounded like myself since I met you. You're . . . bad for me."

"Get Wichita out of your head. This isn't about her. It's about the twelve men at—"

"I'm on my way there. I'm going to evacuate the barrack myself. In the event your story is true. Which it probably isn't."

"What about the trap for Brent and Archer?"

"There is no trap. I'm evacuating, then leaving. Wichita isn't authorizing any law enforcement at the farm."

"She's going to just let them get away?"

"She, like everyone else, still thinks they're in El Cajon. Because they likely are. If your farm theory isn't total BS and they actually show up there, I'm definitely not attempting an arrest. Going up against those two without backup is suicide."

"Do you have any idea what I had to do to get you that intel from Cora? And now you're letting the FBI just piss it away?"

"You're blaming this on me?"

"I wasn't at the meeting with Wichita. You were."

"You mean the meeting about how you're ruining my career?"

"What about my career? Any chance I had left of being a fireman again is gone. I had to tell Stince about pulling the alarm. I'm now a repeat offender. Worse, a perpetrator of a fire crime. No department will ever go near me."

"No department was going near you regardless. Because you're a felon, Tommy. You don't have a career anymore. And you won't have one in the future. But I do. And I'm not going to let you deteriorate it more than you already have."

"Feel superior enough yet, Miss Billionaire? Or do you need to insult me a couple more times for the full effect?"

"You want to hear something sad?"

"By all means."

"I was starting to have feelings for you. But it did nothing but cloud my thinking. I'm really looking forward to you going back to New York and never seeing you again."

"Maybe I was starting to have feelings for you too. But not anymore. Not after I see what you're really about."

"Definitely not anymore with me either."

"Good."

"Yeah. Really good."

"Bye Jordana."

"You're not hanging up first. I am." She hangs up.

He kicks a garbage can, the lid flying off. A couple who just got out of their car gets back in. Tommy stands in the parking lot alone.

SIXTY-EIGHT

Jordana races toward Darrington Farm. A tear flows down her cheek. She makes a call on speakerphone.

"San Diego County Sheriff's Department, Pine Valley Substation," a female voice says on the other line.

"This is Special Agent Jordana Quick, FBI San Diego."

"How can I help you, Agent Quick?"

"I'm part of the Glen Brent investigation. A nine-one-one call came in from a gas station in your jurisdiction earlier. Five one four Prinamack Road."

"Stanton's."

"Stanton's Fuel and Food. Yes. Can you send a car over there for me?"

"For?"

"The phone correspondence from the attendant was brief. I'd like to get more detail out of him. If he's still on shift, have the officers conduct an interview. If he's not there, have them speak to whomever is, find out where the original attendant lives, and visit him at his house."

"All right."

"Have them call me on this number as soon as they get in touch with him."

"Will do."

"Thank you." Jordana hangs up.

She drives in silence for about an hour. Her phone rings on speaker.

"Quick," she says.

"Hello there," a male voice says. "This is Officer Tanner, out of Pine Valley. My partner and I just left Stanton's."

"Was the original attendant still working?"

"He was there. But he wasn't working."

"What's that supposed to mean?"

"We found him in the supply closet."

"Oh."

"Brent and Archer must've forced him to make the nine-one-one call. Before . . . .well."

"Before what, they killed him?"

"They didn't just kill him."

"What?"

"One of them, or both of them . . . I guess it doesn't matter . . . took some liberties with him. Likely while he was still alive, before they slit his throat."

"What do you mean, liberties?"

"His forehead. With the knife. Had these Xs and Os on it. In like a grid."

"Like tic-tac-toe?"

"Yes. Like tic-tac-toe."

A pause. "Thanks for the update, Officer Tanner."

"Wish it were a different update."

"Same. Same. So long."

"Bye Agent Quick." He ends the call.

She gazes at the dark hills on the horizon. Takes some time to process the cruelty behind the gas-station attendant's forehead. But isn't able to. She doesn't understand it.

So Tommy was right about the diversion in El Cajon. But he's still a lying asshole. She tells herself to stay focused. In about twenty minutes she arrives at Darrington Farm. And traverses the property's service roads until spotting a one-story barrack surrounded by acres of shadowy fields and woods. She gets out of her car, bangs on the door.

It opens, revealing a Latin man in boxer shorts and nothing else, his hair tousled as if from sleep. He looks at her with a confused squint to his eyes.

"You and everyone else in there need to leave," she says.

The confused squint remains.

"English?" she asks.

He shakes his head *no.*

She slides her phone from her pocket and taps on it for a while. Pulls up a news article on Brent and Archer with their photos. Shows her screen to him. His expression doesn't budge. She barges into the barrack and flips on the lights, illuminating a space tight with six bunk beds and three metal dressers, its walls covered in posters of pro soccer players and musicians. Heads rouse from the mattresses.

She steps to the nearest bunk, presents the photos to the worker on the bottom bed. "Do you know who these men are?"

No reply. She repeats the presentation and question to the worker up top. No response. She asks the room, "Do any of you speak English?"

A moment. "Poquito," a chubby-faced man says. Which she believes means *a little bit.*

She scampers to him holding out her phone. "Do these two look familiar?"

He glimpses the screen. "No."

"Can you read that headline? Do you know what the word murder means?"

He sits up. "Si. Yes. I know."

"There's a good chance they're coming here. Soon. You and your bunkmates need to get out of here."

He rubs his eyes. Glances at the screen. Then the men

around him. Then Jordana. "Why they coming here?"

"It's a . . . long story. And it doesn't matter right now. What does is staying safe. You need to leave."

He stares at her for a while, skepticism in his face.

"Do you know what the FBI is?" she asks.

"Of course."

She shows him her badge. "I'm an FBI agent. You can trust me."

The skepticism in his face is replaced with fear. He says something in Spanish to the others. It provokes fast side conversations.

"Jesus," she says to herself. Then to the English speaker, "I'm not here to deport anyone."

"You're a federal agent. They nervous."

"They can't afford to be nervous. Neither can you."

"Nobody has reason to kill us."

"It's not a good reason. But I can assure you there is still a reason. Look outside. It's just me, one car. If I was here to deport twelve men, I'd have a team, at least a couple vans."

He peeks out the window at the Blazer. "Then what we in trouble for?"

"You're not in trouble. I'm here for your safety. That's it."

"Promise me?"

"Yes."

"So what you need us to do?"

"Anything but stay here."

"We no have cars."

"I'll . . . bring you somewhere. In mine."

"Where?"

She gazes at the floor for a bit. "Is there another big structure on the farm that can fit you all?"

"Main barn. Other side. About five mile from here."

"I can take you all in two trips. Just . . . stay there for a while. When everything is stable, I'll send someone over to give the okay to come out." She checks her watch. "We have less than an hour. Tell them we need to get moving."

He translates the plan to the others. They throw on

clothes and shoes and follow her outside. Six pile into her car. She brings them to the barn. They push the big door open and enter. She zips back, picks up the second group, and drops them off. They close the door, no external indication anyone is inside. She rests her head on her steering wheel, lets out a long exhale. She did it. They're safe.

She takes a service road toward the property exit. In the woods near the barrack she detects movement. She rolls to a stop. Peers into the darkness. Now just stillness. She glimpses the console clock. Not quite three AM yet. Brent and Archer seem too punctual to arrive early. Probably just a big animal.

She tells herself to keep driving. Even if the movement were human, she already resolved to avoid an arrest attempt. But something in her keeps her from leaving. Maybe it's a desire to prove herself to Wichita. Maybe to her father. She decides the reason doesn't matter. And steps out of the car.

From the trunk she grabs a flashlight. Flips it on. The fingers of her other hand unclip the holster on her waist. Then wrap around the handle of her pistol. Her feet tread the pavement. Then cross onto the grass. A rural quiet pierces everything around her. The barrack. The rows of crops. The trees.

She enters the woods where she saw the movement. Shines her beam ahead. Rocks. Barks. Bushes. No people. She moves the beam ninety degrees to the left. A similar view. She turns to check behind her. A male arm locks around her throat.

She drops the flashlight. A thumb digs into a pressure point on her wrist. She drops the gun. She turns her face toward the man's. She sees one of his eyes. The other is covered in a patch.

SIXTY-NINE

Jordana tries breaking free from the eye-patched man's clutch. But can't. He clearly has some kind of training, a technique to the way he grasps her.

"I'm an FBI agent," she says. "You—"

"I know who you are."

"You're going to be in deep shit if you don't let me go."

He sniffs her neck. "Ah. I've been wondering all day what that would be like. Nicer than I even imagined."

She shudders.

"Why'd you empty the barrack?" he asks.

"What? What barrack?"

"I watched you do it from the woods."

A pause. "I'm just . . . doing my job."

"Doesn't look like you're on the job. Where's your partner? Where're all the other cars? High-profile case like this, I'd think there'd be at least twenty."

"They're on the other side of the farm. They know where I am. They'll be here soon."

He chuckles. "Should I be scared?"

"Yes." She jabs her thumbnail into his eye. Then elbows him in the rib, spins around, and knees him in the crotch.

"You bitch," he shouts.

She wriggles free from him. Scurries toward her gun. Just before she grips it, he tackles her. His bulk crushes her back. He flips her over, his face inches from hers. The nearby beam of her loose flashlight puts a soft glow on him. His nostrils flare.

"What do you want from me?" she asks.

He undoes a button on her shirt. "I just want you."

She attempts to poke him in the eye again. He catches her wrist with one hand, sticks a gun against her throat with the other.

"Try that again and I pull the trigger," he says. "Don't move."

She closes her eyes. Feels him undo a second button on her shirt. His hand lowers to a third. "You piece of shit," she yells. And tries to roll out from under him.

"What'd I tell you about moving?"

Footsteps.

His hand stops on her third button. The gun leaves her throat. She opens her eyes. He is looking over his shoulder at another man's silhouette rushing through the darkness.

Parooh. Her attacker fires his weapon at the second man. Who dives out of the way. He charges at her attacker's legs, knocking him to the dirt. They wrestle. Grunting. Rolling. Her attacker's shooting arm frees. He aims at the second man. Who kicks the gun out of his hand. Then kicks him into a tree, his head whacking the bark. Both men stand. Her attacker reaches back to throw a punch. The second man reaches back too. In the shred of visibility from the flashlight, Jordana sees the shine of metal near his hand.

An axe.

Her eyes jump to his face. Tommy. He whips the axe forward. Its blade cuts into her attacker's throat. His head sags toward his shoulder. A near decapitation. His body plops to the ground.

She stares at the bloody, dead face. Then sits up. And pants for a while.

"Hey," she says.

The sound of the wind. The sound of a bird.

"Hey," he says.

"Why'd you come here?"

"Thought it might be unsafe for one person."

"Guess you were right."

"Guess so."

He sticks the axe handle in his waist. Nods at the corpse. "Who's he?"

"No clue." She nudges the dead man over and slides a wallet from his back pocket. Pulls out a driver's license. "Curtis Hawks." She rifles through the wallet. Her fingers stop. "A VA insurance card. US Army. He's a vet."

"Working with the other two?"

"Had to be. They probably sent him here to check out the property for cops before they showed up. Then he saw me. And ... got distracted."

"Won't be getting distracted anymore."

A pause. "About the phone call earlier, the things I said to you, I'm sorry—"

"So am I. As for ... this ... what just happened ... you okay?"

"Nothing happened. It almost did."

"I'm sure you would've figured out a way to stop it on your own. You were off to a good start. I heard him screaming. That's how I knew where to go."

"I got him in the eye pretty good. Maybe I would've gotten away. Maybe not. Either way ... glad you came."

He kneels beside her. Removes a phone from the dead man's pocket. "Let's see what we got."

"Anything from Brent or Archer?"

"Shit. Need a password."

"Let me see." He hands it to her. She eyes the screen. "Option for a thumbprint." She clasps the dead man's wrist, navigates his thumb onto the screen. Unlocks it.

"Slick."

She opens the text-message history. "Nothing."

"Brent and Archer's MO. How about calls?"

She taps the screen. "A bunch today. No saved contacts. Must be other burners."

"When was the last one?"

"One forty-four AM."

"Did you get here before or after that?"

"A little after."

"That means he didn't tell Brent or Archer about you yet."

"No."

"Which means they still might show up."

"Which means we've got to go." She stands.

He does too. "Or not."

"What do you mean?"

"Text the number from his last call. Got to be Brent's or Archer's. Say the coast is clear."

"Tommy."

"There're two of them left. There're two of us left. If the FBI refuses to end this, we will."

"They . . . don't even text each other."

"He's some new addition to their crew. It'll be understandable if he slipped up and sent one text."

"This won't be a fair fight. You saw them in the warehouse. You know what they're capable of."

"I also know what you're capable of. You saved my life in that junkyard in Mexico."

"Los Hombres del Vacío didn't have decorated military backgrounds. These two are much more dangerous."

He's quiet for a while. "I'm more like you than you'd want to admit. Or, you're more like me than I'd want to admit."

"Okay?"

"My point is, I know me, I know you. And I know if they came here and we didn't do anything about it, and they got away, we'd never forgive ourselves."

"Maybe."

"No. Definitely. We might not regret it today. Or tomorrow. Or in a month. But ... eventually."

She puts her hands on her hips. Stares into the woods.

"What're you thinking?" he asks.

"If I think about the flames, I'll get burnt. Right?"

He grins. "Right."

"So anything but them." She leans forward and grabs her flashlight. Then her gun. She cocks it. "You'll need one of these."

SEVENTY

Jordana opens the trunk of her Blazer to a couple crates of tactical supplies. She hands Tommy a gun. Then grabs a bulletproof vest and says, "I only have one of these."

"You take it."

"But—"

"Non-negotiable. It's yours. Put it on."

She does, then tucks a handful of zip-ties under a strap. "Make sure you're careful. I don't want to see anything . . . happen to you."

He checks the time on his phone. 2:56 AM. And jumps up and down a couple times, psyching himself up. "Let's get at it."

She climbs in the driver's seat of the Blazer, he the passenger's. They drive onto the grass. And stop a couple hundred feet behind the barrack. She turns off the engine, the black vehicle blending into the blackness of the rural night.

They watch the service road. A drop of sweat falls off Tommy's cheek, lands on the leather of his seat. Headlights emerge on the horizon.

"Here we go," he says.

"That's them?"

"Who else would it be?"

"What're they in?"

"Looks like a Prius."

"Where'd they get a Prius?"

"We probably . . . don't want to know."

The Prius winds along the service road. Turns onto a path through the trees. And creeps onto the field toward the front of the barrack. It stops. Two male silhouettes exit.

"Yeah, that's them," Tommy says.

"What're they holding?"

"Rifles."

"They had pistols at the warehouse. We have pistols. Why do they have rifles?"

He places his hand on her knee. "It . . . doesn't matter. Don't think about what they have. Okay?"

She takes a deep breath. "Okay."

The barrack's rear window lights up. Movement inside.

"They're in," Tommy says. "Now. Go."

She starts the engine. Nails the gas pedal. They rip toward the barrack. She hooks the car around the front, thumps the brake, then backs up toward the doorway. The Blazer's hatch butts up against it, sealing most of the opening.

"Ha," she says.

"These assholes are trapped now."

She puts the car in park. She and Tommy leap out. They roll toward the nose. And crouch, clutching guns.

"FBI," Jordana shouts. "You're under arrest."

No reply from the barrack.

"Open the front window," she says. "Throw your weapons out on the ground."

The window does not open.

"What're they doing?" she whispers.

"Hold on."

He inches his head upward. And peeks into the window. "They turned the lights off."

"Why'd they turn the lights off?"

"I don't know."

"There's nobody in there for them to shoot. What the hell is their endgame?"

"Just to . . . escape I assume."

"How does shutting off the lights help?"

"Be quiet for a sec."

"Why?"

A few moments. "You hear anything?"

"No. Why?"

"The back window. It's small. But they could squeeze out of it. You sure you don't hear it opening?"

Neither speaks for a bit.

"Nothing," she says.

"I'll go to the rear. Watch it. You keep your eyes on the front. We—"

"You insane?"

"What if they try to sneak out the back?"

"You'd be in the middle of an empty field there. Without a vest."

A pause. "You're right. We at least need a visual on them. I can't see shit from here."

"How do we get a visual?"

"We get closer. Watch them through the doorway. If they make a move toward the front window or back, we'll have a shot."

"We can't just go up to the doorway. We need the car for cover."

"We can do both. We go in the car. Get to the trunk. Use the hatch for cover."

"We'll be right up in their grill. And they have those rifles. We—"

"I thought we were done talking about the rifles?"

"Let's just . . . wait it out. It's different now. They're here. Right here. Wichita will play ball. She'll send backup."

"Can't hurt. But we're in the middle of nowhere. At three AM. Once she okays the backup, it'll take a while to get here. We need to keep them trapped until then."

"Fine. You . . . I agree."

"You got this, Jordana. We got this."

"Yeah. Okay. Okay."

"If they get out either window, it's their long-range rifles versus our pistols in the open. All we need to do is contain—"

"I thought we were done talking about the rifles?"

He grins. "Right."

"Speaking of containment." She opens fire at the Prius, blowing out the two tires facing them.

"Nice."

"Trunk on three." She holds up one finger. Then a second. Then a third. They dive into the Blazer. And hurry over the headrests into the trunk. Her supplies rattle, clink.

"You good?" he asks.

"Good."

"Stay low."

"I know."

"Call backup."

Her index finger jabs at her phone. She says into it, "I've got them. They're like ten feet away from me. The farm thing was real. Send everyone." A few moments. "I'll explain later." She ends the call. "Wichita's mobilizing all available units."

He nods. "Give me a cover shot. I'll stick my head up, peek in."

"Now?"

"Now."

She aims at the doorway. Pulls her trigger. The bullet splinters the windshield on its way into the barrack.

Tommy's head springs up. He peers through the broken glass. The idling Blazer's taillights bleed a red hue into the barrack's darkness. Jutting out from behind a metal dresser are two rifle barrels.

Tommy ducks back down. "Near the wall to my right."

"What now?"

He thinks for a few seconds. Then shouts toward the doorway, "If you try to climb out the front window, we have an easy angle to shoot you. If you try to climb out the back window, we have an easy angle to shoot you. Even if you got lucky and somehow made it outside, we already blasted your tires. This is over. Throw down your weapons. I spent time in prison. It sucks, but dying is worse."

He listens for the sound of a dropped rifle. It does not come. Instead, he hears the crack of glass. Slivers of windshield hit his face. A heavier object hits his thigh. A metal canister rolls near his leg. White smoke sprays from it.

"Tear gas," Jordana screams. She closes her eyes, sticks her hand over her mouth and nose, and climbs over the headrests.

Through the cloud, he sees her legs sliding out of the car. He follows her, his chest plummeting to the grass. The white smoke wafts out of the car with them, rising toward the black sky.

A sound from the barrack. Tommy looks toward it. The front window is opening. Two heads behind the glass in gas masks. He lifts his pistol toward them. Before he can shoot, a blinding heat consumes his eyeballs, as if hot sauce were rubbed on them.

"Shit," he says. The heat expands into his throat.

He hears Jordana choking. "The smoke," she says. "We've got to get away from it."

He runs toward her voice without seeing her. Nothing visible but a white haze, sporadic black flashes.

A rifle shot thunders through the atmosphere. Hotness in Tommy's rib. A different kind than the tear gas's. He topples.

"Tommy," Jordana says.

He groans, writhes on the grass. "One of them shot me."

"Where are you?"

He pushes himself to his feet.

"Follow my voice," she says.

"My gun. I dropped my Goddamn gun. I need to find—" He coughs. Tastes blood coming out of his mouth.

"Leave the gun. We need to get to cover."

Another rifle shot booms. He braces for his own death.

A miss. All the smoke must mean subpar visibility for them too. He staggers toward Jordana's voice. Her hand finds his. "I have you," she says.

She runs. He keeps pace with her. His legs feel tingly. So do his arms.

The chemical stench in the air lightens. A foggy visibility emerges. The shape of the Prius. The shape of Jordana. She drops to the grass. Crawls behind the car. He does the same.

"Oh my God," she says, rolling up his shirt.

"Is it bad?"

She winces. Rolls the shirt back down. "Do you—"

A bullet annihilates the Prius's front windows.

"Jesus," she says.

Glass shards fall through Tommy's collar, down the skin of his back.

"Dammit," she says. "Looks like they're trying to get into the Blazer. The engine's still on. Keys are in it."

"You have a shot on the driver's seat?"

"Yes."

"Let them know it. Keep them back."

She blasts four rounds. Then takes cover. They shoot back, the car rumbling.

"I put one right through the driver's headrest," she says. "Took out two of the tires."

"Good. But they'll still try to get away on flats." He reaches his arm through the broken window of the Prius, unlocks it, and opens the backdoor, revealing a medley of gear Brent and Archer stashed. "Yes, I knew it."

"What're you doing?"

"We've got to get the keys. And I need something to block me."

"You're . . . what? You can't go over there."

He coughs up more blood. "I'm fine."

"You're not."

He searches through the backseat, finds a folding metal table he assumes they planned to prop the dead farmworkers on when removing their organs. "Perfect."

"Go behind me. Then we go right at them."

"You're pouring blood. You're pale. You're—"

"I'm fine."

"Backup is on its way. And we know what car they're in. We can just—"

"There're woods all over. And we're close to the Mexican border. If they get off the farm, they'll dump the car. Go on foot. They'll be gone."

"We—"

The Blazer starts moving. "Shit, come on." He holds the table like a shield. She gets behind him. He sprints toward the Blazer. She reaches around him, firing at it.

"They stopped," she says.

"Shit yeah."

A rifle round blares. A bullet tip imprints the table inches from Tommy's face. A second shot strikes it, overpowering his grip. The table releases from his hands. "Get down," he shouts.

They hit the earth. Tommy gazes up at the SUV. Brent is in the driver's seat. Archer hangs out the passenger window aiming his rifle at Jordana.

A gunshot.

Then silence.

Archer's big body falls out the window. Jordana must've gotten a round off first. He lies face down in the grass.

"No," Brent screams. The Blazer charges at her.

She jumps out of the way. "Ah."

"You all right?" Tommy asks.

"Just my ankle. Twisted it." She tries to stand, falls back down. "Bad."

Brent stops. Leans out the window. Aims his rifle at Tommy. He picks up the table. Blocks the bullet. Jordana shoots out the Blazer's other two tires. Brent turns to her. Tommy pulls the axe from his waist. Leaps on top of the car, slams the blade into the roof.

Brent's barrel surfaces from the driver's window. Angles toward Tommy. He kicks it, the rifle flying out of Brent's arms. His head vanishes back into the car. It begins moving. Picks up speed. Veers toward the path in the trees to the service road.

Tommy remembers Jordana had a taser in her trunk. If he can slip through the broken back windshield, he can grab it and take out Brent. Tommy lets go of the axe handle, grips the edges of the roof. He shimmies toward the back.

The Blazer goes faster, wobbling from the deflated tires. Tommy ekes ahead. The Blazer goes faster. Too fast for Tommy to reach the taser. He clings to the roof, just trying to stay on. Wind crashes into his face.

Brent hits the brake. Tommy catapults off the car. He's airborne for a couple seconds, then his right shoulder crashes to the terrain, his collarbone snapping. "Son of a bitch," he says.

The glare of headlights. The Blazer barrels toward him. He rolls away from it. His leg doesn't make it. A wheel runs over his shin. He screams. Yanks grass from the ground.

He watches the red shine of the taillights. The car turns onto the service road. Soon it disappears from sight.

"What'd he run over?" Jordana asks. She hobbles toward him on her twisted ankle.

"That lowlife piece of—"

"Your leg?"

"I don't care about my leg. He took off."

"We're alive. We—"

"He's getting away."

"We got Archer. And we saved the farmworkers."

Tommy stands. Pain spikes through him. "We can't let him leave the country. There could be more."

"He's in a car without tires. No way he's going to pull anything off tonight."

"Not tonight. The future. It's only a matter of time

before he tries something again. Either overseas, or back here after getting plastic surgery and a new identity. I have to stop him."

"You have to go to the hospital."

"Not yet."

"You're losing too much blood. If you don't get medical attention ASAP, you will die. I'm calling an ambulance." She reaches for her phone.

"This isn't over."

"He's gone, Tommy."

"Maybe the keys are in the Prius. Only two of its tires are shot. We can go after him in that. Catch up to him."

"We have no idea what direction he'll turn when he gets off the farm. And his keys are probably on him."

"Or Archer."

"I think I remember Brent get out from the driver's side after they pulled up."

Tommy takes an excruciating step. "It's worth checking the car, Archer's pockets."

SEVENTY-ONE

Glen listens to the Blazer's hubcaps grind against pavement. He rolls along a quiet rural road about a mile from the farm. He tears off his mask, plucks from his hip a walkie-talkie paired with one on Bo. Says into it, "I'm sorry Bo. I didn't . . . you stopped moving and I thought you were gone. If you're still alive and you can hear this . . . Goddammit, please know I'm sorry. Respond. Tell me. I'll . . . do something. I had a chance to get out and took it. If I had a sign you were alive, I would've stayed. You know that. I just . . . I'm sorry."

He wipes a tear from his eye. Then calls Hawks. No answer. He tries Cora. No answer. He dials the number of his mother. The line is disconnected. He forgot for a moment she's been dead seven years.

The Mexican border is about twenty miles away. These deflated tires likely won't make it that far. He'll drive south until they give, abandon the car, and hike into Mexico through a wilderness pass. Under the thick treetops of this region, he'll have a legitimate shot to cross out of the US without a chopper spotting him.

He turns on the car radio. Blondie's "Dreaming" plays from the speakers. He sings along, "You asked me what's my pleasure. A movie or a measure? I'll have a cup of tea and tell you of my . . . dreaming. Dreaming is free. Dreaming—"

A bullet rips through the windshield, striking the passenger's headrest. He stomps the brake. Ducks. A red light spins against the night. A cop car.

"Come out with your hands in the air," a male voice says from a megaphone.

Glen glances out the windshield. A cruiser blocks the road, two policemen leaning over the hood aiming guns at him.

He assesses his options, the Blondie song still playing. He could flip the car around, try to lose them on the road. No. His torn tires. They'd catch up to him. A more direct approach is necessary.

He reaches to his ankle, unclips the holster holding a pistol he brought in case of an emergency. He could crawl out of the car, take cover behind it, and blast at the cops. But quite a bit of back-and-forth fire may be needed to take out both of them. By that time, another couple cruisers are sure to show up.

Staying low, his eyes just above the dashboard, he steps on the gas. And rockets toward the cop car, challenging the two policemen to a game of chicken.

The officers fire. The Blazer's windshield shatters. Glass hits Glen's face. But their bullets miss. His foot remains on the gas. The cops dive out of the way, one rolling toward the front of the squad car, the other the rear.

Glen twists the wheel to the right and pounds the brake, the hubcaps screeching. He points his pistol out the window, shoots one cop in the forehead.

On his knees, the other officer unloads on Glen. He ducks. Then fires a close-range round at the officer's mouth.

The bullet explodes out the back of his neck.

"You Goddamn bastards," Glen shouts at the corpses. Then laughs at the sky. He drives around the police car, continues along the road.

A crackle from his walkie-talkie. Bo's voice, it says, "I passed out for a minute there, but I'm alive. Come back and get me."

"Bo. My God. Yes, yes, of course. Yes." He spins the wheel into a U-turn and drives the way he came. "I just ran into a couple cops. Any there yet?"

"Not yet. But they will be soon. So hurry up."

"I am. What about Dapino and the FBI girl? They still there?"

"They searched my pockets. I think they were looking to take off in our car. I played dead, then grabbed my rifle. Killed them both."

"Perfect. Be right there."

Soon Glen turns back onto Darrington Farm. He rides the service road as fast as the wheels allow. The barrack comes into view behind trees. He cuts through them. Stops near the building, says into the walkie-talkie, "I'm here. You hiding inside?"

"Yeah. Still a little weak in the legs from the bullet. You mind giving me a hand walking to the car?"

"No problem. One sec." Glen puts the Blazer in park, steps out, and approaches the barrack's dark doorway. A fist hurtles through the shadows and drills him in the face. He crashes onto his back.

Standing above him is Dapino.

"Don't move," the FBI girl says, stepping out behind him.

Glen gapes up at this surreal sight for a moment, then tries to stand. But he's stopped, the FBI girl whacking him in the forehead with the butt of Bo's rifle. His surroundings oscillate. She flips him over, secures his hands behind his back with a zip-tie.

Dapino kneels in front of him, blood dripping from his torso. Glen looks into his fading eyes, says, "What is this?

Where's Bo? What's happening?"

"You were right about him," Dapino says. The sound of police sirens in the distance. "He is dead. We heard your voice coming from his hip. Dragged him inside. And I took this." He reveals a walkie-talkie in his hand, puts on a voice identical to Bo's, and says, "Bet you didn't think it'd end like this, brother."

Dapino's eyes lose their last flicker of energy. Then close. He crumbles onto his back next to Glen.

"Tommy," the FBI girl says. She shakes him. He doesn't wake up.

SEVENTY-TWO

Tommy lies unconscious on a stretcher in an ambulance. Jordana kneels at his side, holding his hand. A paramedic adjusts the breathing apparatus over his face, then says to her, "Please give us some space ma'am."

Jordana lets go of Tommy's hand and sits on a seat against the ambulance wall. She stares at his eyes, hoping they open. They don't.

The ambulance drives through the farm town for about twenty minutes. Then heads into a small city, passes the closed downtown storefronts, and arrives at a hospital. The EMTs pull Tommy's gurney outside, wheel it through the ER's double doors, and turn it out of sight.

Jordana steps out of the ambulance, limps on her twisted ankle through the hospital's main entrance, and approaches the front desk. The receptionist, a sixtyish lady with a hair bun, peeks at her "FBI" bulletproof vest with an uneasy expression, then says, "Hello there. Is everything . . . all right?"

Jordana explains she's not here for law-enforcement reasons, but visiting a patient named Dapino. The reception-ist directs her to a waiting room. Jordana soon comes up on a cluster of chairs that looks familiar to the one in Mira Mesa where she heard the news of Clyde's death.

Taking a deep breath, she sinks into a seat. Past four AM, the hospital is quiet other than the sporadic beep of unseen medical machinery down the corridor. She folds her arms, drops her head back, and waits.

"Are you a superhero?" a youthful voice asks.

Jordana looks toward a little girl, about six. She didn't even notice anyone else in here. "I'm a . . . regular person. Why?"

"My daddy says your shirt can stop bullets."

Jordana glances at the room's corner. A mid-thirties man smiles. "She's a curious kid. Sorry."

"No," Jordana says. "It's all right." She turns to the girl. "My shirt can stop bullets. So maybe it's a little magic. But I'm not."

"Why do you wear a shirt like that?"

"So I don't get hurt."

"My mommy got hurt tonight. She went to the bath-room in the dark and fell and broke her leg. My daddy took me here with him because I'm not allowed to be at the house by myself."

"I hope your mommy is going to be all right."

"If I wear a shirt like yours, do you think I could stay home by myself?"

"Why . . . why do you think that?"

"Then nobody can hurt me."

"No. You don't want to be alone. It's not fun to be alone."

"Why do people try to shoot bullets at you?"

"They don't very often."

"Why do they sometimes?"

"It's part of my job."

"My mommy has a job. She makes commercials on TV. And my daddy draws pictures they turn into engines for cars."

"Wow. Cool."

"Why do people shoot you for your job?"

"I . . . not everyone is as nice as you. Some people just aren't very nice."

"Why not?"

"I . . . don't really know."

"I think I know."

Jordana chuckles. "Yeah? Why?"

"They're mad because they think God made them a bad way."

A nurse enters. Tells the man he can see his wife. The little girl waves at Jordana. She waves back. Her father and her disappear through a doorway.

A couple hours pass, during which the black of night out the overhead atrium glass lightens with streaks of a new day.

"Hello," a different nurse says.

Jordana, her heart speeding, glances at her. "Yes?"

"Reception mentioned you're here for Mister Dapino."

"Yes."

"Are you his spouse?"

"No."

"Other type of relative?"

"No."

"Technically I'm not supposed to let you into the recovery room." A pause. "But I guess I can make an exception for a few minutes."

Jordana stands. "Appreciate it."

"His shin was severely broken. His collarbone too. We put his leg in a cast, gave him a splint for his shoulder. The bullet tore up muscle in his abdomen. But didn't hit anything vital. He did lose a significant amount of blood. A little bit more and it could've been . . . too much. But we controlled it. And put him on an IV of fluids. He's finally responsive."

"So ... he'll be ... all right?"

"It'll take him a few weeks to heal. But yeah, he'll be all right." She leads Jordana along a hallway, turns a corner, and points at a cracked door. "He's in there." With a smile, the nurse leaves.

Jordana steps inside. Tommy, in a hospital gown, stands on a crutch with his back to her, an IV dispenser beside him, a window in front of him. She walks to his side. His eyes acknowledge her, then turn back to the window.

He gazes up at the sky, filled with the reds and purples and oranges of the morning. She recalls a comment he made on her balcony yesterday, about the image of the black smoke he'd see if he looked at the sky. His eyes don't flinch. She supposes he doesn't see the smoke anymore.

His head turns to her. He kisses her.

SEVENTY-THREE

A man in a hairnet plops a wad of gooey wheat onto Glen's tray in the mess hall of a county jail. Glen approaches the rows of stainless-steel tables, at them packs of loud inmates in the same jack-o'-lantern-colored uniform as him.

He sits on a bench by himself. And has a sip of milk, its scent in his nose not putrid but unpleasant, as if past expiration a day or so. Another inmate sits next to him, on the inside of his light-brown arm a tattoo of a clown face, a common emblem of Mexican gangs. Glen wonders if Los Hombres del Vacio put out a hit for him in here.

"Doctor Brent," a voice says.

Glen looks across the table at a thirtyish man. White, shaved head, veins running down his arms the circumference of pens.

"You're Glen Brent, right?"

"Right."

"Fancy doctor. You probably never been in the clink before this, huh?"

"Excuse me, but have we met? Do I . . . know you?"

"You know me, yeah. Know all about me. My past, what happened to me, what didn't, all the good, all the bad. And you can judge it. All of it. Right Doctor Brent?"

"I'm sorry. I just . . . I'm not sure what you're asking me."

"You really don't recognize me? Look at me. Look at me."

Glen offers him a once-over. "I apologize."

"Let me help you, doc." He straightens his arm, nods down at the juncture between his forearm and bicep. "That's all you need to see. The windows into my soul."

Glen notices three light-pink scars. Which look like track marks from heroin needles.

"I struggled with that shit since I was fourteen," the inmate says. "Screwed up my life, put me in here. I'm clean now. But other people never got that chance. Ill people living on the streets who needed medical help." A pause. "The doctor saw them, all right." He spits in Glen's tray. "Enjoy your breakfast." And joins his friends at another table. They laugh.

After breakfast, Glen wanders out of the mess hall with an empty stomach. In the procession of inmates ahead of him, a large percentage appear Latino, and another large percentage have the young-but-weathered look of drug addicts. A shanking threat from both groups will lurk around everyday corners for the rest of his life. Every meal. Every shower. Every trip to the prison gym.

He returns to his cell, sits on his uncomfortable mattress. At the foot is a paperback copy of the eighth installment of the Prince Troy fantasy series he got from the jailhouse library. He gazes at two photos he taped on the wall, the first of him and Cora on their honeymoon in Hawaii, the second a sonogram of Jade.

His cellmate, a brawny biker, climbs off the top bunk and pisses in the toilet. He glimpses the Hawaii photo. "Great tits."

"That's my wife."

"Word of prison advice, don't hang up a picture of a hot piece of ass if you don't want guys looking at it. Plus, she ain't your wife anymore."

"Is too."

The biker laughs. "Until your lawyer hands you the divorce papers. Any day now. I've seen it happen to a million guys."

"She loves me."

"Maybe she used to. Not anymore. Good luck ever seeing that kid after she pops it out. She'll probably make up some story about who the real father is. Some sea explorer who died trying to rescue dolphins in the ocean or some shit."

"Cora won't do that. She has to bring her in to visit. At least . . . holidays, maybe my birthday."

"No she don't. Why would she want to bring her little girl around you? You're insane."

"No I'm not."

"Hell are you talking about? If I were you I'd embrace that. An insanity plea is the only thing that'll keep you from getting the needle for federal charges."

"My lawyer said the same thing. But I told him no. Because I'm not crazy."

"According to the media, you're responsible for over twenty bodies."

"In hindsight I should've . . . went about things a different way. The head of my hospital had political connections. If I asked him to get me a meeting with a senator, he would've done it. We could've worked together to come up with a bill to help soldiers who needed transplants. I would've made a good spokesperson. Could've gone around the country drumming up support for it. Speeches, appearances, online campaigns. But I was just too . . . fed up to do it that way. That makes me rash. Fine. Not crazy."

"You killed a twelve-year-old kid. For no reason."

"Oh. That. Yes . . . yes I did do that."

"Sane people don't pull that crap."

"Define sane."

"I'm an eighth-grade dropout, man. I don't want to get into some battle of words with a guy like you. You're nuts. The whole country knows it. I'm trying to give you a tip, not make you feel like shit about yourself. Have your lawyer run with the insanity thing."

"I asked him the same question. Asked him to define sane. You know what he said a sane person is?"

"What?"

"Someone who has empathy."

"What's that mean again?"

"It means you can identify with other people. Understand if they're in pain."

"Makes sense I guess."

"So I told him I'm the sanest person in the world then. Because I killed the twelve-year-old boy for that very reason."

"What?"

"That day I thought I lost my wife and daughter. It hurt so much that . . . I just wanted someone else to feel what I felt. Every part of my body was vibrating with this compulsion. To not be . . . alone in that state. The boy's mother. I took her husband and son from her. I knew how it'd make her feel. Exactly how it'd make her feel. I was acting out of empathy. Pure empathy. Nothing but it."

"That shit sounds pretty insane to me."

"That's a contradiction."

"Whatever. I already told you I don't want to get into a big thing over it."

"This is my life we're talking about. It's a big thing to me. You're telling me to declare myself insane. I'm not insane."

"You tell me then. If you're not crazy, who is? If it's not that empathy shit that does it, what does?"

Glen thinks for a while. "Logic."

"What?"

"The ability to follow logic. If you can't, you're insane. It's as simple as that."

"Like math? I suck at math. So does almost everyone I know. So we're all crazy? But you, the guy who shoots kids in the face, is playing with a full deck?"

"Not necessarily math. Cause and effect. A leads to B. And B to C. The basic events of nature. If you can't follow how one yields the next, you're nuts."

"And you follow them just perfectly I'm guessing?"

"Yes. Would you like a demonstration?"

"I've got nothing else on my schedule. Entertain me."

Glen hands him the Prince Troy book. "Hold this please." Then removes the sheet from his mattress. "A sheet."

"Wow. Captivating."

"A leads to B, remember? If I roll up the sheet, I expect to achieve a rope-like object." Glen rolls up the sheet. "There you have it. I was correct."

"I'm blown away. Really."

"B to C. If I attach the rope-like object to the bed frame with a quality military knot, it'll be secure." Glen loops the end of the sheet around a metal bar on the top bunk. Ties it. "Yank on that."

The biker does.

"Sturdy?" Glen asks.

"Once they transfer you to the federal pen, hopefully they have like prisoner talent shows. You'll dominate with this little number."

"C to D. If I attach the other end of the rope-like object to myself, I'll be tethered to the bed frame." Glen stands on the bottom bunk, wraps the loose end of the sheet around his throat.

The smile leaves the biker's face. "Hold up. What're you doing?"

"Continuing the demonstration." Glen tightens the sheet around himself. "D to E. Because of the tether, if I step off the mattress with my legs tucked, my feet won't reach the floor. Well . . . technically the plural, feet, isn't correct. One foot and one prosthetic."

"Brent, what the hell man?"

Glen steps off the mattress. Presses his knees to his chest, circles his arms around them. The sheet digs into his neck, cutting off his air.

"Oh shit," the biker says. "Shit." Arms out, he approaches the bed as if to untie him.

Glen kicks at him, then rolls his legs back up. He feels his eyes bulge. The blood vessels in his face pop. Lightheadedness sets in.

The biker dashes toward the front of the cell, screams, "Guard. Help. Help."

Glen's arms tremble. But he holds on. He numbs. The sound of the biker's voice quiets. The world darkens. Glen's brain starts shutting down. Before it goes, he imagines the sand in Iraq. Infinite sand. He wishes for a heaven. Hopes to see his mother there. Hopes if he does he'll be a child again, not an adult. Black.

SEVENTY-FOUR

Jordana stands at the head of an FBI conference room, at the table in front of her Paul Nash, the Director of the bureau, and his assistant. "Headquarters back in DC is buzzing with your arrest of Brent."

"I couldn't do it alone, sir. This was a team effort."

"Yes, yes. Of course. But make no mistake . . . this is your case, Agent Quick. That's how Washington is seeing it at least. It'll be your face on the newspapers. The sort of face we want representing the future of the FBI. Young, bright, determined. Pure."

"That's kind. Thank you."

"Don't quote me on this, I still of course have to run it by some people in DC, but I see an FBI Medal of Valor heading your way after all this." He stands.

"That would be an honor, sir."

He shakes her hand. So does his assistant.

Nash checks his watch. "I've got to get back up to LA. My people will be in touch."

"Enjoy the rest of your trip, sir."

Nash and his assistant exit the conference room. Now alone, Jordana closes her eyes, smiles. She walks out.

"Quick," Agent Keppler says.

"Hey."

"How'd it go?"

"Seems like a good man."

"Don't be modest. What'd he say? You getting a medal?"

"He thanked the whole team for a job well done."

"Did he mention my name?"

"I think so."

"He didn't mention my name."

Jordana grins. "He knows you were on the team."

"Lunch."

"What about it?"

"You closed your first case as lead. A few of us want to take you out. Celebrate."

A half-hour later Jordana sits with Keppler and three other agents in their thirties and forties at an upscale cafe. The other female at the table leans to her, asks, "So who's this fireman I keep hearing about?"

Jordana feels herself blush. Tommy's slept over the last couple nights. And not on the couch. The shoulder brace and cast haven't held him back. She lost count of how many times they've had sex.

"He's a concerned civilian, I guess is how I'd put it," Jordana says.

"I read the official report. His name isn't even in it. What . . . really happened?"

Jordana smiles. "It's all in the report."

The agent smiles too. "Oh. Okay. I see."

"Can I get anyone a beverage?" a waiter asks.

Keppler looks around the table. "We are celebrating. A real drink or two is in order. I won't tell Wichita on you if you won't on me."

A couple of chuckles.

"I'll have a Michelob," a male agent says.

The waiter takes drink orders around the table, reaching Jordana last. "Ma'am?"

"I'll do a glass of Cabernet. The Velatti."

"Excellent choice. Be right back with those." He walks off.

For the next few minutes the agents ask Jordana questions about the case. The other woman slips in another one about the fireman. Jordana brushes it off.

The waiter returns, placing drinks in front of everyone. "A toast," Keppler says, raising his glass. "To Agent Quick."

"No," Jordana says. "To Agent Gabor."

"Yes. To Agent Gabor."

They all clink glasses. Jordana sips her wine.

"How's that Cab?" one of the men asks.

"It's good. I'm sort of biased though. Velatti is my real last name. My family makes the wine."

He laughs. "Sweet. My real last name is Budweiser."

She doesn't laugh.

"Wait," he says. "You're serious?"

"Yeah."

That felt good. She hasn't said who she was out loud to any agents since getting this job. If anyone judges her because of it, assumes she's spoiled or entitled or whatever else, screw them.

"Oh," he says. "Cool."

"Damn," the other woman says. She's peering at her phone.

"What?" Jordana asks.

"The news. Glen Brent. He was just pronounced dead. Killed himself in jail."

Jordana smiles through the rest of the lunch, but the thought of the suicide lingers. Brent lost everything. She supposes what he did isn't surprising. Then considers why he lost it. All in the name of sick soldiers. All to protect the sanctity of their life. Discarding his own after just a couple nights behind bars doesn't make much sense. Then again, a lot about him doesn't make much sense. Accepting that is difficult. But she does it.

The agents head back to the office. Jordana thanks them for the meal and splits off toward her desk.

"Where the hell is Dapino?" Wichita asks.

Jordana stops, turns to her. Wichita's expression is distant, the same one she's worn since the arrest. She is of course glad they captured Brent, but must still be angry she was proven wrong about the farm.

"I . . . I'm not sure," Jordana says.

"Is he still in town?"

"Yes."

"Where's he staying?"

"That's . . . sort of a personal question, ma'am."

"It's only a personal question if he were staying at your place. Thanks for confirming."

"I don't really see how a private decision I made about someone's accommodations in San Diego has—"

"I don't give a shit where he's been sleeping. Or whom he's been sleeping with. I need to talk to him."

"About what?"

"Is he at your apartment now?"

"He said he was going to check out the beach."

"Call him. Tell him to cut his beach trip short. And meet me here."

SEVENTY-FIVE

Tommy gazes out at the Pacific Ocean on a bench, his crutch beside him. His right hand rests in a sling, his left holding his phone to his face. He says into it, "This is the nutritionist?"

"The one you were supposed to meet the other night," Josh says. "Until you got kicked out of the bar."

"She showed up after I got the boot?"

"I was in a . . . you know, weird headspace, after you laid that guy out. I hung around for just a drink with her and her friend that night. Then everything with Danielle. And you, Jesus, you. Going out there. Everything. I've been a nervous wreck."

"But you did see her again?"

"Last night. We went on a real date. Dinner. Once I knew you were safe, I felt better. Picked up with my social life."

"So how'd it go?"

"Oh. Great."

"Where'd you take her?"

"Lorenzo's."

"Nice."

"T, I looked fresh. Had the pocket square going. The red one. The patent leathers. And she looked . . . I mean, she's a knockout. She'd look good in a tarp."

"Who wears a tarp?"

"I'm just making a point."

"So . . . she's into you? You clicked?"

"Big. Yeah. I dropped the old Yanks story. It went over well."

"You still tell people that load of horseshit?"

"It happened."

"No it didn't. We watched the tape of that entire game twice after you first told everyone. You can see every foul ball. No kid in the stands catches one with his bare hand."

"I was eleven. I looked different."

"We watched the video when we were eleven. In Steve O'Malley's basement. I remember the whole thing. We all knew what you looked like. Nobody in Yankee Stadium that night, not an eleven-year-old, not a thirty-year-old, not a seventy-year-old, barehands a foul ball."

"Whatever. She loved the story."

"I'll put that aside. Nightcap after Lorenzo's?"

"That was my plan. But . . . a little something happened. At the end of dinner. So we parted ways from there. We're going to hang again though. We—"

"Back it up. A little something happened? What do you mean?"

"No. It was nothing."

"Tell me."

A pause. "So I pay the bill. Pick up the whole thing like a gentleman."

"All right."

"Waiter gives me back the Visa. Thanks me. Hits me with a big handshake. I hit him with a joke. It slayed. Smiles all around."

"'Kay."

"Well . . . the asshole at the table next to mine must've spilt a little of his gin and tonic on the floor."

"Oh no."

"I must've laid a heel in this asshole's puddle."

"How bad was it?"

"T, it was fine."

"How bad was it?"

A pause. "Three stitches. But—"

"Where?"

"Little ones. The doctor was a real pro. Cousin of—"

"Where?"

"Forehead. The middle of my forehead, all right? But it was a success. Date was a win, man. A big win."

"You split your head open."

"A little bit, yeah. But she's a nutritionist. She's into . . . health, remedies. She isn't fazed by something like that."

Tommy chuckles. "I miss you, man."

"You too. When am I seeing you back in NYC?"

"Didn't buy a return ticket yet. Guessing I should get on that. I spoke to the head of maintenance in my building yesterday. He's struggling without me."

"You don't want to lose your job. No offense, but with your . . . some of the things from the past . . . you know."

"It's hard for felons to find jobs and I shouldn't blow one I was lucky to get."

"Something like that."

"Yeah. Well, you are right. I do need dough. Got to come up with cash for the fire-alarm fine. Plus I got to pay for a new window for the Halls' house."

"Thought they were rich. They're making a guy like you shell out for it?"

"I'm lucky that's the only headache. The daughter, Cora, apparently talked her dad out of pressing criminal charges against me. If he did, my ass would be back in prison."

"True. True."

Tommy hears a beep on the other line. Scopes the screen. Jordana calling. He says to Josh, "Getting another call. I'll let you know what's up with my flight when I book it."

"Cool. Later."

Tommy switches to Jordana, says, "Hey."

She passes him a vague, ominous-sounding message from Wichita about coming to the office. He enjoys the view of the Pacific for a few more seconds, then takes a deep breath and tells her he'll head over.

In about twenty minutes he arrives at the FBI office in a taxi, gets out on his crutch. He texts Jordana. She texts him back saying Wichita wants him to wait outside.

He looks around. Whistles. A few passing employees glance at him with intrigue in their faces. Soon Wichita's broad body exits the main doorway. Jordana follows her out with an uneasy expression.

Wichita stops in front of him. Eyeballs his cast and sling, asks, "You in pain?"

"I'm good."

A pause. "You could never be a federal investigator. You must know that, right?"

"You dragged me all the way over here just to tell me that?"

"Many federal investigators only last so long. Like you, they're not an ideal fit."

"Great. Can I go back to the beach? Maybe enjoy myself a snow cone?"

"I came up in Quantico with a man like that. Lasted in the bureau three years. Went into private practice after. Lewis Canven. Today he runs Canven Investigative Solutions. One of the most reputable private-investigation operations in California."

"He sounds like a swell guy. Have a good one." Tommy turns around, steps toward the street.

"The reason, Dapino, I asked if you were in pain, is because you have an interview with him today. And I want to be sure you're up for it."

He stops moving. Turns back around. "Interview about what?"

"They only hire candidates with sparkling-clean records. Not ex-cons. You can't blame them for that policy. They have a reputation to maintain. And can't take a risk on some bad apple getting in there and ruining it."

"But I have an interview?"

"It wasn't easy for me to get it for you. I suppose policies like theirs make running any organization easier. I'm guilty of it myself when I hire here. And I'd say a lot of us are guilty of it, in some form, on some level. Dismissing felons as . . . well, just dismissing them."

"What exactly does this company do?"

"Investigate stuff the government can't go near for various reasons. A lot of it high profile. A lot of it sensitive. And they do it well."

"And they want me?"

"I told Lewis the real story about the farm. Not the one in the newspaper. Told him what you did to succeed."

"What was that?"

"Anything." A moment. "I suppose that's the very reason you could never last here. Because a guy like you would do anything to get the job done."

He smiles. "I . . . well . . . thank you, Miss Wichita. I guess I'm lucky to have a friend in a high place."

"Let's get something straight. I'm not your friend. I came here to give you the facts. You have an interview at four PM. Their office is about forty-five minutes from here."

"I can swing that."

"Also, if you get the position, which I have a feeling you will after my endorsement, no more New York. You'll need to move out here. That going to work for you?"

He glimpses Jordana. A smile streaks across her face.

"So," he says to Wichita, "it's sort of like being a fire investigator, but not just fire crimes, all kinds of crimes?"

"Not just any crimes. Big ones."

"Yeah. I can make that work."

"Excellent. I'll text you the details."

"Thanks again."

Wichita paces toward the building. Stops, looks over her shoulder. "One last thing."

"Yeah?"

"It goes without saying, but I'll just say it. I vouched for you, so if you embarrass me in there, I'll break your other shinbone. Got it?" He chuckles. Wichita nods at him, then at Jordana, and marches inside.

Jordana no longer tries to conceal her grin. "I wasn't expecting that. Wow."

"Same. Where should I live?"

"This weekend. I'll take you around the city. Show you all the different areas. See what you like best."

"Josh is going to be upset about this."

"Who's Josh?"

"Well, he'll like visiting, that's for sure. You'll meet him soon."

He looks out at the palm trees in the distance. Silence.

She says, "You seem . . . pensive. Having regrets?"

"You kidding? This is like a dream job. Ten times better than the maintenance gig I have now. This . . . this fits."

"You'll be great."

"I'm just thinking about . . . my sister."

"Yeah?"

"When I was a little kid, she used to tell me stories before bed. She was really good at it. I wish she were around for me to tell her this one."

"You're talking like the story is already over. But it sounds like it's just beginning."

"How do you think it'll end?"

"I don't know."

"I don't know either." A pause. "But I guess that's why we do things. To give them our own ends."

"I like that."

"Yeah. So do I."

ABOUT THE AUTHOR

SKY'S SHADOW is book 1 in Ted Galdi's Tommy Dapino series. Ted is an Amazon #1 bestselling thriller author, featured by *Kirkus* magazine, ABC, FOX, iHeartRadio, and many other media outlets.

For a free book, visit his website at tedgaldi.com.